Praise for the Books of
Amy Patricia Meade

"The first in a new series for Meade features yet another set of bright young detectives . . ."

—*Kirkus Reviews*

"Quaint characters and settings abound in this outing by New Yorker-turned-Vermonter Amy Patricia Meade."

—*Mystery Scene*

"Meade's debut will strike a chord with fanciers of Dorothy Sayers's Peter Wimsey and Harriet Vane."

—*Publishers Weekly*

"If only Katharine Hepburn, Cary Grant, and Jimmy Stewart were still alive. They would be fabulous in the movie version of Meade's debut Marjorie McClelland mystery . . . Meade's kickoff mystery is a winner."

—*Booklist*

"Meade successfully segues from her historicals (*Black Moonlight*) to this snappy yet traditional contemporary. She brings us pitch-perfect dialogue, original characters, and enormous potential for a fun series."

—*Library Journal*

"A fairly straightforward plot with a neat twist at the end, good characters, and a well-drawn location make for a good read."

—*The Bookbag*

Books by Amy Patricia Meade

The Marjorie McClelland Mysteries

Million Dollar Baby
Ghost of a Chance
Shadow Waltz
Black Moonlight

Vermont Country Living Mysteries

Well-Offed in Vermont
Short-Circuited in Charlotte
Game Over at Guild Hall
Foul Play in La Playa

Rosie the Riveter Mystery

Don't Die Under the Apple Tree

Tish Tarragon Mysteries

Cookin' the Books
The Garden Club Murder
The Christmas Fair Killer
The Curse of the Cherry Pie
From Ladle to Grave
Of Mushrooms and Matrimony
Cold Turkey

Evelyn Galloway Mysteries

Death Upon a Star

Foul Play in La Playa

A Vermont Country Living Mystery

Amy Patricia Meade

Foul Play in La Playa
Amy Patricia Meade
Copyright © 2025 by Amy Patricia Meade.
Cover design and illustration by Dar Albert, Wicked Smart Designs

Beyond the Page Books
are published by
Beyond the Page Publishing
www.beyondthepagepub.com

ISBN: 978-1-966322-15-3

Chapter One

"After all that planning, I can't believe we're finally here," Alma Deville exclaimed as she peeled off her boots and socks and cuffed the hems of her denim jeans.

"We're not just here in Playa del Carmen, we're about to celebrate your wedding," Stella Thornton Buckley amended as she too rolled up the legs of her jeans and dipped her feet into the shallow end of the pool at the Caballero Cove Hotel.

Alma sat down and dangled her feet into the pool beside her friend. "I tell ya, if someone had told me three years ago that I'd be remarrying at age fifty-five, I never would have believed them."

"Come now. You're a beautiful, vivacious woman."

"Easy for you to think that way. You're not even forty yet. Me? I'd just about given up on meeting the right man."

"Only to discover that you'd known the right man all along." Stella nodded toward Sheriff Charlie Mills. He was roughly the same age as Alma, with light red hair flecked with gray. He had scoped out a poolside table for four just behind Stella and his fiancée and, upon removing his pullover Nordic-print sweater, began to apply a thick coat of sunscreen to the areas not covered by his navy blue T-shirt and jeans.

"Yeah, thank goodness for Charlie's tenacity. I can't believe he ordered breakfast at my café all those years ago just so he could talk to me. I'm sorry he didn't make his move and that I didn't take the hint sooner. But I'm grateful we finally got the 'push' we needed. Unfortunately, the push we needed was the murder of Alan Weston."

"I suppose you don't really appreciate a person until they're gone . . . or faced with the possibility of a lengthy prison sentence," Stella replied, referring to Alma having once been considered a key suspect in the local contractor's killing.

"Up until that day, Charlie doing his best to keep me from going to jail was the nicest thing anyone had ever done for me," Alma added.

"Well, it's not about where you've been; it's where you're going.

And you and Charlie are destined to have a wonderful life together."

"I'll drink to that. Speaking of which . . ."

Right on cue, a poolside waitress approached bearing a bottle of Veuve Clicquot and four glasses. "Señora Deville? Compliments of Señor Tugores, the hotel manager. He's very sorry your rooms were not ready upon your arrival."

"Champagne? Thank you. I mean, gracias! I looked into this hotel when Charlie and I first got engaged, and it was my first choice, but there was only one room available," Alma explained to Stella. "Then, just a few days ago, I received notice that another room had suddenly opened up. I immediately booked it and canceled our other reservation. I couldn't believe my luck!"

"It was clearly meant to be," Stella said.

"Yes, I love how small and intimate this resort is. It's owned by the same company that runs the big hotel next door, isn't it?" Alma asked of the waitress.

"Sí, Señor Tugores was the owner until he sold to Quintana Hospitalidad last year. They own the Sueño del Mar, the tall white hotel you describe. They asked him to stay on as manager to make sure nothing changed too much. We have many repeat guests who come every year. They don't like things to change." Using a towel, she quietly popped the cork on the champagne bottle and poured both Stella and Alma a glass. "Where is the rest of your party?"

"That's my fiancé, there," Alma said, pointing at Mills, who was cleaning sunscreen lotion from his sunglasses. "And Nick is—hey, where is Nick?"

"He said he was going to make sure they got all our luggage from the taxi, but he should be done with that by now. I'd go look for him, but he doesn't really like cham—"

Before Stella could complete the sentence, Nick arrived poolside, grabbed her glass of champagne and took a swig. "Looks like the celebration has begun!"

"It has, but you don't like champagne," she argued as the server poured another glass.

"I don't, but when at a wedding—" He gave a shrug and proceeded to unzip the bottoms of his trouser legs. "Whew! Hot out here, but it sure beats the five degrees we left back in Vermont this morning."

"Are those—?" Alma asked in disbelief, as she watched Nick convert his pants into shorts.

"Tropicwear. That's what the U.S. Forest Service calls them. I ordered an extra pair just for this trip. They're moisture-wicking too." He stripped off his long-sleeved woven cotton shirt and dove, headlong, into the pool.

"And to think I was worried Nick might not be well enough to enjoy himself," Alma said, referring to the injuries Stella's husband had recently sustained while apprehending Warren Bessette's killer.

"Nick healed quickly, thank goodness. He also caught up on sleep once deer season ended. Talk about putting in extra hours! All his days were spent monitoring traffic, overseeing what was being taken in and out of the forest, tracking hunters and hikers, and breaking up the occasional drunken camp fight. Because most of their time is spent protecting natural resources, U.S. Forest Service employees aren't always seen as law enforcement officers, but they are."

"I can't even imagine. With Charlie being sheriff and all, I worry about him getting shot or injured, but most of his calls are traffic accidents and domestic disputes—usually in the heart of winter when the days are short and everyone's inside getting on each other's nerves. Nick's dealing with people with guns and compound bows. One angry person and kapow!"

"And those domestic disputes couldn't evolve into a 'kapow' moment or two?" Stella challenged. "Let's face it, we both have reason to be concerned. But not this week. Nope, there will be no mention of worries. This week is about fun and celebration and—"

"—and spending some time away from your mother?"

At the mention of her mother, Stella took a large sip of champagne. Since Lila Thornton had been dumped by her boyfriend and moved in with her daughter and son-in-law, she had grown more vulnerable and more loving. As a result, the three of them shared a new sense of closeness. Still, there were moments when the martini-swilling, fashion-conscious matron appeared to take great pleasure in criticizing her new housemates. "I'd be at your wedding no matter where you held it, but I've gotta admit that some time away from Mom before we're fa-la-la-ing around the Christmas tree in a few weeks is certainly a perk."

"What's Lila up to this week, anyway?"

"She's taking care of Bixby for a start."

"I didn't think she liked Bixby."

"She doesn't. She doesn't like any dog, let alone an eighty-pound black Lab. We offered to board him so she wouldn't have the responsibility, but she wouldn't hear of it."

"That's strange, isn't it?"

"Considering she's been working on a line of dog grooming products inspired by designer fragrances for Clyde Perkins's general store, it's not strange at all."

"Designer fragrances? For dogs?"

"Yep, she's calling the line the Posh Pooch. She was putting the finishing touches on the doggie version of Miss Dior last night while I was packing."

"You think she's going to test it out on Bixby?"

"Probably. The ingredients are all natural and organic. She's working with the owner of the natural foods store in town, so there's nothing harmful in it. Apart from the issue of our house and dog smelling like the perfume counter at Macy's."

"Ugh. Poor Bixby."

"That's the thing. Bixby won't mind it at all so long as he gets a treat and a belly rub out of the deal. He's just a hunk of fur and love . . . and drool."

"I still think it's odd that a woman who doesn't like dogs is creating a line of toiletries for them."

"It's an idea she got during our last case. Bixby had gotten wet, and to combat the smell Mom sprayed him with Chanel No. 5. Of course, he wound up smelling like wet dog and Chanel No. 5, but it prompted her to wonder what would happen if she added a deodorizer to the mix. She pitched the idea to Clyde, who agreed to provide financial backing as well as a spot in his shop for the product."

"Huh, doesn't strike me as a product Clyde would normally stock."

"He seems to think it could be a hit with the tourists." Stella shrugged. "My mother has always been rather persuasive when it comes to the opposite sex."

"Lila's powers of persuasion aren't limited to men, honey," Alma noted. "Just last week she came into my Sweet Shop and convinced me to try my hand at French macarons because she thought they'd be popular."

"You've been making macarons? I didn't know that."

"That's because they sold out in less than an hour. An hour! Your mother is persuasive, but she also seems to have her finger on the pulse of what customers want."

"She's always tried to keep up with fashions rather than trends. Those are too flash-in-the-pan, but style has always been her thing. I just hope that this dog project pans out for her. What with her breakup and moving in with Nick and me, she's kind of vulnerable right now."

"You think she might be getting too close to Clyde?"

Noticing that their server had moved on to Mills's table, Stella extracted her feet from the water and moved to join him. Alma followed suit. "Clyde isn't really my mother's type."

"Clyde isn't anyone's type."

Stella laughed. "True, but my mother likes her men more polished, more buttoned-down, more . . . you know, wealthy."

"Well, he might not own a place by the beach, but Clyde's no slouch. I heard that the general store was recently appraised for four million dollars."

"Four million?" Stella silently mouthed. "Are you sure?"

"Yup," Alma confirmed

"How did you find that out?"

"From our old postmaster."

"How did they find out?"

"By opening envelopes and reading people's mail," Mills explained as Stella and Alma drew up a set of chairs and joined him at the table. "That's why we have a new postmaster. The U.S. Postal Service fired the old one. Might even bring him up on charges, too."

"That all happened before you moved into town," Alma elaborated.

Murders *and* a nosy postmaster? Had Stella and Nick known this before moving to Teignmouth, they might have remained in New York

City. "If the store is worth four million, that certainly puts a new spin on my mother's relationship with Clyde. I wonder if she's aware of its value."

"Maybe. Clyde ain't above bragging to impress a woman," Mills stated.

"He sure isn't. He's bragged to me numerous times over the years," Alma said.

Mills was clearly surprised by this confession. "He has? I didn't know that."

"Because I wasn't with you at the time, Charlie. He hasn't done it since we've been together, but it used to be that whenever I was alone in the store, Clyde would make it a point to brag about some new product line or how many shoppers visited over the weekend. At first, I thought he was trying to compete with my café, but then he alluded to the fact that he was pulling in a lot of money and that *some* women might consider him to be a good catch. I left before he could finish because I knew exactly where he was headed with that speech."

"Mystery solved as to why Mom is so captivated by Clyde Perkins," Stella said with a chuckle. "That story also drives home the point that you need to marry this woman, Mills. Stat!"

"Oh, I'm not gonna let her get away. In a few short days, I will be placing a ring on that lovely hand of hers and wondering how I got so lucky."

"No," Alma spoke up. "I'll be wondering how *I* got so lucky."

Stella smiled and raised her glass. "And I'll be grinning from ear to ear because I absolutely love weddings, but I love them even more when those getting married are near and dear to me. Cheers, you two."

The couple raised their glasses to hers and they all took a celebratory sip.

"I couldn't help but overhear," a woman's voice interrupted. The source of the voice was reclining in a poolside lounge chair just a foot or two behind Mills and adjacent to the spot Alma and Stella had recently vacated. She was also in her fifties and clad in a smart one-piece swimsuit and wide-brimmed sun hat. "Sounds as if congratulations are in order."

"Thank you, yes," Alma answered.

"When's the big day? If you don't mind me asking," the woman asked in a strong English accent.

"In five days," Mills proudly announced. "Mexican law requires a waiting period after arrival."

"I never knew that. How lovely! Are you getting married here at the resort?"

"Yes, right on the beach," Alma replied.

"How romantic," the well-tanned woman exclaimed. "I've seen a few beach weddings here. They do a cracking job. There's a gazebo out there just before you reach the pier." She nodded toward the other end of the pool, where an open stage area led to a pristine white sand beach and a wharf where a handful of small passenger boats were moored.

"Then you've been here before," Stella deduced.

"We've been coming here the past eleven years. Twelve if you count the year we missed due to Covid. Being from England, most of our friends go to Spain for their holidays, but you can't beat Mexico, I say. From the beaches to the people to the food, you just can't beat it."

"That's a long flight for you, isn't it?"

"Ten hours nonstop on British Airways, but it's worth it. We come here right around December first and stay through the New Year."

"That's quite a lengthy stay."

"Yes, we combine our annual holiday leave with the Christmas break so we can have a proper getaway. There's no better place to be in December. All the money we'd spend on heating bills and presents and special meals, we spend here. Señor Tugores always puts on a nice light display and a traditional turkey lunch for the guests at Christmas, but he also schedules fun activities in the lead-up to the day. There's a bunch of us who come here every year at this time just to enjoy some cheer . . . without all the other stresses. Is this your first time at the resort? Or just your first time visiting in December?"

"It's our first time here," Alma confirmed. "I was drawn to this place the moment I saw it."

"It's the perfect location," the woman agreed, placing her knitting (what appeared to be an afghan) on her lap. "Right on the beach, a short boat ride away from Cozumel and the ruins at Tulum, and close to town and its various restaurants and nightlife. The food here is so good we rarely venture into town—still, it's nice to have the option for a special occasion. We've also established something of a community here. Speaking of which, I'm Georgina."

Alma introduced herself and her tablemates. "Stella's husband, Nick, is splashing around in the pool. So, you know all the other guests?"

"I've known them for years," Georgina replied as she removed her hat and ran a hand through her aubergine-tinted, dark, chin-length bob. "They're all here at the resort, too, since the boat to Cozumel isn't running this afternoon. Storms in the area. I'll give you an overview, so you know who's who. See the two couples playing cards in the summerhouse?"

The trio followed Georgina's gaze to the far-right end of the pool, where a pink, arched-roof gazebo had been constructed just outside the last of the guest bungalows in the southern wing of the resort. Beneath its rafters, a pair of middle-aged couples clad in swimsuits and cover-ups were leisurely sipping tropical drinks and scanning the cards in their hands for their next move.

"Those are the Horrockses and Banerjees. They're from Chicago, I believe. Or maybe it's Detroit. Somewhere in the Midwest United States, anyway," Georgina dismissed with a wave of her hand. "They're best friends now, but when they first arrived here, they didn't know each other. They lived in the same city, and each had a child the exact same age, but they had to travel here to meet each other. That was nine years ago. Their kids are at university now, but they still come here for the first two weeks of December. Ray Horrocks is in sports medicine, has his own practice. His wife, Diana, is a schoolteacher— science, I think. Manish and Anika Banerjee run two very successful Indian restaurants. High-end restaurants—not like the Mugli Charcoal Pit back in Manchester, but proper Indian cooking. The kind that gets Michelin stars."

"Think Charlie and I will still be coming here with you and Nick nine years from now?" Alma asked Stella.

"I don't see why not," an enthusiastic Stella replied. "Escaping the harsh Vermont winter for a week or two away with good friends? Sounds like an excellent plan to me."

"We might want to move our anniversary celebration a little later in the season, though," Mills suggested. "Help us keep our sanity until spring actually arrives."

"I can't recommend coming here in January or February unless you fancy spending your holiday with elderly snowbirds and families with small children," Georgina warned. "If that sounds rather innocuous to you, I can assure you it isn't. The company that purchased this resort and runs the hotel next door set up the stage you see at the end of the pool." She jabbed a finger in the direction of the beach. "They've provided the perfect entertainment for both lonely widows and weary mothers looking for excitement. Unfortunately, the dramas that ensue from such entertainment can make for some very ugly exchanges."

Stella, Alma, and Mills exchanged puzzled glances.

"You'll understand what I mean when you see the show later this evening," the Englishwoman added cryptically. "In the meantime, the elderly gent in the hot tub is Joseph Penrod. Military background. Vietnam War, I believe. He's been coming to the Caballero Cove Hotel since it first opened nearly sixty years ago, first with his wife and children, then with just his wife, and now since her death, alone."

"Has Señor Tugores owned this resort the entire time?"

"No, it was his parents' place. They opened it in the sixties, I believe. Back when air travel started becoming more popular and affordable. It was a modest little motel then. If you look in the office, you'll see a photo from its opening day. When his parents grew old, they passed the modest little hotel on to Señor Tugores, who updated the facilities and added more bungalows. He's the one who made it the resort it is today. Unfortunately, Covid hit the tourism industry hard and he was forced to sell. Thankfully, the new owners allowed him to remain the manager, otherwise who knows what modifications and improvements they'd have implemented by now.

"Standing outside the hot tub, chatting with Joseph," Georgina continued, "and sporting a bad haircut and a Cheshire cat grin, is our resident captain of industry—or robber baron, depending upon your view—Carlton Ruckert III, better known as Chip. The decorative, highly Botoxed woman standing beside him is his girlfriend, Desirée Hunt. Desirée was a friend of Chip's late wife. The three of them used to come here together on holiday. We were all a bit surprised when less than a year after his wife died, Chip arrived with Desirée *and* they hadn't reserved separate rooms."

"Everyone grieves differently, I suppose," Alma remarked.

"Hmph," Georgina responded with a raised eyebrow. "The last members of our little group are Eloise Sanderson—Ellie for short— and Kendal Chung. They first came here six years ago on holiday and, like everyone else, they made it an annual occurrence. Four years ago, Ellie proposed here, three years ago they got married here, and now as you can see"—she gestured toward the pool, where the two women were relaxing on inflatable pool rafts and talking with Nick—"dear Kendal is expecting their first child. This is their 'babymoon'—I think that's what you Yanks call it."

"We do," Stella confirmed.

"Do you and Nick have children, Stella?"

"No. Someday, perhaps, but not yet. How about you?"

"Me? Heavens no." She picked up her knitting. "Never been the maternal type. Although I love making baby afghans and booties and such, I give them away to friends, you see. But children of my own? No, the mister and I never wanted those."

As if on cue, a man in his early fifties called to her from outside the main office building. He had light brown hair that was graying at the temples and was dressed in a pair of cargo shorts, flip-flops, and a Manchester City football jersey. "Georgie!"

"Over here, Bernard," she replied, placing the accent on the first syllable of his name.

"Georgie, what do you think you're doing? We said we'd go into town at four o'clock. It's nearly ten minutes to and you're still out here sunbathing. And knitting," he added as he glanced at the handcrafted throw with disdain.

"Sorry." She flung the yarn and afghan into an oversized raffia tote bag. "I was just speaking with these lovely people. They're from Vermont—?"

Charlie nodded.

"—in the States. This is Alma, Charlie, Stella, and, in the pool, Stella's husband . . ."

"Nick," Stella provided.

"Nice to meet you," Bernard brusquely greeted. "Georgie, we've got to—"

"Now, now, Bernard. We can take a few extra minutes to welcome some fellow guests to the resort, can't we? I believe you said earlier that Nick is in law enforcement. Is that correct, Stella?"

"Yes, but I don't want to keep you."

"Nonsense," Georgina insisted.

Even Bernard appeared more patient. "Not a problem at all. I get too hung up on schedules back at home. Something I should abandon here in La Playa, but it takes some time to get into the laid-back mood of the place, don't you think? Now, what was this about your husband?"

"Oh, um, he's with the United States Forest Service. Not a policeman, but sort of a protector of the environment. Charlie here is a sheriff though."

"Really? I greatly enjoy American crime shows. I enjoy all crime stuff, actually. Books, television shows—read and watch them all the time. I understand some of those shows are dramatizations, but your job must be fairly exciting—and slightly harrowing—what with everyone packing guns."

Mills chuckled. "I hate to disappoint you, but in Vermont, most of our guns are used for hunting. We also live in a small town, not a big city. My days are spent diverting traffic, conducting welfare checks, and breaking up the occasional fight at the local bar. At least that *was* how I spent my days until this one arrived." His eyes slid toward Stella, who feigned indignation.

"Oh, no. No, you don't. Don't you go there!"

Mills's chuckle grew into a belly laugh. "Hey, I can't help it if life in Teignmouth has become more—colorful—since you and Nick arrived."

Georgina and Bernard's eyes grew wide. "What—what do you do for a living, Stella?" the Englishwoman asked.

"I'm a textile curator. I studied ancient fabrics and methods of weaving. I used to work for the Metropolitan Museum of Art, but now I mostly spend my time on restoration work. By the way, I caught a glimpse of that throw you're working on. It's double knit, isn't it?"

"Y-yes," Georgina stammered. "How did you know?"

"Textiles," Stella said with a smile. "You're an excellent knitter. A master."

"Pshaw! You should have seen our nan. She was the real master. She could knit just about anything, bless her. She taught me everything I know, but not everything she knew." Georgina turned to Bernard. "We'd best get on our walk so we're back in time to shower and change. See you all at dinner tonight!"

As the trio of friends said goodbye to Georgina and Bernard, a young woman dressed in a smart navy blue suit emblazoned with the Caballero Cove Hotel logo arrived at their table. "Señor, señoras, your accommodations are ready."

Alma and Stella let out a tiny cheer. "Time to get out of these winter clothes!" Stella exclaimed.

"And into the resort wear I just bought," Alma rejoined before looking at her fiancé. "You coming?"

"Nah, I'm gonna stay here for a bit, sip my champagne, and maybe check out one of those true crime podcasts I've been hearing about."

"Aren't you warm in those jeans of yours?"

"Yep, but when I think of spending the next few months back at home in the cold, I don't mind it too much."

"Suit yourself," she said with a shake of the head before following the hotel's customer service representative to what would be their home for the next ten days.

"You'll be staying in bungalows seven and nine," the woman announced as she led the two outside the series of lounge chairs that encircled the pool and along a low, interlocking stone wall punctuated every so many yards by black iron gates. Behind each gate, a path led through a miniature garden of marigolds, dahlias, blue agave, cactus, and bougainvillea to a terra-cotta *casita*, or little house.

The casitas known as bungalows seven and nine were located at the end of the horseshoe, with number nine directly outside the hot tub that had been recently vacated by Joseph Penrod.

"Stella, would you and Nick mind if Charlie and I take number nine? The idea of an early morning soak in the hot tub sounds like heaven. Most mornings, I'm up at four to fry donuts and bake muffins."

"Not at all. This is your wedding and honeymoon trip. We want you both to have the time of your lives."

"Thanks, honey. We want you to have a great time too."

"We will," Stella assured her as they came upon the charming structure known as bungalow number seven. It was similar in design to the other so-called bungalows, but the front garden featured a soothing fountain and several rosebushes in bloom. "It's not as if Nick and I will be slumming it."

"Oh, my," Alma gasped. "How lovely."

"This casita may not have direct access to the outdoor hot tub, but it does have a whirlpool bathtub for two as well as a private veranda on the back," stated the hotel employee, who introduced herself as Luciana.

"Ooh!"

"Are you sure you want to stick with number nine?" Stella asked. "Whirlpool, veranda . . ."

"Nope. I already called number nine and I'm sticking with it. I'm not gonna turn into a Bridezilla."

"Number nine has a canopy bed, a refrigerator filled with complimentary soft drinks, and a personal cabana on the beach," Luciana informed them.

"There you go. I'm definitely not going to switch. Can we have visitors in our cabana?"

"But of course. And if you'd like food or beverages, or even a fresh towel, just use the Caballero Cove app on your phone to make a request and one of our staff will bring you what you need."

"Really? Woo-hoo! There you go, Stella. You and Nick can soak in your whirlpool tub and then join Charlie and me on the beach."

"I might never go home. And, of course, you and Mills are welcome to join us on the veranda," Stella replied.

"With a nice chilled bottle of rosé."

"If you're bringing wine, you're welcome anytime."

"Sounds like something you and I should hang over our doors back at home!"

Luciana smiled as she opened the gate leading to Stella and Nick's bungalow. "Or you can use the app and let us bring the wine. You'll find that we have an extensive wine list here at Caballero Cove and that our prices are reasonable."

"That's music to our ears," Stella noted. "Oh, I should probably get Nick to bring the bags over."

"Your bags are already on their way."

With that, two uniformed bellhops arrived on the path behind the three women. Luciana directed the young man bearing the Buckleys' luggage to number seven and the other bellhop to number nine. She then opened the door to number seven and handed Stella a key card. "I hope you find everything to your liking."

"I'm sure I will. Thank you."

"And now bungalow number nine for la señora."

"That's my cue," Alma said with a delighted giggle before following Luciana to the quarters she'd share with Mills. "I'll meet you back here in a few. Then maybe we can rustle up the guys and check out the beach."

"It's a plan." Stella allowed the bellhop to exit before stepping over the threshold and gleefully surveying her accommodations. The casita was precisely that—a comfortable, well-appointed little house consisting of three rooms. To the left of the entrance, the sitting room boasted an exposed beam ceiling, yellow walls, tiled floors, and rattan furniture with luxuriously thick white cushions. To the right of the front door, the bedroom was a soothing shade of turquoise and featured a king-sized bed, replete with pristine white cotton linens, ocean-colored throw pillows, and a headboard that appeared to have been upcycled from an ornately carved church altar. The bathroom, located directly off the bedroom, continued the beach theme with hand-painted local tiles in pale green and blue hues, heavy wood cabinetry, and a candelabra-style light fixture over the deep soaking tub with rainfall showerhead.

Charmed with the resort and her surroundings, Stella did a little twirl in the middle of the bathroom and then danced into the bedroom to change into something more appropriate. Rummaging through her suitcase, she selected one of two new swimsuits and a sarong cover-up she had purchased for the trip and began to get undressed.

Like clockwork, Nick arrived. "Wow, look at this place! Isn't it great?"

"It exceeds all expectations. Hey, how did you get in without a key?"

"Luciana let me in. I passed her on the way back to the office and told her I wanted to check out the place."

"I thought you were busy swimming."

"I was, but when I saw you were gone, I decided to see what you were doing." He stood in the bedroom door and watched as she pulled her jeans down to her ankles.

"Does your phone have an app that notifies you when I'm undressing?"

"I don't need an app for that. I feel it in my gut."

"Uh-huh. Well, switch your gut off for now, because Alma will be back here any minute. She thought we could all check out the beach together."

"Fine with me. Although that bed looks mighty comfortable."

"And it will still look mighty comfortable when we get back here later."

"Okay, okay," he said with a mock sigh. "I guess it is Alma's week, isn't it?"

Stella slipped into a deep blue one-piece swimsuit, hoisting its straps onto her shoulders before tying a coordinating, floral-printed sarong around her waist. "And Charlie's." She reached into the closet and selected one of two garment bags the bellhop had hung there.

"You're not putting on more clothes, are you? It's pretty hot out there."

"No, just getting our wedding outfits out of their bags so they can breathe. I want to make sure nothing's too wrinkled, otherwise I'll ask the hotel to steam them."

As she unzipped the first bag to reveal her matron of honor dress, she noticed an unusual item tucked far into a back corner of the closet shelf. "Nick?"

"Mmm?" He was examining the bedroom thermostat.

"Did you happen to bring a hat with you?"

"Huh? No, why?" He reached a hand self-consciously to the back of his head and ran his fingers through his thick chestnut hair. "Am I getting thin up there?"

Stella rolled her eyes. Ever since Nick had received photos of his twenty-year high school reunion (which he did not attend) and noticed the receding hairlines of his childhood friends, he'd become fearful of going bald. "For the last time, no. Just because your high school buddies are losing their hair doesn't mean you're going to lose yours. Your father still has all his hair and both your grandfathers died with a full head of hair, so unless you're related to those friends of yours, you're fine."

Appeased by this statement, Nick returned his attention to the thermostat. "I can't figure out how to turn on the fan. It feels good in here now, having come in from outside, but seventy-three degrees is a little stuffy for overnight. Don't you think?"

She grunted in agreement. "So, the straw Panama hat on the closet shelf isn't yours?"

He strolled over from his spot in front of the thermostat and retrieved the hat in question. "After all this time together, do you really need to ask?"

"Then it must belong to the previous occupant of this room. He must have left it behind."

"Easy enough to do. It was tucked pretty far into that corner."

"Yeah, I guess. I would have thought housekeeping might have spotted it."

Nick shrugged. "Too busy cleaning."

"True. The bungalow is absolutely immaculate. I just figured staff would check closets and dressers for stray belongings, but no one can do everything perfectly."

"I dunno . . . I come pretty close," he teased.

With a "spare me" glance, Stella snatched the hat from her husband's hands. "I'll give it to a member of the staff before we head to the beach. Someone might be looking for it."

"You really think so? Maybe a wife left it behind on purpose so her husband wouldn't wear it again. You know, kind of like what you did with my old T-shirts."

"You mean like your 'Vote for Pedro' shirt?"

"Yes! I had some real classics."

"I'd hardly call a T-shirt that reads 'Make seven' on the front and 'Up yours' on the back a classic," she stated as she flung the hat onto the bed and continued to unpack their wedding ensembles.

"Oh, come on. That was a terrific ad campaign."

"One you bought into, apparently."

"Not true. I never drank 7-Up."

"But you bought the—oh, never mind."

Alma's voice came lilting from the front door. "Helloooo!"

Stella looked at Nick, her face a question.

"I left the door unlocked. We were both here and all the other guests are on vacation. Didn't seem like I needed to."

"Hey, I'm ready to par-tay!" Alma announced as she stood in the bedroom door. She had changed into a two-piece red swimsuit consisting of a full tank top and skirted bottom. "Well, not really a party. I've never been much for crazy stuff, but I am ready to sink my toes in the sand, eat some good food, and dance into the wee hours. And by wee hours, I mean ten, maybe eleven o'clock."

"We're here for it," Nick cheered. "The dancing *and* turning in by eleven."

"Great!" She eyed the straw hat lying on the bed. "Hey, you trying out a new chapeau?"

"It's a lot different than the brimmed Forest Service hat he wears to work, isn't it?" Stella laughed, snatching the Panama hat from its spot and placing it on her husband's head. It was far too small for the six-feet, two-inch-tall ranger. "Look at that. All you need is one of your old Von Dutch shirts."

"Another classic that you discarded," Nick argued.

"A classic? Maybe twenty years ago."

"Von Dutch stuff will come back. Trust me, it will."

"They'd had better hurry up or you'll be wearing their trucker hats in the nursing home."

"Speaking of hats." He removed the Panama hat from atop his

head. "Who owned this thing? A Keebler elf?"

"It's not Stella's?" Alma asked.

"No, I found it in the closet while I was unpacking," Stella said.

"Maybe it's a courtesy item. Like a hotel room bathrobe," Alma suggested.

"A small man's hat? I doubt it. I'll drop it by the office before we hit the beach."

They locked the door to the casita and made their way through the garden and past the pool to meet up with Mills. Along the way, they passed Luciana.

Stella stopped her and showed her the hat. "I found this in the bedroom closet of our bungalow. I think the previous occupant might have left it behind."

Luciana's face blanched and her jaw fell slack. Several moments elapsed before she spoke. "Oh . . . oh, I am so sorry. The housekeeping staff must have overlooked it."

"Not a problem. The housekeeping staff focused on the important things. The bungalow is lovely and absolutely spotless."

"Oh . . . I'm happy to hear that." The tone of Luciana's voice, however, was anything but happy. "Thank you for turning this in. I shall speak with the staff."

"That was strange," Stella remarked when Luciana was safely out of earshot.

"Well, you kinda called her staff out," Nick noted. "She obviously has high standards for them."

"Maybe, but I don't think that's it. It was as if the sight of the hat frightened her."

"I saw it too. You know, the hotel manager might hold her accountable for keeping housekeeping in line," Alma offered. "Her job might be at risk."

Stella recalled how the color drained from the guest service liaison's face. "I suppose that's probably it," she allowed, although privately she wasn't quite convinced. "Yes, that must be it. Enough talk about hats. Let's get to the beach!"

Chapter Two

The two couples spent the remainder of the afternoon strolling on the beach, wading in the turquoise blue waters of the Caribbean Sea, and lounging in Alma and Mills's private cabana. When the sun began to set, they returned to their respective casitas to shower and change for dinner.

Nick looked handsome in an embroidered white short-sleeve shirt and a pair of well-tailored khakis, while Stella looked cool yet chic in a flowing black sundress with slightly winged cap sleeves, and strappy sandals. They met their friends outside their bungalow gate. Mills mimicked Nick's look with a pair of chinos but topped it with a lively tropical-print shirt and Alma played up her dark eyes and auburn hair with a wrap-waist maxi-dress in a delicate shade of apricot.

Nighttime at the Caballero Cove Hotel was simply magical. The trees surrounding the pool area sparkled with the glow of hundreds of fairy lights, torches lit the stage, and the pumps and filters of the swimming pool itself had been switched off and arrangements of flowers and lit candles were set afloat upon the glasslike surface.

White-gloved waiters passed trays of hors d'oeuvres to the guests as they mingled and drank cocktails before being led to a long table beneath a bougainvillea-covered pergola. Señor Tugores, the hotel manager, was there to greet them.

He was in his late forties and of average height and wore a neatly trimmed beard and well-tailored linen suit. *"Bienvenido . . . bienvenido. Hola,* Señor Mills y Señora Deville. *Hola,* Señor y Señora Buckley. We are pleased to have you with us. There are no assignments of seats for dinner, so please sit where you like. Food is served family-style, with carafes of wine and water on the table. Should you need anything else, our waitstaff is more than happy to accommodate."

The friends thanked Señor Tugores for his warm welcome.

"Do we use the app to call the waitstaff?" Alma asked, glancing at her phone.

Tugores laughed. "No, no. They're right here at the table. In real time."

"Ohhh! Will you be joining us for dinner?"

"I stay for an initial toast and then, I'm afraid, I need to take care of other matters. All of them related to ensuring you have an excellent stay."

"It's been lovely so far. Everything I'd hoped for and more. I can't wait to see the flowers you've arranged for our wedding."

"I hope they, too, exceed your expectations. And if they do, you need to thank Luciana. She is the head of guest services and she's taken great pleasure in orchestrating all the details for your special day. Now, I should commence with the toast. I see some hungry faces staring back at me."

As Señor Tugores stood at the head of the table, Ellie Sanderson and Kendal Chung called to Nick and waved him and Stella to the seats they'd saved for them. Meanwhile, Alma and Mills found a pair of seats at the head of the table, alongside Chip Ruckert and Desirée Hunt.

Couples were seated opposite each other, with the exception of the seat across from Joseph Penrod, who was traveling solo. Manish and Anika Banerjee sat at the far end of the table, closest to the pool area, then Ray and Diana Horrocks, Ellie and Kendal, the Buckleys, Georgina and Bernard Early, Joseph, who sat beside Georgina, and finally, Alma and Mills.

Tugores raised a glass of red wine. "I am so pleased to see four new guests at our table this evening. I hope they enjoy their stay here and, like the rest of you, return again and again. Here's to friends old and new." He glanced, in turn, at Alma and Mills and Stella and Nick. *"Salud, mi amigos."*

Before he could take a sip, the tranquility of the intimate setting was interrupted by boisterous laughter and the bright glow of the clubhouse's motion-activated lights. A young woman, clad only in a string bikini, was dipping her toe into the swimming pool and posing provocatively while a young man in swim trunks and a T-shirt recorded her on his phone. "Oh, yeah! That's it," he egged her on. "We've got a future influencer right here!"

"Perdóname." Tugores excused himself before setting off to address the couple in question and direct them back to El Sueño del Mar.

"That's been happening more often recently," Ellie informed Stella and Nick. "Ever since Caballero Cove was sold to Quintana Hospitalidad."

"There used to be a fence around Caballero Cove," Kendal explained.

"Not along the beach, of course," Ellie clarified.

"No, not along the beach, but the gardens, pool, dining room, and bungalows were cut off from the Sueño del Mar property. The beach was cordoned off as well, with a sign indicating that anything behind that point was private property. During peak beach times, there were Caballero staff patrolling the beach to make sure no one trespassed. It was nice because there was one way in and one way out: through the main lobby.

"Now there's nothing at all on the beach to tell people they can't just come wandering in, so they do. Not all the time, but often enough to be a nuisance," Kendal lamented while gently rubbing her belly.

"We've even had some of the locals stumble in after they've had one too many," Georgina, seated to Stella's right, elaborated. "Remember last year, Ellie, when we found that man, er, 'watering' the hibiscus in the garden outside your bungalow?"

"Oh. My. God," Ellie exclaimed. "How could I forget?"

"It's a wonder we haven't all been murdered in our beds," Bernard complained.

"Bernard!" his wife chastised.

"That's a little dramatic, don't you think?" Kendal questioned. "I saw the guy from the living room window. He was inebriated, but harmless."

"He was, but it's only a matter of time until some riffraff takes advantage of the situation," Bernard insisted.

"There are pickpockets and purse snatchers in this town, but murderers? Come on, Bernard," Kendal argued.

"You don't know that there aren't. I'm telling you, one night, while we're all asleep . . ." He drew a finger across his throat, prompting Joseph Penrod to gaze mournfully at the seat across the table from him.

"Bernard," Georgina again chastised.

Meanwhile, Chip Ruckert clearly hadn't noticed Penrod's expression. "Bernard's right. You never know what people are capable of, especially when cornered. You were lucky the man in Ellie and Kendal's garden didn't become violent when confronted. Then there's the hotel next door—El Sueño, the dream. More like a nightmare, what with the people there partying all the time."

Desirée rolled her eyes as she sipped her martini. "They're young people having fun! Give them a break."

"I thought El Sueño del Mar was a luxury hotel," Alma said as a waiter presented her with a salad of hearts of palm, avocado, tomato, cilantro, and red onion.

"It is," Desirée confirmed. "It's geared to a younger crowd and is extremely trendy."

"Trendy with the sort of kids you just saw a little while ago. Looking for fame on social media instead of pursuing a career," Chip grumbled.

"Says the man who inherited both his money and his business from his father."

"I reinvested that money. I didn't spend it on a luxury trip to Mexico. And what happened? The business flourished. It now earns twenty times what it did when my old man owned it. Twenty times!"

"Uh-huh," Desirée yessed him. She was far more interested in her salad plate.

"Say, you go to that hotel all the time, don't you, Bernard?" Ray Horrocks noted from the other end of the table. "What do you think of the clientele?"

"I don't think of them at all because I don't have much to do with them," the Englishman replied. "I go to the hotel to use the gym because we lack the proper facilities here."

"I'm surprised you don't run on the beach," Anika Banerjee remarked. "Here you are in paradise, away from the winter weather, and you exercise in a gym."

The other guests nodded and chuckled in agreement.

"Bernard's a creature of habit, he is," Georgina stated. "Has his own routine and won't budge from it."

"There are certain exercises I have to do—for my heart," Bernard explained. "You know that, Georgie."

"Yes, yes, I know. Just having a laugh." She turned her attention to the end of the table. "Jogging along the beach just won't do, I'm afraid, Anika. So, it's off to the gym for our Bernard."

"I imagine the hotel gym is state-of-the-art," Nick commented.

"It, er, it suits all my needs," Bernard replied.

"Maybe I'll stop in one afternoon and check it out."

"Again, why?" Anika tittered. "For Bernard, it makes sense, but you can swim in the pool, splash in the ocean, bike ride through town, and run on the beach. Why work out in an air-conditioned gym?"

"I'm with Anika on this one," Stella agreed. "We left minus five degrees back in Vermont. I plan to slather on the sunblock and be outside as much as possible."

"Do you have any activities scheduled during your stay?" Diana inquired.

"Well, Charlie and I are getting married for a start," Alma declared.

"That's fabulous news!"

Alma and Mills's tablemates took turns congratulating the couple.

"If this is a celebration, then you definitely have to get out to the Mayan ruins at Tulum," Anika advised.

Kendal agreed with Anika. "It's a very spiritual place. The temples that look like pyramids and that view of the ocean and the white-sand beach . . . simply breathtaking. We spent an entire day there when we got engaged."

"We did," Ellie confirmed. "It's a bit of a drive, but the hotel runs a shuttle bus. You can schedule a time for the driver to take you out there. There's a flat fee for the trip, which can be divided by everyone in your group."

"What do you think, Charlie?" Alma posed to Mills.

"Sounds great to me," Mills approved. "You only get one honeymoon trip—especially at our age."

"And Stella and Nick?"

Stella glanced across the table at her husband, who gave a nod. "We're in!"

Ellie looked up from her phone, her blue eyes sparkling in the candlelight. "I just reserved the shuttle for tomorrow at noon. You, um, you mind a couple of tagalongs joining you?"

"We'd discussed going to Tulum before this little guy arrives on the scene." Kendal rubbed her growing belly.

"The more the merrier," Alma replied.

"Yeah, you two might be able to point out some things we would normally miss on our own," Nick added.

"I've been to Cozumel, but in all our time coming here, we've never gone to Tulum," Bernard said.

"Why don't you come along?" Ellie invited.

"Oh, no, I couldn't do that," he replied.

Georgina chimed in, "No, touring isn't for us."

"Are you sure?" Kendal questioned. "The ruins are amazing. You should see them at least once. They really are a bucket list item."

"I'm sure, pet. You know I'm not much for gallivanting. When I'm on holiday, I like to stay put and become part of the scenery."

"Giving new meaning to the phrase the hills have eyes . . ." Diana said beneath her breath, much to her husband's and friends' amusement.

Georgina didn't react to the comment, but it was entirely possible that she hadn't heard it.

"You should go, Georgie," Joseph Penrod urged in a thick Southern drawl. "Do you some good to get out of Playa del Carmen for a day."

"And it would do you some good if I were out of your hair for a day." Georgina smirked.

Penrod's face flushed a bright crimson. "I never said that, Georgie. I—I just—"

"Know what it's like to have regrets?" she inserted with a wry smile.

The elderly man fell silent and slid his eyes toward the empty seat on the other side of the table.

"No," Georgina went on, "it would be far better to stay here by the pool with my knitting, looking out at the sea, than to pack my cranky backside into the back of an oversized passenger van. Far better for everyone. Don't you agree, Bernard?"

He looked up from his salad. "You'd be much happier here, love. No doubt about it."

Although the couple were brightly smiling at each other, Stella thought she felt a frisson of tension between the two.

Whatever tension there might have been evaporated with the cheerful voice of Ellie Sanderson. "Sounds like we have a party of four booked, unless someone else wants to make it five. Like Joe perhaps?"

Penrod snapped from his reverie. "Hmm? No. No, I don't think so, Ellie."

"Oh, come on, Joe. It'll be fun," Kendal urged. "We'll order a boxed lunch for everyone and picnic on one of the bluffs overlooking the ocean. The weather looks good for tomorrow, too. Not a drop of rain in sight until late afternoon."

"No." Joe glanced at Georgina. "I appreciate the invitation, but there's something I need to do tomorrow. Something in town."

"We understand," Ellie said. "But you're not getting rid of us entirely. Before this trip is over, we'll show these folks some of the gorgeous cenotes in the area—limestone sink holes filled with the clearest, bluest water you'll ever see—and we'll expect you to join us, Joe."

"Okay, you've twisted my arm," the older man replied with a twinkle in his eyes that belied the melancholy expression on his face.

"Good. We'll make plans for later this week."

"Speaking of plans," Desirée segued as the waitstaff produced the main course, a platter of beautifully grilled local grouper, stuffed with jalapeño, capers, tomato, and olives, and served with a side of cilantro rice and sautéed peppers, onions, and zucchini. And, for the vegans in the group, baked stuffed peppers brimming with saffron rice, coriander, and plump black beans. "Are you folks aware that there's a show tonight?" she asked, her eyes fixed on Alma and Charlie.

"The website mentioned nightly entertainment," Alma replied.

"Yes, tonight there's a Chichimec dancing group, complete in traditional Mexican dress. And then, after the show, there's a dance party."

"There's always a dance party," Chip grumbled. "If you don't like dancing, you'd better brace yourself. There's always someone on stage asking you to shake something and make a fool of yourself."

"Oh, come on. It's fun and keeps you young," Desirée countered as she smoothed her sequined dress over her waist. "Plus, it's good exercise. I'll have you all know that I just celebrated my sixtieth birthday last month."

Whether it was a result of exercise, good genes, or cosmetic surgery—or perhaps a combination of all three—Desirée did, indeed, have a fabulous figure.

"I'll get my exercise on the golf course. Charlie, Nick, do either of you play?"

"No," Mills replied. "I'm more of a hiker myself. I like cross-country skiing and snowshoeing, too. Gives me a chance to observe nature."

"You can observe nature while playing golf," Chip joked. "Especially at the nineteenth hole! How about you, Nick?"

"Sorry, I'm afraid I'm into more outdoorsy stuff too."

"Golf *is* outdoorsy. You should see the views from some of the courses I play here. Beautiful. Absolutely beautiful."

"I have no doubt that they are, but I'd rather be in the thick of those surroundings than looking at them from a golf course."

"Nick is a, um, what do you call it in the States? A ranger?" Georgina asked.

"That's right," Nick confirmed. "A ranger with the U.S. Forest Service."

"A ranger?" Chip exclaimed. "Where do you live? Colorado?"

"Vermont. My wife and I moved there recently, but Alma and Mills here have lived there their whole lives."

"Vermont? You folks oughta move to Texas. Much better weather. You can play golf year-round! Oh, that's right. You guys don't play golf, do you? My late wife, Nancy, used to play golf. So did this one here." Chip indicated Desirée. "Now she seems more interested in dancing."

"I still go golfing, Chip," Desirée maintained as she flipped her platinum hair extensions over one shoulder. "I'm just broadening my interests. You'd play golf every day if you could and you often do. I like to mix things up a little. Some sunbathing, some dance lessons, some tennis lessons . . ."

"I'm paying through the nose for all those lessons."

"You told me to do what I wanted while we're here. Besides, I have some money of my own. My late husband left me a nice sum," she explained to her fellow diners.

"Not enough to cover everything you've been up to. I'm considering counting this trip as your Christmas present."

Desirée shrugged. "Fine with me."

"That's because you go out and buy what you want all the time, anyway," Chip grumbled.

"I've seen you on the dance floor, Desirée, and I must say I can't see why you need lessons at all," Georgina said with a smirk. "You have excellent rhythm."

"Thanks, Georgie," the blonde snapped in reply.

"That's what I say," Chip agreed. "Paying for lessons with these losers is ridiculous. If you want lessons, you can get them back home, from real professionals."

"Sebastián and his team *are* professionals! And what better place to learn to salsa and merengue?"

"You can learn those back home at the club. And probably for less money."

"Really? Your fancy club is going to provide authentic Latin dance lessons?"

"They will if I demand it."

Desirée sighed noisily.

"If they don't, you can always try your hand at swing dancing," Georgina suggested. "I believe some of your friends at the other end of the table might know something about that."

She was met with blank stares from the Horrockses and the Banerjees.

"Oops!" Georgina put a hand to her mouth. "Oh, no, I'm sorry it wasn't swing dancing. I must have confused it with something else."

The couples' vacant expressions rapidly turned sour.

"But I want to learn to dance here, in Mexico," Desirée went on, ignoring Georgina's odd remarks. "I want to enjoy myself while on vacation."

"Well, you're certainly doing that! How many martinis is that today?"

"This is my first. But you can be damned certain it won't be my last."

A dark cloud descended upon the group, dispelled only by the cheerful voice of Ellie Sanderson. "Nothing wrong with a drink or two—or even three! It is vacation, after all. I'm definitely having another glass of wine." She poured herself another serving of red from the carafe on the table. "Anyone else want one?"

Diana Horrocks thrust her glass forward. "Me. I do."

"I wish I could," Kendal said with a laugh.

"You'll be there soon," Ellie assured her wife.

"When are you due?" Alma asked. "Do you know the sex of the baby?"

"March," Kendal replied. "A baby boy."

"Oh, how exciting!"

"Life's about to change for you," Anika noted.

"Big-time," Manish added.

"But in a good way. There will be times when . . . ugh." Anika shook her head. "But it's all worth it. I miss our son being around since he's gone away to school. The house is so quiet."

"Yeah, everyone gives lots of advice on parenting, but no one tells you how to get on with life once they've moved on," Diana sympathized.

"I would think you'd all be happy to have some time to yourselves again," Desirée commented.

"I am. I'm delighted that I no longer hear someone shouting 'Mom' at me while I'm in the bathroom. But that doesn't negate the fact that it leaves you feeling a bit empty, like, 'Okay, I've raised my daughter. Now what? What am I supposed to do next?'"

"Hmph," Georgina grunted from her spot beside Stella. She did not expound upon the reason for the sound, but instead sat with a contented look on her face, sipping a glass of white wine and staring off into the distance.

The remainder of dinner passed without incident. Stella, Nick,

Alma, and Mills chatted happily with the other guests, discussing their hometowns, learning the best places to purchase souvenirs, favorite spots to watch the sunset, and the best things to do while in Cozumel. Which consisted primarily of diving.

After a dessert of lusciously light and creamy mango sherbet with coconut cookies, the group rose from the table. Desirée, despite having recommended the after-dinner show, retreated with Chip to the bar and a gloomy Penrod wandered back to his bungalow to read a book. The others moved to the pool area, where rows of chairs had been arranged in front of the stage.

A few well-heeled couples in formal attire and several middle-aged women in a colorful array of cocktail dresses—most likely guests of El Sueño—were there, sipping champagne in anticipation of the start of the show.

The remainder of the seats filled in rapidly with other well-dressed guests, the majority of whom were female. Within minutes of the poolside seats and tables filling up, the stage lights dimmed. Dancers, some in brightly colored outfits with full skirts and others in crisp white shirts, bolero jackets, tight-fitting trousers, and wide-brimmed sombreros stomped, swished, and twirled about the boards in a highly entertaining demonstration of traditional Mexican dance.

At the end of the hour-long performance, the dancers took a bow to a round of generous applause before the lights dimmed again. "Bravo," Mills cheered while Nick gave a loud hoot.

When the lights came back on, the hotel staff quickly stacked the audience chairs onto waiting trolleys and wheeled them away. "Wow, they're not letting the grass grow beneath their feet, are they?" Alma remarked.

"No," Stella replied as she watched their fellow audience members flood the bar.

"Hey, we're off to our bungalow. Kendal's tired so we're just going to watch some TV in bed," Ellie told them by way of a good night.

"Of course," Alma said. "We might not be far behind ya. We caught an early flight this morning."

"Yeah, good night," Stella bade. "We'll see you in the morning."

"Good night," Nick and Mills echoed.

Before the friends could discuss their nighttime plans with each other, Georgina Early sidled up to Stella. "Sticking around for the, erm, disco part of the evening?"

"Oh, is that what this is?" Alma asked. "Maybe. Might be fun."

Stella nodded. "A dance or two to work off dinner might be a good idea."

"Good lord, yes. Although a little glass of wine as a nightcap sounds good too."

"More of that tempranillo?" Nick confirmed before he and Mills headed off to the bar.

Georgina gave a sardonic laugh. "Well, if you're looking for a cardio workout, you're in the right place."

Alma and Stella exchanged puzzled glances, but Georgina didn't offer an explanation. "Well, I'm knackered. Off to bed with me. You ladies enjoy the rest of your night," she purred before setting off for her bungalow.

"What was that all about?" Alma wondered aloud.

"No idea, but did you notice a little bit of a 'vibe' during dinner?"

"Yeah, I'm not sure people like Georgie very much."

"Well, she does have a strong personality, doesn't she? It always feels as if she knows something you don't."

"Arrogance."

"Maybe. Or maybe . . . maybe she does actually know something."

With that, the lights on the stage went dim and the acoustic guitar music that had accompanied the traditional dancers was suddenly replaced with the booming bass of club music.

"Oh, my . . . perhaps I'm a little old for this after all."

"Nonsense! You're just as young as those women lined up by the stage. Probably younger. Just drink your wine, bob your head to the beat, and dance with your man. And then, when we're all tired and can't dance any longer"—Stella glanced at the time on her phone—"which will probably be in thirty minutes or so, we'll go back to our bungalows and collapse. And I'll probably be the first."

"Nah. Charlie will. He woke up every thirty minutes last night, anticipating the alarm going off. I'm surprised he's still awake now."

If Mills had been feeling drowsy, what happened next was certain to wake him up. As he and Nick returned with their drinks, the lights came up on the stage to reveal a line of a dozen handsome young men, all dressed in fitted black dress shirts, tight black trousers, and matching purple sequined vests. As they bumped, gyrated, and twerked in time to the music, the middle-aged women who had swarmed the performance area squealed in delight.

"Is this the Riviera Maya or Chippendales?" Nick quipped as he handed a glass of tempranillo to his wife.

"I'm no prude, but I hope they're not going to take their clothes off," Alma shouted over the pulsating rhythm.

"I doubt it," Mills said, passing Alma her glass of wine and then taking a sip of his beer. "Didn't the Horrockses and Banerjees bring their kids here?"

"That was a few years ago," Stella said. "Before the hotel was sold."

"Yeah, this doesn't seem like the kind of thing that would have been going on back then," Nick agreed. "The kids would never have gone off to sleep with this noise."

The dancers split off into two groups. The first group remained on the stage and invited audience members to come up and dance with them. The second dispersed into the crowd, where they were bombarded by eager women looking for a dance partner. One of the dancers in this second group pushed past the crowds and headed directly toward Desirée, who immediately threw her arms around his neck and kissed him on the cheek.

"So, about those dance lessons . . ." Mills remarked as Desirée and the dancer began to move in time to the music, their bodies pressed tightly together.

"I don't think she'll get lessons like that at the club back at home," Alma completed the sheriff's thought.

"I don't know about that. You've seen *Dirty Dancing*, haven't you?" Nick teased.

"*Dirty Dancing* takes place at a high-end summer resort, not a country club."

"Resort, country club . . . does it really matter? Bottom line is Chip would have more control over a dancer back at home who he hired than he does over a dancer here in Playa del Carmen."

"Speaking of Chip, where is he?" Stella questioned.

"Over there, by the bar." Mills gestured at the table where Chip was seated. His hands were in his lap and his chin rested on his chest, as though in a deep sleep.

"How can he sleep through this?"

"Judging by the empty glasses in front of him, he probably had some help," Nick noted.

"He was drinking Scotch at dinner," Mills added. "And from the smell of him, a little before too."

"Do you think he's okay?" Stella asked. "Should we check on him?"

"You don't think . . . ?"

"I don't know. You have a lot more experience in these matters."

Before there could be any further discussion, Chip Ruckert jolted awake, folded his arms across his rounded belly, and proceeded to go back to sleep.

"Will you two stop it?" Alma shouted. "I'm not spending my wedding trip listening to the two of you debate whether hotel guests are dead. You do enough of that at home."

"Sorry," Stella apologized.

"Sorry," a sheepish Mills muttered.

"I'm here to have some fun." She took Mills by the arm. "Let's go get a table, put our drinks down, and dance!"

Alma's companions were in no position to argue with the bride-to-be. Likewise, they, too, wanted to enjoy a week of warm weather, tropical beaches, Mayan ruins, and a little not-too-late nightlife, so they followed her to a poolside table, deposited their beverages, and moved to the tiled area in front of the stage.

The DJ, clearly noting the number of couples on the dance floor, switched to a tender ballad. "That's better," Stella stated as Nick put his arm around her waist and pulled her closer.

"Much better," he agreed. "You know, I'm not one for weddings—the same old catering hall food, the oversweet wedding cake, the family drama. But I love this wedding getaway idea."

"Me too. Reminds me of our own wedding—which I loved, apart

from all the stress beforehand. Trying to please my mother, trying to please your mother, trying to make everyone happy. It was a lot of pressure."

"Are you saying you'd have preferred a wedding getaway like this one?"

"No, I wouldn't change a thing. However, if we ever renew our vows, I'll be the first one logging onto my travel app."

"I wouldn't change a thing, either. Everything about that day was perfect. You—you were perfect."

She smiled. "Why do I get the feeling that this whole wedding getaway is making you feel more than a little bit romantic?"

"Because it is." He pulled her closer as they swayed in time to the music. "I might give you a hard time about getting rid of my old T-shirts, but these past eight years with you have been the best years of my life."

"They've been the best years of my life as well."

"And I know we'll have some ups and downs as most couples do, but I also believe that things will only get better. Look how far we've come since that first apartment of ours near the train tracks."

"How could I forget that place? You didn't want to be on the toilet or in the tub when the five forty-five express rolled through," she recalled with a laugh.

"Now we have our own home and my job is secure. We're doing better than we've ever done. But I also realize that my job is only secure because of the sacrifice you made. Giving up your position at the museum and moving to Vermont went above and beyond what I ever expected—what any spouse could expect. I don't want you to ever think that I don't appreciate what you've done or that I take it or you for granted."

"I know you don't."

"Good." Nick smiled at her. "I look forward to the next chapter in our lives."

"The next chapter?"

"Yeah, we have the house, the dog—"

"My mother."

"For once, she'd actually like what I'm about to say."

Stella's body stiffened as she braced herself for Nick's next words. "She would?"

"Uh-huh. Being around Ellie and Kendal today got me thinking. Well, I started thinking about this the moment we learned that we got the house. As I said, we're in a good spot in our lives and we're not getting any younger . . ."

She gave a nervous laugh. "Gee, thanks!"

"You know what I mean. We're in a different phase in our lives, Stell. Leaving our thirties behind us, putting down roots, your restoration business is taking off. You're your own boss now. You work from home and you have a lot more flexibility than you had at the museum, where you worked sixty-hour weeks. And then there's your mother."

Stella raised a questioning eyebrow.

"Lila seems to be putting down stakes in Vermont, meaning that even after she moves out, she'll probably still be nearby, which could come in handy," Nick continued. "What I'm trying—and failing—to say is that I'd like us to consider starting a family."

Nick had blurted out the last sentence so quickly that Stella—despite anticipating it—had to think about what had just been said.

"This is . . . this is . . . unexpected. I mean the timing of it is unexpected. Not the *overall* timing, of course," she explained without taking a breath. "As you said, we're in our late thirties and we probably should be thinking about, you know, families and stuff. But the timing—with us being here for Alma and Mills's wedding—makes this conversation unexpected."

"Yeah, I guess the timing is a little odd."

"I just feel like we should be focused on supporting them right now."

"And we are. Supporting them and discussing our future aren't mutually exclusive, you know."

Stella realized that over the course of their discussion she and Nick had stopped dancing. Alma had taken notice and was watching them. Not wishing to cause her friend concern, she flashed her a broad smile, gave Nick a nudge and the couple resumed their rhythmic swaying. "You know, we very well might be in a new phase in our lives. When we were first together, you never would have used the phrase 'mutually exclusive' in an ordinary conversation."

"I was such a dork," Nick reflected. "I'm still amazed you even agreed to go out with me."

"Maybe I saw a diamond in the rough."

"Or it was Be Kind to Animals Week."

"After all these years, you finally found me out. It *was* Be Kind to Animals Week."

They laughed, embraced, and resumed their dance. When the ballad ended a few moments later, the DJ followed with a high-tempo dance track, spurring Nick to take Stella by the hand and give her an old school disco twirl. Stella happily complied, spinning outward from Nick and then back toward him, throwing her arms around his neck upon arrival.

"Señora Buckley?"

Stella looked up to see Renata, the server who'd poured them champagne upon their arrival. "Yes?"

"Inés sent me to talk to you."

"Inés?"

"She cleaned your room before your arrival. She wants you to know how sorry she is."

"Sorry for what?"

"The hat. The hat from the gentleman who had the room before you."

Stella immediately relaxed. "Oh, that. Tell Inés she needn't worry. I didn't file a complaint, I only turned in the hat so that it could be returned to its owner."

The young woman's face blanched.

"What's wrong?" Stella asked.

"The vicar—the gentleman who owned the hat—he isn't missing it. He's dead."

Chapter Three

"**B**ixby. Bixby! Look at Grandma." Lila Thornton stood in the living room of the Buckley residence and cajoled the black Labrador retriever resting on the hearth of the woodstove. "Bixby, look at Grandma and the camera."

Bixby didn't react. He remained motionless, staring straight ahead, his chin propped up on the edge of his fleece-lined dog bed.

"Prolly misses your daughter and son-in-law," Clyde Perkins suggested.

"Probably. But he should know me by now. I'm not a stranger taking care of him."

"It's the vibes," the college student Clyde had hired to take promotional photos announced.

"Vibes?" an incredulous Clyde repeated.

"Yeah, there's different energy when a family's all together than when they're separated. It's all about the vibes. You should get some pheromone spray to help him relax. Or maybe try aromatherapy."

"My pet deodorizers *are* therapeutic," Lila countered as she placed her hands upon her hips. "They're made with essential oils."

"You could try a calming vest. Or, I know, why don't you take him for a massage?"

"A massage? For a dog?" Clyde shook his head in disgust. "We'll handle this ourselves and let you know when Bixby's back to his ol' self."

The young man shrugged. "Sure. Text me and I'll be here."

"Text? Why don't young people call each other anymore?" Clyde lamented once the student had left.

"I don't know, but they'll probably blame it on their parents. All those times Mom pushed them to call Grandma to thank her for their birthday gifts had a negative effect on their psyches. Yep, it'll be Mom's fault, I bet."

"Can't rightly comment as I've never had kids. Never even had a wife. But I do know that you're a bit of terrific." He moved closer and put an arm around her shoulders.

They made a strange couple. Lila was slim, in her late sixties, immaculately dressed and highly attractive, with perfectly coiffed, highlighted blonde hair. Clyde, on the other hand, was in his mid-seventies, bald, slight-of-figure, and with more than a passing resemblance to the female figure in the painting *American Gothic*.

What they did have in common was a love of money. Given the success of Clyde's general store, he could have afforded the nicest house in Teignmouth, but instead lived in an apartment at the back of the store and saved his cash. Cash that Lila Thornton wouldn't at all mind spending.

Lila had been married twice—once to Stella's father, whom she divorced, and then to a wealthy banker who passed away years later. From there she found herself in a long-term relationship with a real estate developer who lavished gifts upon her, but also kept her isolated from friends and family. That relationship ended just before Thanksgiving, when he threw her out of his house so that he could move his new—and much younger—girlfriend in.

Homeless and alone, Lila rented a car and landed on Stella and Nick's doorstep, where she was welcome to stay until she put her life back on track. A job at the cosmetics counter in Clyde's store was a critical first step in that journey. However, creating a best-selling doggie deodorizer and having Clyde on board to help develop and promote it would make her dream of a new car and a home of her own, without a man's name on the rental agreement, come to fruition that much quicker.

"You're beautiful, creative, dedicated, and whip-smart," Clyde continued.

It had been years since Lila had heard such praise. Toward the end of her last relationship, all she heard was never-ceasing criticism, but Lila wasn't about to let it go to her head. "I'm not always very smart."

"Still ahead of those folks who've never been smart at all."

She couldn't help but crack a smile. "You have a point there."

"So, what do we do about our canine friend? Should we get your daughter and son-in-law on that video calling thing on your phone?"

"No, Stella and Nick don't know that we're going to use Bixby's image for my products." She cast him a sideways glance. "They don't know you're here either."

"Should prolly keep it that way for now. I sold 'em an air mattress without a pump when they first arrived. Not sure they're over that yet."

"Why would you have done such a thing?"

"Thought they were flatlanders."

"Flatlanders?"

"Folks from the flat states: New York, New Jersey, Connecticut . . . you know, not from around here."

"By that definition, they *are* flatlanders."

"Yup, I just didn't know they were *your* flatlanders."

"But I'm a flatlander, too."

"Yup, but you're not like other flatlanders. You make Vermont a better place."

"Clyde," she sang in warning.

"Don't 'Clyde' me. It's true. You bring style to Teignmouth. Charm. Class."

"And a dog who won't listen," she lamented as Bixby began to snore.

"Looks fine to me. Maybe he needs obedience training."

"He usually listens. Besides, we can't get him trained in less than a week."

"Maybe you should call the vet."

She shook her head. "His appetite is fine and he enjoyed his evening walk. Also, if I make an appointment, the vet might call Stella and Nick."

"Hmm. I can ask some of the farmers who come to the store. They know a lot about animals."

"Maybe. Let me spend some time alone with him first. Stella and Nick just left and, although I love having you here, Bixby doesn't know you very well. It's only natural that he might be nervous."

Clyde pursed his lips. "Suppose that makes sense. I don't like most folks when I first meet 'em either. 'Cept you, of course, Lila."

"That's very sweet, Clyde. I liked you straightaway, too."

He grinned from ear to ear, but his smile quickly faded. "Say, if that dog is nervous around people, how's he gonna react to a whole crowd of new faces?"

Lila frowned. "Oh, you mean the launch party?"

"Yup. Are we still on for Friday?"

"Yes, twelve dogs and their owners will be here at ten in the morning to test our Posh Pooch products. I've alerted the local papers."

"Good." Clyde made his way into the kitchen and to the door that opened onto the driveway. "Good night, Lila. I sure hope Bixby comes 'round soon."

Lila bid him good night and returned to the living room, where the black Lab was snoring in his bed. "I sure hope he does, too."

Chapter Four

Stella slept fitfully that night. The combination of a new bed, the overly long day, and an extra glass of red wine had certainly played their part, but there was something else nagging at her.

Waking at dawn, she wrapped herself in a turquoise floral satin kimono, exited the bedroom, and wandered barefoot into the front garden, where she stood and watched the sun rise over the beach. Apart from the hotel staff cleaning the pool and placing cushions in the surrounding chairs and chaises, the resort grounds were empty. Stella relished the quiet, the soothing sound of the waves as they lapped upon the shore, the promise of a new day.

Yet she was still haunted by the images of the vicar's hat as it rested upon the closet shelf and the expression on Inés's face when she informed her and Nick that the owner of that hat was dead. Why did Inés appear so fearful?

Then there was the matter of Joseph Penrod. Stella had assumed that his emotional state at dinner was due to being, once again, at the resort where he had vacationed with his wife and children. Indeed, he might have, but what if he had also been reacting to the loss of a good friend? What if the seat opposite Penrod, in addition to being occupied all those years by his wife, had recently been vacated by the deceased vicar?

Stella's thoughts were interrupted by the presence of a waiter in full uniform, bearing a silver coffee service and a white ceramic cup. "señora?"

The staff setting up for the day must have alerted him to her presence.

"Gracias," she gratefully accepted. Sipping coffee in a lush garden while watching a Mexican seaside sunrise? This must be a dream. A dream she was ruining with unfounded suspicions about a deceased vicar.

Inés would, quite naturally, be afraid to tell a guest that a former guest passed away in their room. Likewise, if the vicar was friends with Joseph Penrod, then it stood to reason that he was most likely also rather elderly. Although his passing was tragic and certainly an event to mourn, there were worse places to spend one's last days.

She drew a deep breath and vowed not to allow her thoughts to spiral out of control. They were on vacation—in paradise, no less!—to celebrate Alma and Mills's wedding. There were no cases to solve, no restoration work to perform. This was a rare opportunity to clear her mind and thoroughly relax. Taking the coffee cup from the waiter's tray, she sat down at the teak bistro set just outside their bungalow gate. From there, she had a perfect view of the beach, pool area, and the other guest bungalows.

She was nearly finished with her coffee when Ray Horrocks, fresh from a jog along the beach, stopped by. "Mornin'. How'd you sleep?"

"Oh, fine. It takes me a little while to get adjusted to a new bed."

"Yeah, Diana's the same way. Sleeps like a log on the second night though."

"I'll probably do the same. Hey, someone mentioned to us last night that the gentleman who stayed in our bungalow prior to us . . ." Stella stopped herself. Ray Horrocks was on vacation. *She* was on vacation. What was she doing asking questions about the vicar?

Ray, however, didn't seem to mind. "Ah, you heard about Reverend Bailor, huh? No one wanted to mention him, what with your friends getting married."

"I appreciate that. I'm not going to mention anything to them, either."

"Yeah, the vicar—no one ever called him Reverend—died four days ago. It was real sudden, but not a surprise, I guess. He was up there in years. Heart attack, local police said. The vicar was a super nice guy. He was English, loved to lie out in his cabana on the beach and read, but he also liked shopping in town and visiting the local restaurants. Everyone liked him, but Joe probably was closest to him, them being the same age and all."

"That's why Joe was so downcast during dinner."

Ray nodded. "The two of them were always talking about books and wines and places they'd traveled. It's too bad for ol' Joe. Having the vicar around made this place more like home after his wife died. With the vicar gone, I'm not sure he'll come back again next year."

"That would be unfortunate. How long had the vicar been coming here?"

"About three or four years. Long enough for Joe and him to become close and for all of us to feel like we've lost a friend."

Stella expressed her sympathy. "I'm very sorry."

"Thanks. I'm sorry for the people in his community. The vicar was retired from preaching, but it sounded like he did a lot of work in his neighborhood food bank. No doubt they'll miss him even more than we do."

"A food bank? What a loss for them."

"Mmm. Hey, I'd better get moving if I'm going to reserve some seats for Diana and me. See you later, okay?"

"Yeah, yeah. Have a good rest of the morning."

As Ray jogged a couple of laps around the pool area, Stella returned her attention to the shoreline. It promised to be a beautiful day, perfect weather for an outing to Tulum. But what to do until then?

Remembering the book she'd brought along—one she'd been wanting to read for months—Stella went inside and retrieved it from her bedside table. As anticipated, Nick was sound asleep.

Upon her return to the garden, she found that the sun had fully cleared the horizon and was shining brilliantly on the bistro table and hotel buildings. Realizing that the blinding rays would make reading difficult, if not impossible, she switched chairs and sat, instead, with her back to the sun and beach and facing the clubhouse.

After his jog, Ray covered two of the lounge chairs with beach towels before disappearing into the office/clubhouse. He emerged several minutes later in a pair of swim trunks, sunglasses, and a clean T-shirt and proceeded to stretch out on one of the towel-clad chairs. As Ray read from a tablet, the waiter who had served Stella coffee presented him with a tall glass of green juice and a white ceramic dish bearing a single muffin. Ray looked up from his tablet just long enough to accept his post-run repast, then returned his attention to the device.

Stella was about to return her attention to her book when she noticed that the same waiter was headed her way, this time carrying a carafe of coffee and a small pitcher of milk. She took note of his name tag. "Pedro, you're spoiling me."

"Sí, señora. That is what we are supposed to do."

"Well, you're doing an excellent job."

"Es un placer, señora."

He poured some coffee into Stella's empty cup, added a splash of milk, and left both carafe and pitcher on the table in anticipation of future refills, before heading back to the clubhouse. What Pedro hadn't anticipated was walking headlong into Georgina Early as she emerged from the garden of her bungalow.

"Oi," she shouted to the head of the pool, ignoring the fact she'd hit poor Pedro with the garden gate. "Oi, Raymond! What's all this about? You know that's my spot!"

"There are plenty of other chairs around, Georgie. You have your pick."

"I have picked. I pick the one you're sitting in."

Ray sighed noisily. "Georgie . . ."

"Georgie, nothing. How many years have you been coming here? You know that's my spot."

"I'm well aware that this is 'your spot,' but had it ever occurred to you that the rest of us might also like to enjoy the best view of the pool and the beach?"

"You can get a view of the pool and the beach from any of the lounge chairs surrounding the other sides of the pool. You simply have to turn your head."

Ray's wife, Diana, had emerged from their bungalow and had joined her husband poolside. "What's going on here? I could hear you two shouting from our casita."

"I should have known you were behind this," Georgina exclaimed.

"Behind what?"

"Taking my chair."

"That's ridiculous," Ray asserted. "No one's behind anything. We simply wanted to watch the shore this morning. You can have your chair back after breakfast."

"I never eat breakfast. You should know that after all these years. You two can watch the shore from the beach," Georgina instructed. "There are loungers and cabanas there."

"There's no waitstaff on the beach until noon."

"So, wait until breakfast for your coffee or whatever that stuff is." She waved a finger at Ray's glass of green juice. "Or if you're really desperate, get the juice yourself from the clubhouse. You're into fitness, Ray, all the back-and-forth from the beach will take a lap off your routine. Especially the way that one eats." Georgie hiked a thumb at Diana, who let out a shriek.

"The way I eat? Maybe *you* should sit on the beach, you'd look exactly like a beached whale!"

"A whale, am I?"

"That's right. That's probably why you like that chair of yours so much. The waiter's always nearby."

"Okay now, let's lower the temperature here," Ray suggested.

"Lower the temperature? You're going to let Georgie talk to me like that?"

"No, I'm not. Georgie, this is unacceptable. You're making a huge fuss out of nothing. We'll be heading into breakfast in a few minutes, anyway."

"More like an hour than a few minutes. They're not even serving yet! Listen, I always get up at dawn and come out here and knit in my favorite spot. It's what I do."

"Just because we're sitting here doesn't mean you can't sit here too. You're welcome to sit beside us and knit. Even though you've been outrageously rude, we still invite you to join us."

"Join you? The seat beside the two of you isn't my spot!"

"My God, Georgie, you have some serious issues," Ray accused.

"*I* have issues? You're trying to keep me—someone you've known for years—from enjoying my holiday to the fullest."

"That's not true, Georgie. You could be just as happy in any other chair. You're just being unreasonable."

"I couldn't be happy somewhere else. I wouldn't be. I've sat in that spot in all my years of coming here. I've never sat anywhere else."

"Maybe it's time for a change," Diana replied.

"This place has already changed enough for my liking. It seems to be overrun by insensitive clods!"

"Insensitive clods? You're the one who's insensitive, Georgie. How about giving someone else a chance to enjoy the view and some early morning coffee?"

"You do have a chance to enjoy the view . . . just not in my seat!"

Diana clenched her fists. "Georgie, you are absolutely the most infuriating, most stubborn, most—"

Señor Tugores, alerted by his staff and, most likely, the shouts of his arguing guests, emerged from the clubhouse. As usual, he appeared cool and collected in a perfectly pressed white linen suit. "What is the problem?"

"These two"—Georgina pointed accusingly at Ray, who had finally risen from his seat, and Diane, who stood beside him—"took my seat without even asking!"

"Señora Early, I sincerely doubt that Señor y Señora Horrocks meant any harm. They are your friends."

"The hell they are. They conspired to be out here this morning, before I'd even gotten out of bed."

"Now, Señora Early, please stop accusi—"

"No, señor, she's right. That's what we did," Diana confessed. "Today is our wedding anniversary and we decided to spend the start of the day together, here by the pool, quietly sipping our drinks, enjoying an early breakfast, and reading the morning news. Together. And yes, we did it before you got up, because we knew if you were around, you'd throw a fit. And we were right. You're throwing a fit."

"If you knew I'd be upset, why do it at all?"

"Señora Early does make a very valid point," Tugores said diplomatically. "If you knew it might bother her, why do it?"

"Oh, I'll tell you why, Señor Tugores—because they *wanted* to upset me."

"Señora Early, you go too far!"

"She always goes too far," Diana asserted. "We honestly didn't want to upset you, Georgie, but you know what? Now that you mentioned it, I'm tired of tiptoeing around you, trying to stay in your good graces."

"Diana," Ray warned.

"No, Ray. I'm done. I'm tired of trying not to make Georgie angry, for fear of what she might do. I'm tired of it all, but most of all, I'm tired of you, Georgie, you old shrew!" Diana stormed off.

"Señora Horrocks!" Tugores shouted after her.

"Diana didn't mean all that," Ray attempted to apologize. "She has a bad temper. She reacts without thinking, but she'll come to her senses."

"You and I both know that's not true, Ray. She meant every single word of it."

"No, she—she's just going through a rough time right now, Georgina. Don't hold it against her."

"She should have thought of that before she started calling me names."

Stella, who'd been peeking over the top of her book, cocked her head to one side. It was Georgina who'd started the name-calling. Why didn't Ray set the record straight and correct her obvious lie? And what about Señor Tugores? If he really wanted to mediate, he would have urged Georgina to accept Ray's apology, but he didn't. Instead, he remained oddly silent as Ray tried to appeal to the Englishwoman's better nature.

If Stella didn't know better, she'd say both men were frightened and intimidated by Georgina Early. But why?

"Georgie, please, don't do this," Ray pleaded.

"Don't do what? You sound completely unhinged, Ray. Isn't that what you called me? Unhinged?" Georgina ripped the beach towel from the chaise lounge in question, sending Ray's tablet tumbling onto the terra-cotta tile.

"Georgina!" he screamed before bending down and retrieving the device from the ground beneath the chaise. Fortunately, it appeared to still be working. "You could have broken it. What the hell is wrong with you?"

"You call me unhinged, I'll act unhinged. Be happy that's the worst of it." She plopped down into the chair with her knitting and looked out at the beach, leaving Ray to collect his belongings and retreat to his bungalow, where Diana was no doubt waiting for him.

Once Ray had gone, Señor Tugores lingered behind Georgie, as if weighing the decision to speak to the woman. Silence eventually won out as he turned on one heel and walked back into the clubhouse.

Stella, unaware of her immediate surroundings, suddenly felt a pair of hands on her shoulders.

"What was all that about?" Nick asked softly.

"How long have you been watching?" she asked.

"I came out here right about when Diana took off." He sat in the chair opposite his wife. "The shouting woke me up."

"Ray and Diana took Georgie's seat by the pool."

"Like with force?" He opened the lid of the coffee carafe and peered inside.

"No." She pushed her now-empty coffee cup toward him. "Here. I'm done for now. Use that for yourself."

"So then why was Georgie so upset?"

"That's just the thing. Ray put their towels down before Georgie was even up. It's weird that she should react so strongly. I mean, I'm sure if she'd asked nicely, they might have moved, but she came out here ready for a fight."

"Guess she's not a morning person." He filled the cup with coffee and added a splash of milk.

"I'm not a morning person either, but I don't stumble out of bed looking to verbally attack people."

Nick put his hand out and rocked it from side to side. "Meh. That's debatable."

She tossed her bookmark at him, prompting him to nearly squirt coffee from his nose.

"Okay. Okay. I'm joking. Although your reaction kinda validates what I said."

Stella held her book aloft as if she was about to throw it, too.

"You're bluffing. You'd never throw a book," Nick said calmly.

She placed the book onto the tabletop. "You know me too well," she said with a sigh.

"I do. As you know me."

"If only we'd known what kind of resort Alma booked us into."

"I don't know . . . seems nice. The food was delicious last night. And this coffee is good." He held the cup aloft and smiled.

"You're right. It's a beautiful place and the food and service are both terrific, but you have to admit there's a weird vibe around here. Dinner last night was pretty tense."

"The guests said they're like a family. Families argue."

"I suppose . . . but an awful lot of those vibes seem to coalesce around Georgie."

"Probably because she's kind of a diva," Nick suggested as he drank his coffee. "She's been coming here for decades and obviously feels as if she owns the place. Or that she should at least be treated as if she owns the place."

"She is quite a formidable character, isn't she? Maybe that's why both Tugores and Ray Horrocks seemed to be intimidated by her just now."

"Georgie and Bernard are probably two of Tugores's best customers. He's not about to upset either one of them. And Ray . . . from what I can tell, he's a pretty laid-back guy. He's not the type to get into it with another hotel guest, especially one he's known for so long."

"The other source of last night's vibe is the vicar. Ray told me he died just a few days ago."

"That's a shame."

"Yeah."

"Was he ill?"

"No, it happened suddenly. Heart attack or something like that. Reverend Bailor was his name. He was an older gentleman."

"So, the poor guy died unexpectedly and the staff was in a hurry to clean the room so it could be rented to someone else. That explains the hat being left behind."

"But it doesn't explain why Inés was so terrified last night."

"Hon, she was worried her friend might get into trouble for not cleaning thoroughly," Nick explained.

"With all due respect, I don't think that was it."

"Of course you don't. Your brain is always looking for darker motives and explanations. I'm not judging you, it's just how you work."

"I can't argue with that, except this feels less like my brain and more like my gut."

"Is that why you're out here so early? Because your gut woke you up?"

She sighed noisily. "You really are annoying. You know that, don't you?"

"I try," he said with a smirk.

"Well, stop it. Okay, perhaps it was my brain working overtime. I just felt so bad for Inés and our housekeeper. Oh, and for Joseph Penrod. You saw how despondent he was."

"Yeah, I thought it was because of his wife."

"I did too."

"But I guess Joe was friends with Reverend Bailor, huh? They were around the same age probably."

She nodded. "Yeah, they'd grown close through the years."

"Poor guy. That's rough."

Stella looked up to see the man in question talking to Georgie. Although he was speaking softly—too softly for Stella and Nick to hear what was being said—his expression was dour. "Don't look now, but Mr. Penrod is having a discussion with Georgina."

"They're guests at the same resort. That's hardly unusual."

"This isn't a lighthearted chat. Penrod looks genuinely displeased."

"All that shouting between Georgie and Diana probably woke him up."

"Looks a bit more serious than that."

"More drama?"

"Maybe. Georgie's smiling."

"Smiling?"

"Smirking might be a more accurate description," Stella noted as she peered over the top of her book. "She looks smug about something."

"Probably the chaos she caused this morning. Penrod's ex-military, isn't he? He's organized, orderly and, whether he was woken by the argument or not, I'm pretty sure he's none too thrilled to witness such emotional scenes take place at his family's beloved vacation spot."

She watched as Penrod waved his arms in the air furiously. He was certainly giving Georgie a piece of his mind about something. *Or was he?* Stella wondered as the man suddenly placed the palms of his hands together as if to pray.

Georgie laughed loudly. Loud enough that Stella and Nick could clearly hear its sneering tone from their casita.

Nick stopped in mid-sip. "What did Penrod say to her?"

"I'm not sure, but he looked as if he might be begging or pleading."

"Pleading? For what?"

"Your guess is as good as mine."

Penrod left the pool area for the beach, his hands tucked into the pockets of his Bermuda shorts, and a look of despair upon his face.

"Mornin', Joe," Ellie and Kendal greeted him as they emerged from the front gate of their casita, which was situated on the opposite side of the pool area, just across from Stella and Nick's bungalow.

The older gentleman kept his head down and murmured a vague reply as he trudged along the path to the shore.

With a shrug, the couple, both dressed in swimsuits and cover-ups, draped their towels over the set of lounge chairs nearest yet perpendicular to Georgie's and settled in to enjoy a couple of deep pink smoothies brought to them by a member of the waitstaff.

Nick felt safe enough to turn around and glance at the three women by the pool. "Looks like the storm has passed."

"Here's hoping."

"Well, we're both awake and sufficiently caffeinated. What do you feel like doing this morning?"

"I don't know . . . how about a walk on the beach?"

He raised an eyebrow. "Because you want to walk on the beach? Or because Joseph Penrod decided to take a walk on the beach?"

She leaned back in her chair and folded her arms across her chest. "Okay, you've got me. Both."

"Stella, we're here for a wedding."

"I know, but Penrod looked upset. Between the vicar dying and whatever happened with Georgie just now, he might need a friend." She smiled at her husband. "Or two."

"Alright," he capitulated. "I'll go get changed."

She put her book down on the table and rose from her seat. "I'll join you. I can't exactly go strolling along the beach in my nightgown and robe, can I?"

"Hey, you're on vacation. Anything goes."

"Yeah . . . not quite. I'm going to pop into the bathroom. I'll be just a minute." She leaned down to give her husband a kiss. As she did so, angry shouts rose from just outside the clubhouse.

"Uh-oh. Round three comin' up."

Stella stood up and looked in Georgie's direction. This time, she didn't bother to hide behind a book.

Kendal was perched on the edge of her lounger and in great distress. "I've known for years that you were difficult and cantankerous and a terrible gossip, yet I've always defended you to other guests. But all this time, I never imagined you were homophobic!"

"Because I'm not homophobic," Georgina maintained. "Me not giving you the afghan I'm currently knitting isn't a reaction to your—your lifestyle."

"Lifestyle? Our marriage and soon-to-be family isn't a style choice."

Georgina gave a highly exaggerated sigh. "You *know* what I meant!"

"No, I don't. I told you that the afghan you're knitting is the perfect color for our nursery. It matches the wallpaper on the accent wall exactly."

"That's all well and good, but I've already told you this afghan isn't for you."

"No, you didn't. When I asked who you were knitting it for, you told me it was for no one in particular."

"What I meant to say is that I'm knitting it with someone in mind, but that I'm not sure whether or not they're going to like it."

"If you're uncertain, then why not give it to two people who've already told you they'll love it?" Ellie exclaimed. "Two people who would have treasured it because it was made by someone they considered a friend?"

Stella hadn't known Georgina for very long, but this was the first time the woman had ever appeared even remotely flustered. "It—it isn't as simple as all that!"

"Yes, it is as simple as that," Ellie said sternly.

Meanwhile, Kendal, with more than a bit of difficulty, rose from her chaise lounge. "I cannot believe we're having this conversation with you, Georgie. I simply can't! I thought you were an ally. I thought . . . I guess I should have known better. Those with closed minds always seem to have their mouths open!"

As Kendal shuffled away in tears, Ellie sprung from her seat. "How dare you! How dare you upset Kendal right now. This pregnancy has been incredibly difficult for her."

"I'm sure she'll be fine, Ellie. Women have been having children for years."

"What! Why you heartless, two-faced bitch. How can you be so cold-blooded? Kendal's health could be at risk because of the stress you just caused her."

"Because you're perfect, eh?" Georgina challenged. "I know some things about you that could really cause Kendal stress. How'd you like me to share them with her? How you behaved a few years back was disgusting!"

"You . . . I hope you rot in hell!" Ellie rushed off in pursuit of her wife, leaving behind their towels, water bottles, and other sunbathing paraphernalia.

Meanwhile, Georgie threw the afghan down into her lap and drew a deep breath—whether of relief or annoyance, Stella could not tell—before burying her face in her hands.

"Well, that was brutal," Nick said softly as he rose from his spot at the table.

"I'm glad Alma and Mills weren't here to see all this."

"Yeah, the mood around here could suck the joy out of a school group at Disney World."

She nodded. "Let's get dressed and take that walk."

"Still want to check in on Joe?"

"And Kendal."

"Then can we have breakfast?"

"If Alma and Mills are up by then. Alma said they wanted to eat with us."

He rolled his eyes. "Then we'd better include a stop at the clubhouse before the walk on the beach. I'm going to need a smoothie or a slice of toast or something before we do all that talking."

Chapter Five

Stella and Nick never saw Joseph Penrod while on their beachside walk. The senior must have either gone to town or back to his casita. They did however meet Kendal, who was feeling tired, drained, and slightly achy, so she and Ellie had decided to forgo their trip to Tulum in favor of a relaxing day in their cabana on the beach.

They left the two women lounging in the shade with their books, electronic devices, and a tray of fresh fruit and granola set before them and met Alma and Mills for breakfast in the clubhouse. Unlike the evening's communal gathering, the morning meal was taken at individual tables, allowing the guests to partake of the buffet as early or late as they liked and with whatever company they chose.

After enjoying a repast of freshly made omelets, orange mango juice, and locally grown figs, the quartet walked into town to browse some souvenir shops. Playa del Carmen was a bustling resort town, the main street of which was lined with open-air restaurants, nightclubs, and stores selling everything from scuba gear to lingerie and from brightly colored beachwear to handmade pottery and cheap, made-in-China trinkets and T-shirts.

The two couples meandered along the foot-traffic-only, brick-paved road—the appropriately named Fifth Avenue, or Quinta Avenida—basking in the scent of authentic Mexican cooking, watching as local women wove raffia baskets and handbags, and enjoying the laid-back, friendly atmosphere. At one end of the road stood a large shopping mall boasting the most popular American retail stores: Sephora, Pandora, Starbucks, American Eagle, and Levi's.

"I'm not too interested in shopping in a mall," Alma stated. "How about you folks?"

"I'd rather shop in Mexican stores," Stella agreed.

"Yeah, I've never been a fan of shopping malls," Nick concurred.

"I don't like 'em either, but this one has a smoke shop. I wouldn't mind checking in to see what sort of pipe tobacco they have. You know how I enjoy a good pipe when I sit by the woodstove," Mills said to

Alma.

"I do. Go on, Charlie, and treat yourself. I'll just have a seat out here." She indicated an empty bench in the square just outside the mall entrance.

"I'll join you," Nick replied.

"I'll be with you in a minute or so. I'm almost out of my SPF face cream and there's a pharmacy just across the way." Stella pointed to the row of shops opposite the mall. "Does anyone need anything while I'm there?"

"No, thanks, honey. I've packed most of our medicine cabinet," Alma said with a laugh.

"Yeah, I did too. I just didn't realize my makeup was low. I'll be right back," she shouted over her shoulder as she rushed off.

She swung open the pharmacy door, only to find herself face-to-face with Joseph Penrod.

"Oh!" she exclaimed. "Hello. Sorry, I didn't see you coming out, otherwise I would have—"

An obviously startled Penrod said nothing, but pushed past Stella and hurried out the door, clutching a white paper bag to his chest. Shaken by the encounter, she wandered around the store in a daze before finally finding her brand of BB cream and purchasing it. "Hey, you'd never guess who I ran into leaving the drugstore," she said to Alma and Nick as she met them in the square.

"If you mean Joe Penrod, we saw him, too," Nick said.

"Yeah, he ran through here like he'd seen a ghost," Alma corroborated.

"It was the strangest thing. I opened the door and there he was. It was as if I'd caught him doing something . . . wrong."

"He was probably buying something embarrassing. You know, laxatives or hair remover or something."

"Are those things still considered embarrassing?" Nick challenged. "I mean, you see ads for them all the time."

"Maybe not for most people, but for an old school sorta guy like Penrod, they could be. My dad was an army man. He never wanted anyone to know when he was sick or had a medical problem. Thought it made him look weak."

"Okay, but wouldn't running away make him look cowardly?" Stella questioned.

Alma tossed her head from side to side. "My dad wouldn't have done it."

"Maybe it's like Alma said. He was buying some stomach or cold remedy and took off because he didn't feel well and didn't want to answer questions," Nick suggested.

"I guess," Stella allowed. "He just looked frightened. That's what was so weird about it."

"After his argument with Georgie this morning, he's probably at the end of his tether. Remember, he's grieving the vicar, too."

"The vicar?" Alma asked. "Who's the vicar?"

Stella made a face at her husband before answering. "Oh, he's the gentleman who left his hat in our room. He was a friend of Joseph's. Unfortunately, we received word that he just passed away."

Nothing in Stella's explanation was untrue, it simply left out one simple detail: that the vicar had been at the resort when he died.

"Oh, that's too bad. Poor vicar. And poor Mr. Penrod, losing his friend so close to Christmas."

"Yes, it's a shame."

"But why was Penrod arguing with Georgie?"

"Oh, she seemed to be in a bit of a bad mood this morning."

"How can anyone be in a bad mood on a day like today? And here, of all places? It's absolutely beautiful."

"That it is." Stella glanced at her phone. "It's eleven o'clock. Once Mills is done, we should head back to the Caballero. We don't want to miss the bus to Tulum."

"Hey, did I hear someone take my name in vain?" Mills joked as he rejoined the group, a pouch of pipe tobacco stuffed into the top pocket of his tropical-print shirt.

"You did," Alma confirmed. "It's time for us to get back to the hotel."

Mills nodded. "I got that vanilla-scented tobacco that you liked."

"That was pretty nice stuff."

"Yeah, and this was at a pretty nice price, too. Bought as much as I'm legally allowed to buy before I'm hit with duties."

"You actually know how much tobacco you're allowed?"

"Yep. The equivalent of one hundred cigarettes, which is approximately one hundred grams."

Alma shook her head. "Lawmen."

"I thought it was pretty common knowledge," Nick said in defense of his friend.

"Of course it is," Stella teased. "Two cups equal a pint. E equals mc squared. A squared plus B squared equals C squared. One hundred cigarettes equal one hundred grams of tobacco. Elementary."

"Lawmen," Alma repeated.

"Yep," she commiserated.

As the couples walked hand in hand along the busy, palm tree-lined road, Stella saw a familiar face at one of the open-air cafés, only the person she saw wasn't with the person one might have expected.

Giving Nick a nudge, she quietly directed his attention toward a corner table beneath a large purple-blossomed jacaranda. There in the shade sat Diana Horrocks being tenderly held not by her husband, but by Manish Banerjee.

After the initial look of surprise had run away from his face, Nick leaned in to his wife and whispered, "I'm guessing I probably shouldn't wave."

"Yeah," she softly replied. "I wouldn't."

● ● ●

After a quick trip to their bungalows to freshen up and retrieve their sunscreen, hats, and water bottles, Stella, Nick, Alma, and Mills assembled at the Caballero Cove Hotel clubhouse to await the arrival of the hotel's passenger van.

As opposed to the tense atmosphere earlier that morning, the hotel's midday mood was tranquil, if a bit too quiet for a resort full of holiday-makers. Chip Ruckert and Desirée Hunt, both wearing dark glasses and looking a bit worse for wear, were soaking in the jacuzzi. Ray Horrocks and Anika Banerjee, occupying two inflatable pool rafts, chatted and laughed while floating and enjoying tropical drinks. Señor Tugores was standing outside the pergola, reviewing the evening menu with Inés. And Georgina Early was still in her chaise knitting away, glancing up every few minutes to look at the sea.

As the two couples waited for word that their transportation had arrived, a uniformed server bearing a tray rushed past them as he checked his phone. Stella noticed that the device displayed an order for two veggie burgers to be delivered to cabana number six. Kendal and Ellie were apparently serious when they said they intended to spend their day at the beach and away from Georgina.

A figure appeared at the back door of the clubhouse. It wasn't the van driver, but Joseph Penrod, newly returned from his shopping trip and clutching the white paper bag he'd been carrying when he left the pharmacy.

Stella didn't attempt a second hello. Instead, she stepped back and allowed the man to pass. Penrod walked in front of the group without making eye contact with anyone. However, before reaching the pool area—and Georgina—he paused and glanced backward as if to say something. Thinking the better of it, he turned his head and marched forward toward the pool, where he sat at the table near the jacuzzi.

"Exactly like my father," Alma told Stella. "Suffering but can't bring himself to ask for help."

They watched as Penrod stretched his legs out in front of him as if to sunbathe, then sat upright again and, after taking several glances in Georgina's direction, picked himself up and meandered out onto the beach.

"How is everyone?" came the booming voice of Bernard Early from the doorway of the clubhouse.

So focused had Stella and Alma been on Penrod, that they jumped at the sound it.

"Sorry to sneak up on you," he apologized. "I'm quite glad I didn't miss the van."

"Oh, are you coming with us?" Stella asked.

"I am. I decided I should finally see the ruins. Been coming here long enough."

"I thought you weren't much for sightseeing," Alma questioned.

"Nah, that's Georgie. I enjoy getting out and about. I walk into town on a regular basis and enjoy talking to the fishermen down by the docks. I've also ventured to Cozumel and Puerto Morelos several times and even Chetumal, four hours from here, but never Tulum."

"Bernard? Is that you?" Georgina called from her poolside seat.

"Yes, love," he replied.

"I'm glad you're back in time to accompany our new friends to Tulum. Seeing how you gallivant, I thought you'd be late and miss the van."

"I told you I was going with them, pet. I'm a man of my word."

"Hmph," she scoffed, throwing her knitting into her bag and joining Bernard and the rest of the group by the clubhouse door. "Bernard and I thought it best that you travel with someone who knows these parts."

"That's very nice of you," Nick said. "But isn't our driver a local?"

"Of course they are, but then there's Tulum itself. It's a tourist attraction. No doubt there will be people there hawking all sorts of rubbish."

"Really? It's a national park. I wouldn't think that sort of thing was allowed."

"As if people pay attention to rules." Georgina waved her hand. "All I know is that wherever I go in the state of Quintana Roo, someone is trying to get your money."

"That's pret' near like everywhere else in the world," Mills noted with a chuckle.

"Yes, I suppose it is," an amused Bernard agreed before turning to Georgie. "And what are you up to this afternoon, my pet?"

"Me? Just a spot of lunch and maybe a nap." She stretched her limbs and yawned. "I don't know why, but I'm a bit knackered. Although it was a bit of a tiring morning. If only some people respected other people's routines . . ."

The beep of a vehicle horn came from the front of the clubhouse. Moments later, a woman in a Caballero Cove uniform appeared at the entrance to the pool area. "The van to Tulum is here. All passengers for Tulum."

Bernard bid goodbye to Georgie. "Enjoy that nap, love. And be good, will ya?"

Georgie grinned. "I can promise one of those two, but not both."

• • •

The van left the Caballero Cove Hotel and set its course along Mexico's Route 307 to Tulum. Stella and Nick sat together on one side of the van, Alma and Mills on the other, with the two men seated upon the van's center aisle and the women by the windows.

Bernard Early availed himself of the aisle-facing handicap seat just behind the driver and directly in front of Stella and Nick. "Well, that's more like it," he proclaimed as he stretched his legs and folded his arms behind his head. "Georgie's been in a bit of a mood this mornin', if you hadn't noticed."

"I'm not sure any of us know Georgie well enough to have an opinion of her mood," Alma stated.

"Diplomatic, eh?" Bernard remarked with a smile. "Bless you for that. Georgie was in a proper state. I'd say she was a prime example of getting up on the wrong side of the bed, except it can happen at any time during the day. She's made enemies of most of the guests with her behavior. Some of the staff as well."

"That's unfortunate. Has she seen a doctor?" Stella asked. "Not that I wish to pry . . . but if she's not feeling well, it could be affecting her mood."

"She's seen our doctor dozens of times. She never mentions a thing to her, but I have. All her blood test results and other exams have come back normal. It's a puzzle, a frustrating and embarrassing puzzle."

Stella examined Bernard's profile as he looked out the window and watched the scenery. He was not overtly upset or shocked by his wife's behavior, nor did he seem saddened by it either. If anything, he seemed resigned to accept the situation as part of his fate, a reaction that made complete sense in the overall scheme of things. If Georgina was publicly rude to fellow hotel guests and staff, how must she have treated Bernard when they were away from prying eyes?

"I must say," Bernard spoke up, "this little trip gives me a chance to find out more about the work you gentlemen do in law enforcement."

"I'm afraid the trip is going to take a lot longer than that," Nick replied.

"Yup, like I told you yesterday, I'm a small-town Vermont sheriff,"

Mills rejoined. "Not much more I can tell you."

"Nonsense. You must have so many stories, and I have so many questions. For instance, how many people have each of you arrested? Have you ever arrested someone you were certain was guilty, only to see them acquitted by a jury? Or is that a lot of rubbish used by television writers to bolster ratings?"

"I wouldn't know," Nick answered. "My arrests so far have led to fines, not trials."

"The folks I've arrested usually want to pay their fine, do their time or probation, and move on with life. Like I said, it's a small town. Not a lot of high crimes being committed."

"I thought you said there'd been an uptick in crime lately . . ." Bernard folded his hands on his lap and glanced at Stella, who purposely avoided eye contact.

"Oh, that? Well, there have been a few murders lately . . ."

"Murders? Plural? As in more than one?"

"Yup . . . but the job is usually pret' routine."

"A murder is anything but routine! And here you've been trying to pass yourself off as the sheriff of a small town where nothing happens. Meanwhile you're an absolute superhero."

"Now then, I wouldn't go there. I have a great team who works alongside me."

"Including Mrs. Buckley, I believe?"

"I, um, I acted as deputy on a case or two," she replied.

"And yet you're busy talking about textiles."

"Because that's my job."

"But you're a crimefighting machine."

"I don't believe I ever referred to myself that way." She went back to looking out the window.

Bernard didn't take Stella's hint. "You have to admit it's pretty extraordinary, solving murders in your spare time. Say, you lot aren't on a case right now, are you?"

"Yep, a case of champagne," Nick joked. "This is a wedding party, not a search party."

"A destination wedding would be an excellent cover for an investigation."

"What would we be investigating?"

"Oh, I don't know . . . a smuggling ring? Oh! I have it—someone at the hotel next door. There are a number of luminaries staying there, including some foreign dignitaries."

"And we're investigating these luminaries from a van headed to Tulum?"

Bernard chuckled. "Good point. My apologies. I have an overactive imagination. Georgie's always on me about it. Of course, having an overactive imagination, I wonder, have you lads ever conducted an international investigation before?"

"No," Nick was quick to answer. "Although I haven't been in the field for very long. I used to hold an office position in New York."

"How about you, Charlie?"

"Once. I worked with the Royal Canadian Mounted Police in the search for a convicted felon who escaped prison and fled across the U.S. border. They'd traced him to our area. I worked with them and the sheriff of a neighboring town to help bring him in."

"That's brilliant stuff!"

Mills shrugged. "That was nearly twenty years ago."

"More like twenty-five," Alma corrected. "I remember we were all terrified to go out of our houses."

"So, what crime novels do you enjoy, Bernard?" Stella asked.

"Oh, all of them, really. Drives Georgie batty how many I read. Although to be fair, I think most of what I do drives Georgie batty. I guess I'm just not an easy person to live with." Bernard fell silent—a silence that lasted until they reached Tulum.

The passenger van came to a halt in the gravel-lined area designated for taxis and shuttles. With their admission to the park arranged by (and later paid to) the hotel, the group presented their passes at the front gate and entered the grounds of the ancient Mayan city.

One of the last cities occupied by the Mayans, Tulum was built high upon a cliff overlooking the Caribbean Sea. Achieving its greatest prominence between the thirteenth and fifteenth centuries, Tulum became wealthy by engaging in the trade of jade and obsidian. When the Spanish arrived, Tulum's population diminished and the city was abandoned, but its buildings—some of the best-preserved ruins in all of Mexico—remained, a testament to the glory of the only coastal Mayan city.

After a stop at the visitor center, which provided a history of the site, the group traveled a gravel path through the thick stone walls that encircled the city and into the ruined metropolis itself.

The sight was awe-inspiring. In a vast and grassy clearing surrounded by jungle stood a myriad of gray stone buildings in a remarkable state of repair. But by far the most impressive was El Castillo—"the castle"—a twenty-five-foot-tall pyramid set directly on the bluffs, with its back to the turquoise waters of the Caribbean.

"Wow," Nick uttered aloud.

"You got that right," Mills remarked.

As Alma and Stella snapped photos, Bernard followed the path to the right and a flat-topped, thrown stone pyramid structure with a narrow keyhole entranceway. "What's this? Some kind of food storage building?"

Nick referred to the sign outside the structure. "It's a *platforma funeraria*. A burial crypt. The Mayans buried their dead facing the west, as the setting sun signified death and the underworld. Leaders, however, were buried facing the east, to meet the rising sun and be resurrected with the dawn. You can see murals depicting the three worlds—the world of the dead, the world of the living, and the world of the gods—in the Temple of the Frescoes just behind the tomb."

"I didn't know you spoke Spanish, Nick," Alma said admiringly.

"I do. So does Stella. When you live and work in New York City, it helps to be bilingual."

"Although Nick is the only one of us who's truly bilingual," Stella clarified. "I didn't speak much Spanish at all when I worked at the museum. As the saying goes, if you don't use it, you lose it."

"It will come back to you," Nick replied. "A week here and you'll find yourself remembering all sorts of words and phrases."

Stella read the sign to herself. "Mmm, they're starting to come back to me already. Say, that's rather an interesting thought, isn't it? That your soul is linked to the rising and setting of the sun. I know other cultures buried their dead facing a certain direction, but not for the same reason."

"Yeah, it's a great concept . . . if you're royalty," Mills countered.

Bernard had remained silent during this exchange, his eyes fixated first on the tomb and then on someone—a man, well-dressed, and bearded—standing outside the Temple of the Frescoes. "Excuse me, but I see a friend of mine just over there, on the other side of the tomb."

"A friend?" Alma questioned. "From the hotel?"

"Yes, he's staying at El Sueño. The guests there book private tours. If you'll pardon me, I need to say hello."

Bernard left the group to join the man, who seemed pleased, yet extremely nervous, to meet with him. The pair greeted each other and then set off on the trail that led down from the bluff and onto a white sand beach. He rejoined their group approximately forty minutes later as they were about to climb the steps of El Castillo. "Sorry about that. I'd have been back sooner but I couldn't find you. This place is vast, isn't it?"

"We probably should have exchanged phone numbers before you left," Stella said.

"Ah, that wouldn't have helped. I left my mobile back at the resort, the 'nana I am. I use it so much back home that I try to unplug while I'm here. Stupid, really, but true."

"It's not stupid. I should actually try that more often," Nick offered. "But now that you found us, let's check out El Castillo, huh?"

The group continued their tour, pausing at two o'clock to sit on the beach and enjoy the light and refreshing boxed lunch provided for them by the hotel. Energized by the repast, they finished their explorations a few minutes before they were scheduled to meet the van in the drop-off area at four p.m.

As they waited in the area of the car park designated for buses and shuttles, Stella noticed Bernard's friend several yards away with what appeared to be his wife and two teenage sons. The friend and his family boarded their private shuttle without a glance in Bernard's direction.

The ride home was a quiet one. Although it had been a thoroughly enjoyable afternoon, it had been a tiring one and the van's passengers soaked up the air-conditioning in silence as they looked forward to cool, refreshing showers, a change of clothes, and an opportunity to relax before convening for predinner drinks at six o'clock.

They arrived back at the hotel shortly before five o'clock, just as the sun had begun to cast long shadows. The hot, tropical sun and azure skies could easily fool one into believing that it was the height of summer, but the early sunsets and cool evening breezes served as tangible reminders that winter and, with it, the shortest day of the year were well on their way.

As the hotel staff readied the pool and pergola area for the evening's festivities, Kendal and Ellie returned to their bungalow with their beach gear. The two women gave the group a friendly wave before disappearing into their casita. All the other guests had already vacated the area and retired to their villas to change for dinner, save for one.

While standing at the clubhouse door, Stella could see the dark head of Georgina Early resting against the back of her favorite lounge chair. She wasn't knitting, but appeared to be staring off through her dark glasses toward the sea.

"Hiya, love," Bernard greeted. "Hey, did you chain yourself to that chair? It doesn't look as if you budged an inch since we left."

She didn't answer.

Bernard approached his wife. "Georgie, darlin', you'd better get up. Dinner's in an hour and we all need to get ready."

Again, she did not respond.

"Georgie, wake up, love," he repeated, this time with an anxious tone in his voice. "Ceviche's on the menu tonight. Your favorite. You don't want to be late, do ya?"

When the woman remained uncharacteristically silent, Bernard reached over and gave her shoulder a nudge. "Georgie?"

Her head fell forward, sending her sunglasses sliding off the bridge of her nose.

"Georgie!" Bernard shrieked as he dropped to his knees beside the lounger, knocking over her insulated water bottle and bag of knitting as he did so. "Georgie, wake up. Wake up, Georgie!"

Suspecting that the Englishwoman was suffering from more than a bout of narcolepsy, Nick and Mills rushed forward to assist.

"Let me take a look at her," Nick urged as Mills placed his hands on Bernard's shoulders to both calm the man and guide him away from Georgina so that Nick could assess the situation.

Alma, meanwhile, went into the clubhouse to alert the management to call for an ambulance.

"Does your wife usually sleep this soundly?" the sheriff asked.

"No, she's usually at me for snoring. Says I keep her awake."

"Does she have diabetes or any other medical condition that might make her lose consciousness?"

"She has high blood pressure, but that wouldn't cause—cause this. Could it? Could she have had a heart attack? Georgie!" Bernard lunged forward, but Mills kept him firmly in check.

Nick leaned over the unconscious woman and placed his fingers on her wrist and then her neck. He looked up at Stella before speaking. The expression on his face told her everything she needed to know. "I'm very sorry, Bernard," Nick said as he stood up. "But I'm afraid Georgie's dead."

Chapter Six

Stella and Alma watched from the pergola while, in the last fading rays of daylight, the body of Georgina Early was lifted from the lounge chair and onto a waiting gurney.

"But royalty, in death, were positioned to face the sun, so that they could be reborn with the dawn of each new day," Stella whispered.

"Huh? What's that?" Alma questioned.

"Oh, nothing. I was just thinking about how Georgina considered herself the queen of this place."

"She did, didn't she? It's such a shame. She wasn't very old. But I suppose at least she spent her last days in her favorite place."

Stella eyed the lounge chair and recalled the fuss Georgina had made that morning. Had she known it was her last day on earth, would she have stirred up such an argument? Or would she have taken the chair alongside Diana and Ray and chatted with the couple over juice and coffee?

What about Georgina's run-ins with Kendal and Ellie? And her quieter, yet still far from pleasant, interaction with Joseph Penrod? Would Georgina, faced with her own mortality, have behaved differently toward them? Would she have tried to enjoy her final day with friends? Or had raising such disputes become so ingrained in her behavior that she could no longer see the upset she caused others?

Given Bernard's account of his wife's conduct, Stella suspected it was the latter.

And what of Joseph Penrod? He was only just recovering from the loss of his friend, Reverend Bailor. He may not have gotten along with Georgina, but another unexpected death at his beloved Caballero Cove Hotel would, no doubt, put him in a tailspin.

Unexpected. The word caused Stella to catch her breath.

Georgina's was the second unexpected death at the hotel in less than a week. For a resort consisting of just ten bungalows, the odds seemed stacked against such an occurrence. Still, Stella was well aware that life was full of seemingly impossible coincidences. And yet . . .

"Uh-oh, I know that look," Alma said with a shake of her head.

"What look?"

"The look that says your brain is working overtime."

"My brain is always working overtime," Stella replied with a nervous laugh.

"Yeah, I know. Thinking of things I don't want to talk about during my wedding getaway."

"Then we won't talk about them," Stella promised. "Like you said, my brain works overtime. Therefore, I have a tendency toward blowing things out of proportion."

The two women fell silent and watched as Georgina's body was wheeled into the clubhouse to be loaded into the ambulance that waited outside the front door.

"'Cept that you don't," Alma noted after a minute or two had passed.

"I don't what?"

"You don't blow things out of proportion. If you think something's wrong, it usually is."

"I don't think something's wrong, per se . . ."

"You don't? Didn't you say that the man who had your bungalow died a few days ago?"

"I did."

"And now Georgina's dead."

"That's right."

"And you don't think that's odd?"

Stella chose her words carefully. "Well, Reverend Bailor was quite elderly."

"Georgina wasn't."

"No, but . . ."

"But two people dead in one week in a resort this size?"

"Yeah, and Georgina wasn't exactly well-liked."

"I barely knew her, and I wasn't exactly enamored with her."

"Same, but there's a big difference in finding someone obnoxious and wanting to kill them," Stella pointed out.

"But you gotta admit, your Spidey-senses are tingling, aren't they?"

"They are, but I could be wrong. We need to wait and see what the police list as her cause of death."

After giving their statements to the Quintana Roo police, Nick and Mills joined their partners beneath the pergola.

"What's going on?" Stella questioned.

"Police suspect a heart attack," Nick answered.

"Given Georgina's history of high blood pressure and the fact that she was over fifty—" Mills started.

"Hey," Alma objected. "You and I are over fifty. I refuse to believe that we're simply coronary events waiting to happen."

"We aren't. Not since you've broken me of my jelly doughnut habit. But Georgina wasn't as fortunate as I am."

"That was the correct answer," Alma purred.

"So, that it's then?" Stella questioned. "Georgina suffered a heart attack?"

"The police are waiting for the coroner's report, but a heart attack seems most likely," her husband answered.

"If Georgina's blood pressure was extraordinarily high, that might account for her volatile behavior this morning," Stella reasoned. "Well, Alma, either my Spidey-sense is broken or it's picking up a signal from somewhere else."

• • •

Lila put in a long day at the general store. A fresh layer of snow brought with it an influx of skiers, snowboarders, and out-of-state visitors in search of the quintessential New England Christmas experience. Tourists and sports enthusiasts, of course, equated to sales. As the largest of just three retailers in the town of Teignmouth, Perkins' General Store was the biggest recipient of those sales.

Lila stood post at her counter serving a steady stream of customers looking to take advantage of Vermont's lower sales tax to purchase gifts of perfume and high-end cosmetics, or simply seeking a new holiday beauty regime.

Having used her brief lunch break to drive home, check in on and walk Bixby, Lila found herself both exhausted and completely famished by the time the store shut its doors at six p.m.

Walking into the Buckleys' farmhouse kitchen at ten minutes after six, she flung her car keys onto the center island and knelt down to give the black Lab who greeted her a thorough scratch beneath his ears before taking him outdoors for a quick romp in the fenced-in backyard. With Bixby's business completed and his fur completely drenched from rolling in the fresh snow, Lila brought him back inside for food and fresh water before heading upstairs to her bedroom.

After stepping out of the day's clothes and slathering her skin with her favorite cherry blossom body cream, Lila donned her favorite satin pajamas and was prepared to slip on a pair of terry-cloth slipper socks when she looked up to see a black snout pushing its way through the crack in the door.

"Bixby, you know you're not allowed in here," she admonished, albeit in a gentle tone.

Bixby paid no mind and instead barged into the room with an onslaught of nose and face kisses for Lila.

"Okay." She laughed as she held up her hands to protect her face from Bixby's tongue. "Okay, that's enough from you. You got your dinner, now it's time for Grandma to be watered and fed."

She rose from her bed with a grimace. She had long laughed at other women her age who spoke glowingly of grand-pups and grand-kitties, and now she was one of them. Well, she reasoned, at least no one else heard her use the phrase apart from Bixby.

With the click-clack of Bixby's paws leading the way, Lila descended the hardwood staircase into the living room, where she debated starting a fire in the stove. Realizing that the task would require her to go outside and retrieve wood from the pile in the backyard, she shook her head and adjusted the thermostat instead.

As the furnace roared to life, Lila moved into the kitchen, preheated the oven and, removing the cocktail shaker from its spot in the cupboard, set about making a seasonal martini.

It would be her very first Christmas alone. Yes, she had Stella and Nick and now Clyde at the store, but for the first time since she was at college, she wasn't cohabitating with a man. She didn't need to report her whereabouts to a man. She didn't have to share her income with a man. She wasn't arguing over household chores with a man.

It was quite liberating . . . if a trifle intimidating. Still, she was optimistic for the future. She enjoyed her work at the store and felt valued for both her fashion and sales savvy. And she was incredibly optimistic about the new pet deodorant line, even if Bixby was having difficulty mustering enthusiasm.

Therefore, this was a holiday season to celebrate. And celebrate Lila would. Once Stella and Nick were home, there would be a tree to trim and shopping trips, but for now, she would take seasonal comfort where she could find it.

Lila wasn't much of a cook—hence, why she'd stockpiled meals from a gourmet deli in Burlington for the week—but she was a terrific mixer of cocktails. Grabbing the bottle of vodka from the freezer and the bottle of pomegranate juice from the refrigerator, she added four parts of each to the shaker and then topped it with two parts orange liqueur and some ice and shook the contents.

All the while, Bixby watched intently.

"This is Grandma's treat," she explained as she poured the contents into a martini glass.

At the word *treat* the dog gave a soft bark.

"Oh, boy, I did it now, didn't I?" Taking a sip of martini first, Lila wandered into the living room and grabbed a dog biscuit from the treat can on the mantel above the stove.

She presented it to the patient canine, who chomped it down eagerly.

Lila moved back into the kitchen and took another sip of martini. Bixby's appetite for treats had thankfully returned since the previous evening. When she and Clyde were trying to get him to sit still for the photographer, Bixby completely snubbed the treats Lila had offered him.

She thought perhaps the presence of strangers in the house had dulled his appetite, but the offer of a treat just before bed ended in the same result. Perhaps Bixby was growing accustomed to being in her care, for he seemed to be his usual happy-go-lucky self.

Lila popped her food in the oven and set about lighting some candles. "How about some atmosphere, Bixby?"

The black Lab wagged his tail.

"I'm having a beautiful boeuf bourguignon tonight, with celeriac and potato mash and baby carrots. If you're good, I'll give you a little bit of my beef."

Bixby reclined under the kitchen table, as if in anticipation.

She took another sip of her martini. "Atta boy. You and Grandma are going to get along just fine this week. Maybe I'll ask Clyde if I can bring you into the store one day, this way you're not alone."

Bixby's tail wagged.

She sat with Bixby, scrolling through her phone as she awaited her meal. The Buckleys had a microwave, but Lila preferred slow heating. "Nuking" might be fast and easy, but it often sacrificed food flavor and texture and she was all about enjoying her evening repast.

She gazed out the window at the falling snow. Fresh powder meant tomorrow would be another busy day, but Lila didn't mind. She had a job she enjoyed, a renewed sense of purpose, and, thankfully, a warm home where she could rest and relax.

The oven timer chimed, indicating that dinner was ready. Lila grabbed a set of potholders and carried the steaming aluminum takeaway dish to the table, where she had a fork and knife at the ready.

Lila discovered that the knife was completely unnecessary as the beef was succulently fork-tender. "Mmm . . ." she moaned. "Oh, Bixby, you're in for a treat. This is absolutely delicious."

Stabbing a piece of the beef with her fork, she took it to the sink, where she rinsed off the thick, luscious gravy. After drying it with a paper towel, she placed the meat in Bixby's empty bowl.

Instead of leaping to his feet and gobbling the much-desired table scraps (Bixby was frequently chastised for begging at the table), he heaved a heavy sigh and rolled onto his back, his legs bent at the knees.

"Bixby," Lila called. "Bixby, treats. Yummy treats."

The Lab yawned and rolled onto his side, his face turned away from his food dish.

It was Lila's turn to sigh.

Returning to her seat, she took a sip of martini and texted Clyde:

Bringing Bixby to the store tomorrow. Worried about him.

Chapter Seven

Deeming the poolside pergola too close to the scene of Georgina's death, Señor Tugores and his staff gathered the Caballero Cove guests in the clubhouse for an informal and rather gloomy supper. Bernard, for obvious reasons, did not attend. Kendal Chung and Joseph Penrod were also absent, stating they felt too frail to join in and were ordering room service.

With the evening show and subsequent dance party relocated to the hotel next door, the guests retired to their casitas after dinner. Alma, Mills, Nick, and Stella had toyed with the idea of gathering in one of their living rooms for a glass of wine and quiet conversation, but given the circumstances, meeting in any sort of social capacity felt disrespectful.

And so, the friends said good night to each other and retreated to their respective accommodations to shower, unwind, and eventually sleep. Stella, however, was less than successful at accomplishing the last task on the list. Nodding off to sleep shortly after turning in for the night, she awoke at three in the morning with the awful sense that something was wrong.

Unable to shake the feeling, she rose from the bed and wandered into the living room to read. Before she could switch on the light, she noticed something moving outside the garden gate.

She crept forward, as if the person outside might hear her, and hiding behind the drapes, peered out the front living room window. In the light of the full moon, Stella could make out the figure of a woman tiptoeing past the pool area. She held her high-heeled sandals in one hand and a small evening bag in the other and was skulking through the dark like a theatrical—possibly drunken—prowler or burglar

It was Desirée Hunt.

As she passed the Buckleys' bungalow in search of her own, Stella stepped out from the obscurity of the drapes. Unlike the other guests, Hunt had clearly been out on the town, most likely—Stella was willing to wager—at the hotel next door.

The clubhouse motion light suddenly switched on, illuminating

Desirée in silhouette as she fumbled with her keys before eventually admitting herself to the casita she shared with Chip Ruckert.

Stella frowned. She couldn't imagine Ruckert being incredibly pleased with either the state of Hunt upon arriving home, nor the time of her arrival, but then again, having seen Ruckert falling asleep at the bar, it was questionable whether or not he would even be awake enough to know when Desirée came home.

She shrugged. Although interesting fodder for gossip, Desirée and Chip's relationship was none of her business. Besides, at the moment, what she wanted most was calm and quiet—something she'd never find if she sat around speculating about the personal lives of their fellow guests.

Stella switched on the floor lamp near the front window and prepared to snuggle onto the sofa with her book, but something outside caught her attention again. A shadowy figure could be seen moving near the far end of the pool nearest the beach. The person was dressed in a black hoodie and dark shorts, which made it impossible to determine whether they were a man or woman, adult or older child.

The only thing that stood out about the figure was the Q-shaped silver reflective strip of their running shoes as they stealthily picked their way along the row of bungalows on the other side of the swimming pool. Were they looking for a particular casita? Or were they searching for one with an open door or window so that they could climb inside?

Stella was watching the dark figure so intently that she had completely forgotten she was illuminated by the living room lamp. She quickly reached over and switched off the light, but it was too late. The figure turned to face her, their face obscured by the hood they wore, and beat a hasty retreat.

Stella's heart was racing. A person would only run if they were up to no good. But what, precisely, were they up to? They didn't approach any of the casitas and try their doors or windows. No, if anything, they walked with a sense of speed and purpose that made her think that the individual knew exactly where they were going.

Feeling a sudden chill, she checked the lock on the front door and rushed to the bedroom to tell Nick.

"Ellie said the management was seeing a lot more foot traffic trouble since they took down the barricade to the beach," he said when Stella had finished describing everything she had witnessed.

"At three in the morning?"

"The clubs close around then. Whoever you saw might have been drunk and suddenly found themselves at the wrong resort."

"The person I saw wasn't drunk. Desirée Hunt on the other hand . . ."

"Desirée Hunt was out there too?"

Stella nodded. "She toddled home just before the mysterious figure arrived. She was shoeless and slightly worse for wear."

"Hmmm . . . think she was taking 'dancing lessons'?"

"I do, but enough about Desirée," she quickly dismissed. "Should we call the police or call the management?"

"You didn't actually see this person do anything, did you?"

"No, they just walked . . . suspiciously."

"So, they were simply trespassing."

"Yeah, I guess so."

"They didn't try anyone's front gate or walk through their garden to test a door handle or peep through a window?"

"No, they just kind of walked along, hands in pockets, until they saw me standing in the window with the light on like a blooming idiot," she said with a sigh. "Then they stopped and ran in the opposite direction."

"So, again, all this person did was trespass."

"Yes, but . . . well, they moved as if they knew where they were going."

"You think they had a target in mind?"

"I do. I'm not sure exactly where they were headed, but they stopped immediately after passing casita number eight, Ellie and Kendal's."

"And you said they'd come in from the beach, correct?"

"That's right."

"So, they'd already passed number ten, the Horrockses' casita."

"Leaving just the Earlys' bungalow at number six and the two next to it." Stella pulled a face. "Wait a minute. Who's staying in those bungalows?"

"Joseph Penrod is staying in casita two. I saw him go in there tonight."

"And number four?"

"No idea."

"Huh. I must be on vacation because I've only just realized something is off. This place is supposedly booked, but the math doesn't add up. The casitas on this side are occupied by Alma and Mills in number nine, us in number seven, Chip and Desirée in number five, the Banerjees in number three, and . . ."

"Señor Tugores in number one," Nick stated.

"Really? He lives at the resort?"

"That's what the bartender told me last night. Tugores has never lived anywhere but here."

"Wow. That's dedication."

"A tiny bachelor's bungalow near the beach? I can think of worse things."

"You'd think maybe he'd move so he could rent it out and make more money," she said with a shrug. "But it still begs the question: who's staying in number four?"

"That, sweetie, is an excellent question. And one we need to ask Señor Tugores tomorrow morning."

"Then you don't think we need to call the police tonight?"

"No. I'm not sure about the laws here, but I'm reasonably certain they're similar to ours. If all this person did was trespass, then there's not much the police can do unless Señor Tugores decides to file charges. In order to do that, of course, the police would have to find the person first and I'm pretty sure they have their hands full with other matters. As for waiting until morning to speak with Señor Tugores, there doesn't seem to be any urgent reason to wake him right now. You successfully scared off the intruder and, quite honestly, given what happened to Georgina Early, the man could probably use the sleep."

"We all could," Stella agreed. "Hey, you don't think . . . ?"

Nick raised a questioning eyebrow in Stella's direction as he checked the thermostat.

"It's odd, isn't it? This trespasser showing up less than twelve hours after we discovered Georgina Early dead. You don't think the two could be linked, do you?"

"You think a drunk person trespassing on resort property is somehow connected to a fifty-plus woman with a history of high blood pressure suffering a fatal heart attack?"

She climbed into bed and pulled the blankets up over her. "Well, when you put it that way. But I maintain the person I saw wasn't drunk."

He slid in beside her and kissed her on the forehead. "I'm not dismissing you, hon. I also think it's strange that a resort this small has lost two of its guests in the course of a week, but Reverend Bailor was old and Georgina had a health issue, so it kinda makes sense."

"No, you're right. And I'm sure it will make sense to me too, once I get a good night's sleep."

"You never sleep well the first night of vacation," he noted.

"You know, you're right. I'd completely forgotten."

"That's because it's been so long since we've been on a vacation. But, yeah, you even had trouble sleeping the first night of our honeymoon, although you'd been up nearly the entire night before."

"Because I also don't sleep well on planes. Huh, I'm kinda like a thermos of milk, aren't I? I really don't travel well."

He smiled and pulled her closer. "Maybe, but you make up for it once you arrive at your destination."

• • •

Nestled closely to Nick, Stella drifted off to sleep rather quickly and remained so for the next four and a half hours. Waking at eight o'clock, she discovered Nick had already risen and had ordered coffee, fresh fruit, and croissants to be delivered to their casita garden.

"What a nice surprise. Thank you." She gave her husband a kiss as she tied her kimono around her waist and then yawned. "Sorry I slept so late."

"You needed the sleep. After what you witnessed last night, I'm glad you slept as well as you did."

"I admit I do feel refreshed." Stella sat down at the bistro set, opposite her husband. "But we were going to meet with Señor Tugores first thing this morning."

"I already went to his office."

"Oh? What did he say?"

"I didn't have a chance to speak with him. He was having a heated discussion with a woman. It sounded like Luciana, the head of guest services."

"Really?" She helped herself to the carafe of coffee. "What were they talking about?"

"I don't know. I wasn't there for long, but I did hear Georgina Early's name mentioned."

"Georgina? I wonder why."

"I couldn't make out everything Tugores was saying, but it sounded as if he was unhappy about the way something was handled."

"Whatever it was, Georgina's hardly in a position to complain about it, so why would Tugores be upset?"

"Like I said, I couldn't catch everything. Nor did I really try. I leave the eavesdropping to you."

She smiled. "I am pretty good at it, aren't I?"

"Pretty good? I expect you to be recruited by the CIA any day now. Or subpoenaed."

As Nick presented Stella with a croissant from the basket on the table, she noticed Renata approaching. She was pushing a housekeeping cart and looking utterly miserable.

"*Buenos dias*, Renata," Stella greeted. "*Como esta?*"

"Oh, Señora Buckley, not good."

"It is a dark day, isn't it? I suppose you knew Señora Early well, since she's been coming here for years."

"*Sí*. I mean, no. I did not know her well, but how she dies is . . ." Renata threw her hands in the air.

"Yes, it was very sudden. And so soon after Reverend Bailor."

"*Sí*, the padre. You are right. It *is* too soon. *Too* soon," the housekeeper said excitedly. "That is what worries me."

"Oh?"

"La policía say Señora Early died of the same thing as the padre, but this is not so. It cannot be so." She leaned in close to Stella and said softly, yet firmly, "The padre did not have the heart problem."

"He didn't?"

"No, I clean his casita all the time. I clean the casitas on that side of the pool; Inés cleans the ones on this side. We clean when guests are out, but the padre, he stay because he like to talk. The padre did not have the high blood pressure. He had the low blood pressure."

"He told you this?"

"*Sí* and he showed me the medicine he take. But the medicine, it went away after he died."

"What do you mean it went away?"

"I went to show it to la policía and it was not there."

"You mean it disappeared?"

"*Sí.* The padre kept it in the *baño*—the bathroom. He never moved it, but when he died—poof!—it was gone. Same with Señora Early."

"What do you mean the same thing happened?"

"Señora Early had the medicine, too. She keep it by her bed, but when I went there just now, it was gone."

"You saw Georgina's bedside table this morning?"

"*Sí.* I was cleaning."

"Cleaning?"

"*Sí,* Luciana told me to."

Stella glanced at Nick. Could the order to clean the Earlys' casita have been at the root of her argument with Tugores? "But Luciana's in guest services. Why would she tell you to clean?"

"So that the casita is ready for the next guest who stay there."

"The next guest? Is Señor Early going home?"

"I do not know. I do not think so. I was not asked to clean his casita."

"*His* casita? He and Señora Early had separate accommodations?"

"*Sí,* since about three years ago."

"So, what do you think happened to Señora Early and Reverend Bailor?"

"I do not know. The padre was a kind, gentle man, but Señora Early, nobody liked her. Even Señor Tugores got into a fight with her the day she died." Renata invoked the sign of the cross. "Señor Tugores would not lose his temper with a guest who spend money like la señora if he did not have a good reason."

• • •

Stella and Nick dressed hastily and set off on foot for the local police station. "I predict there might be another murder," she said to him en route.

"Another? We don't know that these actually are murders, hon."

"Don't we? Everyone hated Georgina Early. Sounds like even Bernard was on the outs with her."

"And Reverend Bailor?"

"I confess that I can't come up with a motive for that one. Maybe he knew something and had to be silenced. Or maybe his death was legitimately due to old age." She paused. "But then why was his medication missing? No, his death has to be linked to Georgina's. It just has to."

"Who's the third murder?"

"Me. When Alma finds out I'm sleuthing during her wedding getaway, she's going to kill me."

Stella and Nick arrived at the whitewashed two-story police station on Benito Juarez Avenue shortly after nine o'clock. They were greeted by a friendly uniformed officer named Lenzana.

Nick began to explain their situation in Spanish, but the young inspector held his hand in the air with a smile. "Please, señor. I speak English."

With this request, Stella and Nick described the strange circumstances surrounding the deaths of both Reverend Bailor and Georgina Early.

"This housekeeper, you trust her?" Lenzana asked when they had finished.

"Yes, we do," Stella asserted.

"But you only just met her."

"I know, but her fear seemed genuine last night, as did her concern this morning."

"Would she be willing to make a statement?"

"I doubt it. She made it clear that she's not supposed to clean rooms while the guests are occupying them. Once she told me what she knew, she also sped away before the manager could see her."

"And you? Have either of you spoken to Señor Tugores about the housekeeper's discovery? Or about the mysterious figure last night?"

"No," Nick replied. "We thought we should speak to you first."

"Me? Don't you think this is of concern to Señor Tugores and his business? We cannot go after a trespasser without his permission or the resort's surveillance footage."

"We realize that and we had planned to talk to him this morning, but after learning that Mrs. Early's casita had been cleaned, we weren't sure we could trust him."

"Trust him? Señor Tugores didn't order the housekeeper to clean the casita. His employee did."

"I know that—we know that—but it seemed suspicious to us that Tugores had both argued with Mrs. Early on the day of her death and with the employee who ordered the cleaning."

"Some hotel guests are extremely difficult," Lenzana said, still smiling, as if he found Stella and Nick's presence amusing. "And could it not be that Señor Tugores was arguing with the employee because she ordered the dead woman's casita to be cleaned before the proper time had passed?"

Stella and Nick looked at each other. Here in the institutional gray walls of the police station, Lenzana's words made complete sense, but when viewed from within the context of Caballero Cove, his explanation failed to take into account the emotionally fraught environment that had prevailed the few hours prior to Georgina's death.

"You don't understand," Stella argued. "Something strange is going on. For starters, Caballero Cove only accommodates twenty visitors at a time, yet two of them have died in the matter of a week."

"I believe that is what is known as a . . . coincidence. Is it not?"

"Possibly, but Reverend Bailor didn't suffer from high blood pressure. He suffered from low blood pressure."

"They are both heart issues, are they not? And low blood pressure can be just as deadly in elderly people. You are also once again assuming the housekeeper is telling the truth."

"But Georgina died of high blood pressure."

"Yes, two different causes of death. That should put your mind at ease about them being connected."

"But supposedly they both died of a heart attack."

"No, they both died of cardiac arrest. That means the heart stopped suddenly. I do not wish to sound insensitive, but when someone dies, their heart stops, so cardiac arrest is often cited as cause of death."

"But everyone disliked Georgina Early. She argued with just about everyone the morning of the day she died."

"Just because people are on holiday does not always mean they leave their troubles behind, Señora Buckley. Some people"—he took turns looking at Stella and Nick—"have difficulty clearing their minds and relaxing."

"What about the room being cleaned so quickly?" Nick asked. "Don't you find that at all suspicious? Especially after Señor Tugores was seen and heard arguing with Georgina Early yesterday?"

"I do not find it suspicious. Miguel Tugores has lived in Playa del Carmen all his life. He is a stellar member of our community. Believe me when I say that he is above suspicion."

Stella frowned. "Don't you believe in intuition?"

"I do, but I also know that intuition can be influenced by negative feelings. You already said Señora Early angered everyone at the resort. This could be influencing your judgment."

She sighed noisily, but Lenzana quickly calmed her. "I will add your findings and the notes of this meeting to Señora Early's case file and, if anything comes back from Señora Early's autopsy and toxicology report, I will let you know. Until then, go out and enjoy the sunshine, the waves, the food. If you've learned anything about this case that is without dispute, it is that life is short."

• • •

The pair exited the police station and turned onto Fifth Avenue heading back toward the Caballero Cove Hotel. "Well, that didn't exactly go the way we'd anticipated."

"No, it didn't, but I have to say I'm relieved."

Nick was surprised. "You are?"

"Yes. I'm glad Georgina Early and Reverend Bailor weren't murdered. I'm also extremely glad that Alma's and Mills's wedding won't be marred by a murder investigation."

"So, you're satisfied with Lenzana's explanation of the situation?"

"I am. I still have a feeling that something is wrong, but he made an excellent point about the power that toxic personalities can have over us. We can begin to feel what they feel and think what they think, simply by being in their presence."

"You mean that Georgina's suspicious and argumentative nature might have made you unduly suspicious, if not argumentative?"

"That's precisely what I mean. In the course of one morning, she accused the Horrockses of intentionally stealing her chair, she withheld an afghan that Ellie and Kendal wanted to purchase for their newborn, she had words with Joseph Penrod, and we learned that she didn't treat her husband very well, either."

"Don't forget the night before, over dinner, she made some interesting allegations against Desirée Hunt."

Stella smirked. "Yeah, after seeing Desirée come home at three o'clock this morning, I'm going to refrain from commenting on that one. But, you're right, Georgina had something negative to say about nearly everyone."

"In other words, the 'something wrong' you've been sensing was Georgina Early."

"Yeah, that's an excellent way of putting it."

"But even though Georgina's gone, you still have that feeling," Nick challenged.

"I do, but now that I've recognized the source of that feeling, perhaps it will fade."

From inside her straw cross-body bag, Stella's phone rang.

"Probably Alma wondering where we are," Nick remarked.

"No, I texted her before we left, saying we were taking a walk." She retrieved the phone to find the police station number displayed prominently on its face. "It's Lenzana. You didn't leave your wallet or phone at the precinct, did you?"

Nick checked his pockets and shook his head while Stella swiped the phone screen to answer. "Hello?"

"Hola, Señora Buckley." Inspector Lenzana's voice sounded clearly on the other end of the connection. "I shouldn't have been in such a hurry to relinquish you. A few moments after you and your husband left, I received the coroner's reports."

"Oh?"

"Señora Early died of cardiac arrest."

Stella cast her eyes heavenward so quickly she wouldn't have been surprised if Lenzana could hear them over the phone. "Not to be rude, Inspector, but wasn't that already a foregone conclusion?"

"It is not surprising, no, but the rest of the report is. Señora Early's heart failure was caused by an overdose of oxycodone."

"Opioids?"

"I am afraid so. Sadly, it is not uncommon these days. Many of your countrymen choose to blame us for the epidemic, but we're struggling with it, too. The drug cartels kill our people in many ways—not all of them with guns. Although some drugs are produced here, the majority of cocaine and opioids come in from Central America via the sea. Cozumel is one such entryway—with Cancun being a party town, you can imagine the demand."

"No, I do understand. How does this report impact the Early case?" she asked, trying to bring the inspector back on topic.

"As most overdose deaths are accidental, that is how we are treating this case. Señora Early did not appear to have been depressed."

"No, quite the opposite. She was surly and argumentative."

"Yes, as you say. As illegal substances were involved, I need to report her death to Los Federales so they can track the supplier of the oxycodone. I also need to speak with Señor Early about the circumstances surrounding his wife's overdose—did she leave a suicide note, for instance, or talk about ending her life?—and work with him to register her death with the UK authorities."

"What if there was a suicide note and the note was inadvertently discarded when Georgina's casita was cleaned?"

"Once again you're implying that the cleaning of Señora Early's casita was for nefarious reasons."

"I'm not implying. I'm simply questioning why there was such urgency in cleaning the dead woman's room. I realize that as a small resort, casitas are always in demand, but Georgina's things were still in it. Why not wait until they were moved out? That's premature on many levels. Also, perhaps I'm wrong, but an order to prepare a casita for rental should come from Señor Tugores himself, not the head of guest services. The head of guest services would only direct a housekeeper to clean if a specific guest has requested it."

Lenzana was quiet. "You do share some very valid points, Señora Buckley. Me and my men will be at Caballero Cove shortly. No doubt I will see you there."

"Yes, we're heading back now."

"And no doubt you'll have more to say then."

"I think you already know the answer to that," Stella replied with a grin.

Chapter Eight

"An opioid overdose?" Alma questioned as the four friends sat at a poolside table enjoying a round of cold drinks. "I never saw that coming."

"Neither did we," Nick replied.

"That's the thing about opioid addiction, unless you know someone intimately, it's largely invisible," Mills lamented.

"Maybe it wasn't invisible," Stella suggested. "Georgina's volatility, the bad behavior Bernard spoke about, her reluctance to leave the resort—they could all have been caused by addiction, couldn't they?"

"Sure could," Mills confirmed. "Bernard would know best what was going on."

"Bernard said she'd been to a doctor about her troubles," Alma recalled. "Can't believe they couldn't help her."

"Addicts have gotta be willing to help themselves. We see it all the time in law enforcement. Folks go to jail for drug possession, get out clean, then do it all over again. It's a crying shame. Also, who knows how Georgina got started on that stuff. Most doctors are fine, but there are some out there who are too eager to pull out their prescription pad."

Nick nodded. "Not to mention a few pharmacists out there willing to fill those prescriptions, no questions asked."

"It all makes me wonder," Stella started. "Was the medicine Renata saw on Georgina's bedside table every day the oxycodone? Or was it the blood pressure medication Bernard mentioned?"

"If Georgie was poppin' them like candy, it was probably the oxycodone," Alma said.

"That would make sense, wouldn't it? She would want them to be accessible."

"She might even have brought them out to the pool in her knitting bag, just so they were nearby."

"Which would explain why they weren't on the bedside table when Renata cleaned the room."

"This is all speculation," Nick reasoned. "Why don't you ask Renata?"

"Renata doesn't know the difference between an opioid and blood pressure medication."

"No, but she might recognize the name on the bottle. I'm sure she dusted around it, moved it, and saw it dozens of times since the Earlys arrived."

"She's probably cleaning the even-numbered casitas. I'll see if I can track her down," Stella announced, taking her phone with her.

As she rose from the table, Lenzana and a handful of officers from the local headquarters emerged from the clubhouse and was led by Señor Tugores to Georgina's casita.

Stella went the long way around the pool to avoid them, finally spotting the housekeeping cart and its user outside casita number eight. "Renata, hola!"

"Hola, Señora Buckley. Can I help you?"

"Yes, actually you can. Do you remember telling me about the missing medicine bottle this morning? The one on Georgina Early's nightstand?"

"Sí."

"Did that medicine bottle have a label on it?"

"Sí, it had a label from la farmacia."

"Do you remember the name of the medication on that label?"

"No, señora. I do not."

"If I were to show you a name of a medication, would you recognize if it was a match for the medication on the nightstand?"

The housekeeper responded positively. "Sí, I have seen that label many, many times."

Stella typed something into her phone and then held it aloft. Across the display was the word *oxycodone*. "Is this the name of the medication Georgina Early took?"

Renata gave a firm no. "The name was longer and it started with *hache*."

"The letter *H*?"

"Sí. I cannot try to pronounce the word it is so long. Sorry."

"That's fine, Renata. No apologies needed."

Stella looked up to see Inspector Lenzana approaching. "Buenas dias. Are you Renata Torres?"

The housekeeper's eyes grew wide. "Sí."

"Señor Tugores tells me that you cleaned Señora Early's casita this morning."

Renata glanced at Stella with panic in her eyes.

"It's okay, Renata. I'm sure you aren't in any trouble," Stella assured her as she looked at Lenzana, her face a question.

"She is not in any trouble at all—not with la policía or with Señor Tugores," the policeman responded.

"Can you stay with me?" Renata asked Stella. "I do not wish to answer questions alone."

"I'm certainly willing to stay, if . . ." She looked again at Lenzana.

"It is permitted," the inspector allowed. "Señorita Torres. Why did you clean Señora Early's casita this morning?"

"Luciana, the lady in charge of guest services, told me to do so."

"Did she say why?"

"Sí. She said it needed to be cleaned so it could be rented to new guests."

"With Señora Early's belongings still there?"

"Sí, her cases and clothes were still there along with all the knitting she'd done."

"Is it usual to clean a casita for new guests while the old guest's things are still there?"

"No, it never happened before."

"Did you ask why it was happening now?"

"Sí. Luciana told me it was a scheduling issue. That Señor Early might leave after housekeeping had gone for the day, so she wanted the hard cleaning done right away and she would take care of the last details herself."

"When you say 'hard cleaning,' what does that mean?"

"Scrubbing the *baño, la cucina,* cleaning and mopping all the floors, dusting, changing the linens, and getting rid of the trash."

"This trash, did you notice any letters or scraps of paper Señora Early might have written?"

"No, but I don't look at everything. I just throw things away when I clean for new guests. If I look and examine everything I find, I never get done."

Lenzana nodded. "And you placed this trash in the dumpster?"

"Sí. Just outside the clubhouse there is a high fence and gate, so guests cannot see it."

"Gracias. One last question. Do you recognize this?" With a gloved hand, Lenzana displayed a prescription pill bottle for Renata's review. The label, from the pharmacy in town and dated a week earlier, listed the medication inside as hydrochlorothiazide. A few pink tablets remained in the bottle.

"Sí!" Renata replied excitedly. "That is Señor Early's medicine. Where did you find it?"

"On the table beside her bed."

"No! That cannot be. It was not there this morning when I cleaned."

"You're positive it wasn't there?"

Renata invoked the sign of the cross. "Absolutamente."

"Did you see anyone go in or out of Señora Early's casita?"

"No. No, I did not, but I have been in and out of other guest casitas all morning."

"And you, Señora Buckley?"

"Nick and I only just got back a short time ago and we've been chatting with our friends ever since. If someone entered Georgina's casita, I'm not sure I would have noticed. I have a question for you," Stella volleyed. "Are you certain that the contents of the bottle match the label?"

"I need to have our medical examiner confirm their chemical makeup, but the tablets do appear to be marked as hydrochloro-thiazide."

"If they are, then where have they been?" Stella asked. "And why did someone find it necessary to take them?"

Chapter Nine

"Just because the dog wouldn't eat your dinner don't mean he's sick," Clyde Perkins said as Lila plopped Bixby's dog bed behind the cosmetics counter of the general store. "He might not have liked the smell of that beef. Cooked in wine, isn't it?"

"It is, but I don't think that's the problem. Bixby's an infamous scrounger and counter surfer. Not a meal goes by that Nick doesn't reprimand him for begging at the table, even on curry night."

"Well, we have some dog treats here that no dog can refuse. They're made from peanut butter and organic chicken by a fella up in Weston. He tried to sell them to the Vermont Country Store, but they weren't interested. If Bixby snubs these, then we know he's sick." Clyde grabbed a packet of said treats from the pet care section of the shop and popped it open. As if on cue, Bixby rushed forward, tail wagging, and devoured a handful of the canine snacks.

"Ain't nothing wrong with this dog," Clyde proclaimed.

"That doesn't prove anything," Lila argued. "Putting peanut butter treats in front of a dog is like putting a chocolate cheesecake in front of a menopausal woman."

"I'll have to remember that. About the cheesecake, I mean."

Lila flashed a self-conscious smile. "It's true. If you ever find yourself in the doghouse—no pun intended—it's not a bad place to start. Wine helps, too."

"I already took note of that one." He returned the smile. "So, you still think there's something wrong with our boy, here? Something other than missing Stella and Nick?"

"I do. I gave him lots of affection last night, practically my undivided attention. I gave him his dinner, took him out for a run in the backyard, lit some of my relaxation candles, and gave him lots of pets and hugs and kisses."

"Lucky Bixby."

Lila ignored the remark, but she felt her face go slightly warm. "He seemed to be his normal self again until I offered him part of my dinner. Instead of lapping it up, he rolled over and went to sleep."

"Well, the change of scenery will prolly do him some good. We get lots of folks with dogs in here, too. He might make some four-legged friends."

"Oh! I didn't even stop to think how he might get on with other dogs."

"He seems like a mellow boy, but just keep him on a leash until you get a better idea."

"I didn't bring one. I opened the door at home and he just followed me out."

"Don't worry. We stock those, too," Clyde said with a grin as he handed Lila an extra-large dog harness with leash.

"Thanks, Clyde. I'll pay for it out of my next check."

"Nah, consider it part of my investment in the pet deodorant project. Can't have an advertisement without a spokesdog."

"No, I suppose you can't." She fastened Bixby in his harness and tied his leash to a column that stood behind the cosmetics counter. The black Lab didn't seem to mind. He sniffed at the new harness and then yawned, stretched, and sprawled in his bed.

Clyde opened the store's front doors to a throng of shoppers waiting to purchase everything from groceries, sandwiches and household products to outdoor gear, winter clothing, and holiday gifts.

Lila helped several customers with fragrance and cosmetic gift purchases, ensuring that with each interaction she mentioned her new pet product line and sprayed a small sample in the air.

The feedback for the line was overwhelmingly positive. Most people said they liked the idea of a pet deodorizer that didn't smell like a pet deodorizer—that is, too flowery, stringent, or antiseptic. A deodorizer that not only possessed therapeutic qualities but smelled like a favorite fragrance was something they'd definitely be interested in purchasing. Some customers even went so far as to suggest an expansion for the product line with the addition of a pet deodorizer for carpets and soft furnishings.

Pleased with the response, Lila broke for lunch. Not having to drive home to take Bixby for a walk meant that she could enjoy a sandwich and a hot drink of tea from her insulated jug while watching the dog play in the snow on the village green.

After grabbing her lunch bag from the shelf beneath the counter, she reached behind her for Bixby's leash. "Come on, Bixby. Ready to go outside?"

The leash was in Lila's hand, but it was no longer connected to the dog's harness and Bixby was nowhere in sight. Not wishing to disturb the customers in the shop, she silently, albeit frantically, searched the aisles for the missing canine.

Ultimately, she came up empty. "Clyde," she whispered to the proprietor as he stood at the till awaiting the next purchase. "Clyde, I can't find Bixby."

"He prolly wandered off to the stock room for a nap. It's warm and quiet back there. Been known to go back there myself on slow days."

Lila followed Clyde to the stock room, but alas, there was no Bixby.

"Maybe he followed one of our customers outside," Lila suggested.

"One of us needs to stay here for the customers. You go. Bixby won't come to me if I call him."

Fraught with worry, she dashed outside without even stopping to put on her coat. "Bixby," she called once in the slushy store parking lot. Thankfully, the speed limit on Main Street was capped at twenty-five miles an hour, but the idea of Bixby running into heavy tourist traffic was still terrifying. "Bixby!"

From a parking space at the far end of the lot, a man's voice echoed, "Ma'am! Ma'am, are you looking for your dog?"

She looked up to see a man dressed in a Carhartt jacket, heavyweight canvas pants, and work boots. "Yes! Yes, he's a black Lab. A big boy named Bixby. Have you seen him?"

The young man summoned her to his truck, which bore the logo of White's Tree Farm. The flatbed was piled high with freshly cut netted trees, in the midst of which lay a black lab, sound asleep and loudly snoring. "Is this him?"

"That's him, alright," Lila confirmed. "Oh, thank you so much for finding him."

"I'm pretty sure he found me," the young man said with a smile. "Just glad I spotted him before I left. I'm on my way to deliver to a Christmas market in White River Junction."

"I'm glad you spotted him too! I'm watching him for my daughter and son-in-law. I don't know what I would have told them, had I not run into you. What on earth possessed him to climb in the back of your truck? The smell of the pine?"

"Doubt it. Most dogs aren't attracted by the smell of pine, probably because they know it's toxic to them."

"Really? I never knew that . . . but I never owned a dog before, so I suppose I wouldn't."

"We have three Goldens back at the farm. They never bother the trees. Retrievers are usually smart that way."

"Clearly, they're very smart. This one managed to get out of his harness."

"Classic retriever trick. They'll drive you nuts if you don't let them burn off some energy, but they're great dogs."

"Poor Bixby's been not-so-energetic lately. He just spent the morning asleep in the shop, so I'm surprised to see him sleeping so soundly here."

"Maybe he's depressed your daughter and son-in-law are gone?"

"I wondered about that. Oh! My son-in-law works for the U.S. Forest Service and frequently takes Bixby with him to work. Do you think maybe the pine scent reminds him of his time in the woods with my son-in-law?"

"Could be. If I've learned anything, it's never to underestimate a dog."

"I'll take your advice, but I wish someone had told me that sooner. We wouldn't have been in this mess. Thank you so much for all your help." She called Bixby to join her back in the store.

"Not a problem. It was nice meeting you both."

Bixby didn't move a muscle.

"Bixby," Lila called again.

This time the dog replied with a loud snore.

"I'll carry him into the store for you."

"Oh, thank you! I'm so sorry to bother you."

"No bother. They're like big babies sometimes," the young man said with a smile.

He hopped into the back of the truck and lifted Bixby with a groan. "Come on, bud. Let's get you back inside with Grandma."

The reference to her as Grandma made Lila cringe. It was one thing to refer to herself as such in the privacy of her own home, but having a virtual stranger refer to her as a dog's grandmother was another matter entirely. Still, the young man was doing her a tremendous favor by helping with Bixby, so she smiled gratefully and lumped it.

"Here you go, pal," the young man said as he eased the dog into his bed behind the cosmetics counter.

Bixby woke briefly and sighed before rolling over.

"You've been such a tremendous help. No pun intended—tree-mendous—get it?" Lila snorted. "Hey, I need a Christmas tree and you've been such a dear, I'd like to purchase one of yours."

"Oh, you don't need to do that." He shooed away the idea with a shake of his head.

"But I want to. It would be nice to surprise my daughter and son-in-law when they get back and I'd much rather buy our tree from someone honest and fair. How much for a six-foot tree?"

"Seventy, but . . ."

Lila grabbed her handbag from a locked drawer in the counter and extracted seventy dollars from her wallet. "Money well spent. Thank you."

"Thank you, ma'am. Where do you want it? I can tie it to your car."

"No, just leave it by the back door. Clyde Perkins has a truck. I'll have him bring it home for me."

"Okay. I hope Bixby gets to see his parents soon."

"They'll be back next week," Lila assured him.

"Glad to hear it. Happy holidays."

"You too." She fastened Bixby's harness and reattached the leash. She probably should take the dog for a formal walk outside, but seeing as he'd only just come back in, she decided to eat her sandwich first.

"I see you found our boy," Clyde remarked as he sidled up to the cosmetics counter.

"Making a run for the New Hampshire border in a Christmas tree truck."

"New Hampshire? Knew there was somethin' funny about that dog. I'll check that harness to make sure he doesn't get loose again."

"Will you, Clyde? Thank you. Also, there's a Christmas tree by the back door of the shop. If you could bring it home for me in your truck later?"

"You got a stand for it?"

"Oh . . . um, I don't know."

"I'll throw that in the truck too. Now, you just eat your lunch and don't worry about the time. When you're back on shift, I'll go out and take care of that tree."

"Thanks, Clyde. You're a peach."

"You ain't so bad yourself," he answered with a wink.

Lila made her way to the small area adjacent to the stock room to eat her lunch. Although not a break room in the traditional sense, it possessed a table, a couple of folding chairs, and an old radio that was constantly tuned to VPR.

She had just taken a seat when the phone in the outside pocket of her handbag began to ring. "Stella?" she said aloud, noticing the name on the display as she accepted the call and placed the device to her ear. "Stella? Stella, honey, are you okay?"

"I'm fine, Mom," came her daughter's voice after a few seconds' delay. "I just wanted to check in and see how you're doing."

"Bixby and I are terrific. We're getting on famously. He's here at work with me."

"Really? Oh, that's so good to hear. I'm not disturbing you, am I?"

"No, just grabbing a quick lunch. Bixby's on lookout at the cosmetics counter."

"That's good. I hope he's being a good boy."

"He's . . . he's great." Lila opted to omit Bixby's attempted escape. Why trouble Stella on her vacation? "Just great."

"Aww, Nick will be happy to hear that."

Lila broke off a corner of her sandwich and nibbled it. "So, you must have called for something other than to check in on Bixby and me."

"No, not really. I just . . . well, it's nice to hear your voice."

She pulled the phone away from her face and glanced at it. "Why?

Are you sick, dear? You didn't drink the water or use ice cubes, did you?"

"No, Mom, I'm not sick. Nick isn't sick. We're fine. Everyone's fine."

"Whew! You had me worried. Then what is it?"

"Nothing, the resort is fabulous. Right on the beach. And the weather has been perfect."

She broke off another corner of sandwich. "I look forward to seeing the photos," she said before consuming it.

"I'll send some later today."

"I'll keep an eye out for them."

An uncomfortable silence fell between them, one that couldn't be explained by the lag in their connection.

"Are you sure everything's okay, Stella?" Lila asked.

"Yeah, I'm just a little edgy. A, um, a woman died here yesterday."

"Stella! You're on vacation. Don't you think you should give it a rest?" Lila scolded. "Your friends are getting married."

"Mo-om!" Stella stretched the word to two syllables as she so often did as a teenager. "It's not like I'm responsible for her death."

"Of course you aren't, but you are responsible for your reaction. And from the tone of your voice, it sounds as if you're hot on the trail again."

"No, not really. Okay . . . maybe a little. I just have the feeling something's wrong and a few of the details surrounding this woman's death justify that feeling. However, I wanted to make sure my intuition isn't picking up on something else, like you or Bixby being ill or the pipes in our house freezing."

"No, everything here is fine. I mean . . . Bixby does miss you both."

"Is he okay? He's not sick, is he?"

"No, no, he's eating normally. He played in the backyard last night like he usually does. He's just a little sad, that's all. When we finish our conversation, I'll let you talk to him and see if that perks him up."

"Absolutely. I hope it helps."

I hope so, too, Lila thought, but she kept her fears to herself. "I'm sure it will. Now, tell me, what does Graham think about this feeling of yours?"

"Nick," Stella emphasized in an attempt to get her mother into the habit of referring to her son-in-law by his chosen name rather than his given one, "is as confused as I am. You see, this woman is the second person to have died here in the past week."

"*Two* people have died? In one week?"

"Yes, and it's a small resort."

"My God, darling, are you sure that feeling in your gut isn't food poisoning?"

"Positive. It wasn't at all like that. The first person—a minister—died from heart issues, only according to one of the housekeepers, he didn't have heart issues. And the second—the woman I've already told you about—died from an overdose, only the police can't find the substance she overdosed on, but they can find her heart medication, which went temporarily missing."

"I'm sorry, darling, but I didn't understand a single thing you just said. I heard what you were saying and I understood the words just fine—so don't think I'm having a stroke or aneurysm—but none of it made any sense."

"That was pretty much the point."

"Well, I admit it all sounds suspicious, but who would want to murder these people, Stella? You said the resort is lovely, but is the surrounding area sketchy?"

"Sketchy? What year is this . . . ?"

"Okay, okay," Lila said with a sigh. "Is there a lot of crime in the area?"

"No, it's fine. A few pickpockets and lots of timeshare salespeople, as can be expected in touristy areas, but otherwise, it's perfectly safe. But to be honest, I don't think this was an outside job. The woman died poolside in broad daylight, with only the other resort guests around her."

"Hmm . . . you said everything there is perfect, but how is the food?"

"What?" Stella sounded shocked by the question.

"How is the food at the resort?"

"Delicious. What does that have to do with anything?"

"Everything! Travelers don't go around killing other guests in beautiful beachside resorts with delicious food, do they? Now, you're positive that no one broke in and killed these individuals?"

Stella hesitated. "Reasonably positive. I saw someone prowling around last night, but it seemed to me as if they were looking for something or someone."

"A prowler? That sounds dangerous! Are you certain you're safe there?"

"As safe as I can be at a resort where two people have died in the past week," Stella deadpanned.

"That isn't funny. You have your father's gallows humor."

"Sorry, Mom. Yes, I feel safe. Nick, Alma, and Mills are here. I'm not alone."

"Good. Your dead woman—I feel terrible calling her that. What was her name?"

"Georgina."

"Was Georgina married?"

"Yes, she was."

"Well, there you have it! It was her husband. When these things happen it's always the spouse."

"Georgina's husband was out sightseeing with us when she died. Also, what about the minister? Why would Georgina's husband want to kill him?"

"Simple. The husband confessed to the minister about the killing."

"He confessed prior to committing the crime?"

"Huh?"

"The minister—or vicar, as he was called—died first."

"Well . . . yes. The husband was overcome with guilt about the murder in his heart and confessed to the vicar."

"Do vicars in England even hear confession? I don't think they do."

"Does that matter? People talk to clergy members all the time."

"Hmm . . . I don't know, Mom, I still think it was a resort guest. Everyone hated Georgina. On the day she died, she argued with just about everyone here."

"That is interesting," Lila mused. "But I still can't see someone committing murder while on vacation, darling. If you hate a fellow guest that much, you simply pack up and head home. Or book into another resort."

"It's not quite that simple. When you cancel a reservation like that, you're still billed for the entire stay. No one wants to lose money. Also, this resort has a lot of good memories for many of the guests staying here."

"In that case, the guests would band together and threaten to go home unless the horrible guest was forced to leave. That's a much more reasonable solution than murder."

"Perhaps. But even the manager got into a scrap with Georgina."

"Really? She *was* bad news, wasn't she? Every hotel manager I've encountered was willing to bend over backward to accommodate their guests," Lila said with a sniff. That Lila had traveled in more expensive circles than Stella was evident. "Ah, well, that was another lifetime ago. Anyway, I gave you my two cents. Did it help you, darling?"

"Umm, maybe. But I will say that I've enjoyed talking to you. And you certainly helped to put my mind at ease about you, the house, and Bixby."

"Happy to help. Oh, speaking of Bixby, before you go, I'll bring the phone out to him." Lila hurried from the break room to the front of the shop, where Bixby still slumbered behind the cosmetics counter. "Bixby. Bixby."

The dog lifted his head and sniffed the air, his eyes still closed.

Lila knelt beside him and, lifting a floppy black ear, placed the phone close to his head. "Listen, Bixby." She was about to tell him that his mommy was on the line, but she refused to publicly participate in such precious behavior.

"Hi, Bixby," Stella greeted the dog. "I heard you're being a good boy. Are you a good boy?"

At the use of the phrase "good boy," Bixby's tail wagged.

"We miss you, our good boy, but we'll be home soon. Until then, be good for Grandma."

Lila cringed and tried to avoid the eyes of shop customers looking for "Grandma." "Bixby's tail is wagging," she told her daughter upon returning the phone to her ear.

"Terrific. If you think he needs to talk to us again this week, just shoot me a text and we'll call you."

"Sounds good, sweetie. You and Gra—er, Nick, stay safe. Give my best to Alma and Sheriff Mills."

"Will do. Love you, Mom."

"Love you, too."

Lila disconnected the call and glanced at Bixby. Although momentarily excited by the call and the sound of his owner's voice, he had returned to a lounging position, with his head propped on the side of his plush bed and a vacant, far-off look in his eyes. "Oh, Bixby," Lila whispered to herself. "What am I going to do with you?"

Chapter Ten

Lila's words stayed with Stella the remainder of the afternoon. Watching her fellow guests as they basked in the sun, swam, and played cards, she agreed that people on vacation were unlikely to commit murder. And yet, it was difficult to ignore that the mood was far lighter than it had been when she, Nick, Alma, and Mills first arrived.

Indeed, the mood at Caballero Cove was practically jubilant. Far closer to that of a typical coastal resort approaching the holiday season than that of a small hotel that had seen the loss of two longtime guests over the course of a week.

The lighthearted ambiance lasted through right until cocktail hour and dinner. Bernard was absent again, choosing to take his evening meal in his bungalow, but everyone else was present, including Joseph Penrod, who, although not exactly carefree, was a great deal more cheerful than he had been during that first dinner two nights ago.

Señor Tugores called the group to the dining table beneath the pergola and raised his glass. "To Señora Early."

The group raised their glasses and joined in a moment of silence before taking a sip in the late guest's honor.

"And now on to a bit of business. As you all know, our annual costume party is scheduled for this time tomorrow evening. I was going to cancel it due to Señora Early's passing, but Señor Early spoke with me this afternoon and has insisted that we move forward. I told him I would speak to the rest of you before making a final decision. So, tell me what you think," Tugores presented.

Ellie was the first to speak. "It feels wrong to be partying when a woman is dead."

"A woman who nearly pushed me into early labor," Kendal snapped. "I feel no need to show her any respect."

"I'm not acting out of deference to Georgie, but I do respect life and the power of nature. We'll soon have a child of our own to raise and I think we need to set an example."

"We also need to teach our child to stand up for itself and not to let bullies push them around."

Desirée spoke up. "I'm with Kendal. If any of us were on that slab instead of Georgie, you can bet she wouldn't be deliberating whether to go ahead with a party. She'd go on with her life as if nothing happened."

"She was an addict," Ellie argued.

"Just because she overdosed doesn't mean she was an addict," Ray Horrocks said. "As you know, I work in sports medicine. Accidental overdoses occur all the time, but they don't always prove to be fatal. That's why we focus on pain management and prescribe opioids only as a last resort."

"So, what are you trying to say, Ray?" Diana challenged. "Should we hold the party or not?"

"I don't know. Addict or not, her death is unfortunate in that it probably could have been prevented. If she was struggling with pain, she could have come to me or any other therapist in the UK or here in Mexico and they might have been able to help her."

"And?" Diana urged, clearly annoyed with her husband's vague response.

"As sad as her passing might be, she surely caused a hell of a lot of unnecessary grief and aggravation for a bunch of folks who only wanted to be her friend. I say we go ahead and have the party."

"I second that," Diana rejoined, clearly pleased with Ray's decision.

"In Indian culture, we mourn the loss of a loved one for thirteen days. There is no dancing, no music, no singing. I shall not be mourning Georgina Early," Anika Banerjee stated blankly.

"I will not be mourning her, either," Manish echoed. "However, her existence reminds us to partake of the joyfulness in life that always appeared to elude her."

"Well said," Diana praised.

"I don't go in for flowery speeches," Ruckert chimed in, "so I'll just say it as plainly as possible: Georgina Early was a bitch. She tried to ruin this place for us every chance she got. And I'm happy she's gone. I know everyone else here—including Ellie—feels a sense of relief at not having to see her face again. Why should we hide our sense of elation by canceling a party that she never seemed to enjoy anyway?"

All eyes turned toward Joseph Penrod.

"I agree with what everyone has said. I, like Ellie, was taught to respect both the living and the dead. I joined the military, where I fought for them both—their honor, their safety, their memory. Yet, I also agree that Georgina could be terribly cruel. If Georgina's overdose is, in fact, proof that her cruelty stemmed from addiction or chronic pain, then I am truly sorry. If only she'd told us the situation she was in. I believe that if she had told us, that we as a group would have responded with kindness. You were all very understanding and kind when my wife passed away . . ." He hung his head and slowly swung it from side to side. "But she didn't talk to us. Didn't open up. Instead, she reveled in bitterness and propagated misery. She leveled caustic remarks at all of us. *All* of us, including my best friend."

Penrod stared at the empty seat across the table. By emphasizing the word *all* it was abundantly clear that Georgina had taken aim at both Reverend Bailor and Penrod's late wife.

"Sorry to be so long-winded, Señor Tugores." Penrod smiled wanly at the hotel manager. "To answer the question, if the woman's own husband sees no reason to cancel tomorrow night's festivities, why should we?"

A cheer went up from the tablemates who'd spoken before him, with the exception of Ellie, who rose from her seat and gave the man a hug.

"Then it's been decided, unless our new guests are opposed?" Tugores looked at Alma, who sat at the end of the table, across from Mills.

She eyed her fiancé and then with a nod said, "No. We're all very sorry about what happened, but you folks knew the deceased far better than we did, and if you and Bernard all think it's okay . . ."

Another cheer went up from the table.

"Ellie doesn't like to admit it, but she's been looking forward to the costume party," Kendal announced with a sly grin in her partner's direction.

Ellie accepted Kendal's comment in good humor. "It's true. Our costumes are completely on point this year. We spent the past month perfecting them. I just didn't feel right about going ahead with the party tomorrow."

"Your sensitivity is one of your finest qualities. Our baby is lucky to have you as a parent," Kendal praised as she blew Ellie a kiss.

The table erupted in a prolonged "Aww," prompting a smile from Tugores before he left for his office.

"I suppose you brought your old standby costume, huh, Joe?" Ellie teased.

"My army uniform? You betcha. It isn't a Caballero Cove costume party without it."

"We thought you might spice things up for a change. Maybe dress as a matador," Diana joked.

"Or something Bollywood-inspired," Anika rejoined, prompting giggles.

"What? Me in a vividly colored turban?" Penrod played along. "Can you just picture it?"

"I think you'd look handsome in anything, Joe," Ellie said earnestly.

"It's that regal, military bearing," Desirée noted.

"It is, isn't it?"

"Now, ladies. If you're finished having a laugh at my expense . . ." He had blushed a bright crimson.

"We're being serious, Joe," Desirée replied. "You should branch out a little more. Wear some printed shirts, a few youthful pieces. You could definitely pull it off."

"And what about me?" Ruckert demanded. "Can I pull off some more youthful styles?"

Diane, Anika, and Ellie pulled faces at each other and tried not to laugh.

"A little bit of youthfulness could benefit everyone, Chip, be it fashion, music, or mindset."

An awkward silence fell over the table—a silence broken by the arrival of the waitstaff with the first course. As the group settled in to enjoy their dinner, various small conversations broke out.

Ellie leaned in toward Stella. "Desirée's getting tired of him," she whispered, casting a glance in Chip Ruckert's direction.

"They do seem like very different people," Stella noted in an equally hushed tone.

"They didn't always. They and Chip's first wife, Nancy, were thick as thieves. The three of them did everything together. If you didn't know who they were, you'd have a difficult time discerning who was the married couple and which one of them was the proverbial 'third wheel.' Nancy died a couple years back—at home, not here." She laughed uneasily. "Not everyone who vacations here, dies here."

"That's a comfort to know."

Ellie laughed again. "Ha! I know. Anyway, one summer we all received an email from Señor Tugores stating that Nancy had died at home rather suddenly. That December, they"—she slid her eyes toward Desirée and Chip—"arrived here as a full-on couple. It all happened so quickly that it was . . . disconcerting."

"Are you saying you suspect foul play?"

"No," Ellie was quick to deny. "Although that rumor has flown around here plenty of times. Still does on occasion."

"Like now?"

Ellie shook her head. "No, but watching Desirée with those dancers has raised some questions."

"With whom?"

"Well . . . Georgina, not surprisingly. She was obsessed with those dancers, convinced that something illegal was going on. I guess that was the drugs talking."

As Ellie shrugged and turned her attention toward her dinner, Stella glanced at the empty chair beside her. Was Georgina simply trying to make trouble? It wouldn't have been shocking if she was. Or did the woman truly suspect the resort's dancers of wrongdoing?

She looked up to see Desirée glaring at her, or more accurately, staring through her.

Stella gave a shudder and, like Ellie, concentrated on the dish that had been placed before her.

"So, if Bernard gave his blessing for the party tomorrow night," Diana said loudly enough for the entire table to hear her, "does that mean he's attending?"

"He should," Desirée answered. "God knows, Georgina held him back from doing anything fun all these years."

"I hate to say it, but it's true," Ellie said. "I was actually shocked that she let Bernard go to the ruins yesterday."

"She was always finding something for him to do. 'Bernard,'" Kendal added in an uncanny impersonation of Georgina, "'could you go into town, pet?'"

Chip spoke up. "If I were him and finally rid of that horrible woman, I'd party like there was no tomorrow."

"He won't be at the party," Penrod announced, much to everyone's surprise.

"What?" Anika cried. "How do you know he won't be here?"

"Because," Penrod explained in between quiet slurps of gazpacho, "he has other things he needs to do."

"Oh," Diane replied as the weight of Bernard's burden—beyond simple grief—finally dawned upon her. "I do suppose he has to file paperwork and arrange to bring Georgina back home."

"I'm sure there's a lot of red tape, too," Manish added.

"Shame," Desirée lamented. "The guy needs to cut loose for a while."

As the table continued to discuss Bernard Early's unfortunate situation, Penrod enjoyed his cold soup, a vague smile upon his face.

• • •

After a delicious dinner of shrimp aguachile with mango over rice (*calabacita con elote* for the vegetarians) and a decadent and creamy vegan coconut flan, the group retired to the pool area for music from a local string quartet. Drinks were courtesy of Caballero Cove Resort management.

It was a dignified and fitting way to cap an exceedingly pleasant and delicious meal. Unlike the night of the four friends' arrival, Penrod decided to extend the evening with a glass of excellent Scotch whiskey. Even Señor Tugores took a break from his duties and joined the group for a glass of wine and conversation.

"What a difference a couple of days make," Nick observed after providing their drink order to a member of the waitstaff.

"This place sure is a helluva lot livelier," Alma agreed.

"More like what the website promised us," Mills said with a smile.

105

"And all because of one woman," Stella replied.

"Mm-hmm. Well, I hate to say it, but if this place is happier, then so be it. This place is so beautiful I'll enjoy spending our honeymoon here, no matter what. But, it sure is nice to spend it surrounded by happy people," Alma confessed. "And on that note, I'll be a lot happier after a visit to the little girls' room."

"Is there room for a little boy to join you?" Mills asked, much to Alma's amusement.

"Sure is. Let's swing by the bungalow. We'll be back in a few," she told Stella and Nick.

As Mills and Alma departed, Diana and Ray Horrocks stopped by, each toting an umbrella-garnished glass. "Hey, you two, Ray and I feel like we haven't had a chance to really talk and get to know you."

"Probably because we haven't, what with everything." Stella gestured wildly with her hand.

"Oh, I know. I assure you this place is usually a lot more relaxed," Diana said to Stella as their husbands began their own conversation. "Not quite this relaxed, but a lot mellower than the past two days."

"So, this is over-the-top?"

"Um, no, not really. Not for us guests, but I've never seen Señor Tugores hanging out and having a few drinks and laughs after dinner. He's usually busy elsewhere."

"Must be nice for him to break free for a change. I heard somewhere that he's lived at this resort his whole life."

"That's right. His parents built the place before he was born. He took it over and updated it to what you see now."

"No wonder he's so dedicated to the place."

"Mmm . . . although from what I've heard, he wasn't always so focused. He supposedly fell for a girl a few years back. Not only was the girl several years younger than he was, but she was an employee of the resort. When her parents found out about the romance, they threatened to notify the police and sue for sexual harassment. Tugores's parents were in charge back then and completely freaked out. Rumor has it Tugores hasn't dated since."

Stella whistled. "That's quite the story."

"Yeah, it is, isn't it?" Diana laughed. "Very *Romeo and Juliet*. Taboo young love and all that."

"Definitely. Who told you that story?"

"I honestly can't remember. It's been so long."

"What are you girls laughing about?" Ray asked.

"I told Stella about Tugores and his ill-fated love affair," Diana replied.

"Oh, that. Di, you don't even know if it's true or not. It sounds so dramatic." He recounted the tale for Nick's benefit.

"Where did you even hear that story?" Stella asked.

Ray sucked his teeth and cast his eyes heavenward in an effort to remember. "Jeeze, I don't know. Penrod, maybe? I'm not certain, but he's been coming here forever, so he probably knows more about this place than anyone else here."

As a waiter delivered Nick and Stella's drinks, the couples were joined by Manish and Anika Banerjee.

"Hey, what a great evening! It's like old times again, isn't it? Before—" Anika stopped herself and glanced self-consciously at Stella and Nick. "Before a certain someone started ruining the place for us."

"I'm surprised you all kept coming back," Nick remarked.

"We have such fond memories of Caballero Cove," Manish said. "Our kids would spend hours playing in the sand on Bandista Beach and we'd snorkel Cozumel or, if it was raining, visit the planetarium. There's nowhere else we'd rather be, even if Georgina made things difficult at times."

"We were just discussing the old days," Diana told them. "We told them that rumor about Señor Tugores."

"Which one is that?" Anika asked. "There have been so many rumors through the years. Most of them complete nonsense."

"The one about Tugores and that girl. Years ago."

"Ah, that old story. If you're going to share gossip, why not choose something juicy? Like how Joseph Penrod might be a secret millionaire."

"What?" Nick and Stella exclaimed simultaneously.

"I overheard Joe's conversation with Georgie yesterday morning. You know, the one that led to their argument by the pool. I was in the pool house getting a towel and an inflatable raft and could hear just about everything they said. Joe kept mentioning their 'deal' and how Georgie needed to honor it."

"Deal? What kind of deal?" Stella asked.

"I didn't get the details, but Georgie worked in wealth management, so I assume they had some sort of business arrangement."

"Wealth management? So, Georgie was probably making investments on Penrod's behalf."

"Manish and I are not wealthy, so I can only guess, but that sounds about right. Neither of them mentioned the word *money* or even numbers, just some 'deal' they had arranged and that Georgie somehow was meeting the terms."

"Hmmm . . . that is a pretty juicy story."

"What's even juicier is how does a veteran manage to wind up with a million dollars in the bank?" Ray questioned. "Most lifers I know do okay, but their spouses still work."

"If Penrod was a lifelong officer and made some wise investments, he could easily be in the millionaire range," Nick stated. "And don't forget, he might have come from a wealthy family."

"I don't care how he got it, but I do want to know what Georgie did with it." Anika took a final swig of her drink and gestured toward the bar. "We'd better grab another round before the dance party starts."

"Wait." Nick put his hand in the air. "There's another dance party tonight?"

"There's usually a dance party every night. Tugores canceled last night's party because of Georgina's death, but he resumed the party tonight because *someone* didn't want to walk home from El Sueño again," Ray explained.

Stella's eyes grew wide. "You mean you saw Desirée last night too?"

"Not last night, no. But we've all seen her toddling home whenever the party's been moved next door."

"There's something shady about that woman," Diana warned before heading off to the bar. "That might be the only thing Georgina was ever right about. She's up to something with those dancers."

Shortly after the two couples left, Chip Ruckert approached Stella and Nick. Just twenty minutes had elapsed since dinner and he was already well on his way to complete inebriation. "You folks need to be careful."

"What do you mean?" Nick questioned.

"That bunch you were just talking to." He gestured wildly toward the Horrockses and Banerjees.

"Why? They've been coming here for years, just like you, haven't they?"

"They have and I had my reservations at first."

"I bet you did," Nick replied, suppressing a knowing laugh.

Stella looked at her husband and rolled her eyes.

"But then they were so invested in their children that you couldn't help but like them," Ruckert, oblivious, went on. "Now that their children are grown . . . well, they've become swingers."

Stella nearly spit out her drink for laughing. "Pardon me? Did you say swingers?"

"I did. Swingers, wife-swappers. I've seen Manish and Diana together and Ray and Anika together."

"I've seen them together, too," Stella admitted. "At a café and in the swimming pool. Where have you seen them?"

"In town, shopping, and here at the resort. Last year, Ray and Anika went to Tulum without Manish and Diana."

"So, when you say 'together,' you don't mean 'together-together'?"

"No, but you don't need to be a detective to know where it all leads. The bedroom."

Nick closed his eyes and shook his head in disbelief.

"Did Georgina Early happen to tell you they were swingers?" Stella asked.

"No . . . no, I deduced it myself, but she agreed."

"Uh-huh."

"And I think it's obvious why they made a beeline over to see you tonight," Chip said while eyeing Stella. "You're very attractive."

Nick cleared his throat, loudly.

"I mean you're both very attractive people. Not that I find men attractive. I don't function that way. Not to put down people who do, but—"

"Yeah, yeah, we get it," Nick interrupted. "Thanks for the warning. Enjoy the dance party."

"Oh, I don't dance. That's Desirée's thing. Speaking of which, where she'd go?"

As Chip shuffled back to the bar in search of his significant other, Desirée was seated poolside fixing her makeup in a compact mirror.

"Swingers? He's about sixty years too late on that one, isn't he?" Nick said to Stella.

"His whole mindset is about sixty years too late," she quipped.

"No arguments, there. Wife-swapping? Jeeze Louise. You know I love Alma, but why do I have the feeling that she found this place in an ad in *Soap Opera Weekly*?"

Stella watched Penrod as he sat by himself, sipping his Scotch and surveying the chaos around him. "Because this place is full of drama."

"You know, you're right. I'd never really thought about it before, but there is a lot of drama going on. With just about everyone." He took a sip of beer. "Hey, why did you ask Chip if Georgina had come up with the swingers theory?"

"Because Georgina was looking into the dancers—she felt there was something odd about them. Georgina called Desirée Hunt shady. Georgina had a deal with Joseph Penrod—a deal she was obviously trying to renege upon. Georgina told Chip Ruckert that the Horrockses and Banerjees were swingers. I'm willing to bet it was Georgina who dug up that odd bit of dirt about Tugores, too."

"But why? Why would she do that?"

"I haven't a clue, but Georgina was at the heart of every rumor and personal drama occurring in this resort. And I can't help but think that her fatal overdose isn't a coincidence."

Chapter Eleven

Lila was awakened at six in the morning by the sound of heavy snoring. "Oh, honey," she said wearily. "Could you please roll over? That's my ear you're breathing into."

The only reply to Lila's request was an abrupt grunt followed by a yawn. The snoring resumed moments afterward.

Lila rolled over and endeavored to drown out the sound by pulling the covers over her head, but her bedmate had wrapped himself tightly in the comforter and sheets. "Ugh. The only reason you're here is to prevent you from being lonely, but if you're going to be rude, you can go sleep downstairs."

She had hoped her words would spur Bixby to either go to his own bed or, at the very least, change position, but the dog remained in his spot, head propped upon the extra pillow and his body entangled in Lila's very favorite Yves Delorme comforter.

Seeing no point in trying to continue to sleep, she slung her feet over the side of the bed, slid into her slippers, and decided that she could at least enjoy a quiet cup of coffee before Bixby woke up and excitedly demanded food and a trip to the backyard.

Such optimism was cut short, however, when the black Lab passed her on the way down the staircase and stood by the kitchen door.

"Oh, Bixby. You're not cutting me any slack today, are you?"

She donned her coat and shuffled out the back door. Standing on the back porch, she watched as Bixby ran happily through the snow before stopping and doing his business. Once finished, he ran straight back toward Lila and butted her hand with his head. "At least one of us is excited to start the day."

She held the door open for him and he rushed inside and directly to his bowl. Instead of retrieving the kibble from the pantry, Lila set about making herself coffee, much to Bixby's chagrin. "Listen," she replied to his whines and whimpers, "if you're going to get me up while it's still dark, you're going to have to wait for me to start the caffeination process before you eat."

With the automatic drip machine working its magic, Lila set about getting Bixby his breakfast. "Here you go, your lordship," she said while presenting it to him.

She eyed the coffee carafe and, noticing the machine had produced enough for one cup, seized it and filled her mug. While she drank, Bixby finished his breakfast and moved into his bed by the woodstove for a nap.

"Oh, *now* you go to sleep." She rolled her eyes and sat down at the kitchen table with her phone and coffee. As soon as she switched the display on, she noticed a text from Clyde. The time stamp read five thirty-six a.m.

Perhaps Bixby should stay with Clyde. They were already on the same sleep schedule, she thought as she clicked on the message.

How about breakfast this morning? Bring Bixby. I have a surprise.

Lila bit her lip. She wasn't sure what surprise Clyde might have in store, but breakfast sure sounded good.

Okay, she replied.

I'll meet you at the store at 7:30.

As promised, Lila pulled into the general store parking lot at seven twenty-four in the morning, with Bixby in tow. Clyde's pickup was already in its usual spot at the back of the building.

Using her key, she let herself into the front door of the shop, whereupon smelling food, a leash-free Bixby ran straight not for the sandwich counter but for the break room. Lila followed him to find three foil-wrapped parcels of food on the folding table, as well as three insulated cups with plastic lids.

Clyde pushed one of the cups toward her. "Black with one Splenda."

"You remembered."

"I made it a point to remember. I once dated a gal who couldn't even speak until she had her first cup of coffee. I decided to surprise her one morning with coffee and donuts, but I accidentally forgot to add the milk to her coffee. Hoo boy, there went that relationship. I'm not gonna make that mistake again."

"Don't worry. I'm not the type to throw someone over because they got my food order wrong."

"Still not takin' any chances. That's why I prepared you a turkey sausage, egg white, and spinach sandwich with pesto." He handed her one of the hot, foil-wrapped packages. "On whole wheat bread to boot."

"Perfect!" She took the package and unwrapped it. "Oh, this looks wonderful, Clyde. I didn't know you could make such sandwiches."

"Who do you think ran the lunch counter when we first opened?" He stabbed his thumb into his chest. "My father hated cooking, so as soon as I could reach the stove, that was my job."

"He trained you well," she praised before sinking her teeth into the sandwich. It was hot, perfectly cooked, and delicious. "Mmm . . . this is great. Thank you."

"Don't thank me until you see the stovetop. It's going to need a good scrub."

"I'm in the cosmetics department," she replied. "I don't do dishes."

"That's my girl," Clyde cheered with a chuckle, before tearing into his bacon, egg, and cheese sandwich.

Lila took a sip of coffee and sat down at the table. "So, are you particularly hungry today? Or does that third sandwich have somebody's name on it?"

"That's my surprise. That's why I wanted you to bring Bixby."

"He already ate, Clyde. And I'm not sure we'll want him in the store after he's eaten an egg sandwich, if you know what I mean."

"I'm not feeding the breakfast sandwich to Bixby. I'm feeding it—I mean, I'm giving it to a customer of mine who breeds dogs."

"Breeding? I'm afraid that boat's sailed, Clyde. Bixby's already been fixed. And even if he hadn't been, I shudder to imagine dealing with him and a litter of puppies right now."

Clyde sat down at the opposite side of the table. "I'm not suggesting that Bixby be used for breeding, although he is a handsome pup. Alice, my breeding friend, is an expert on dog behavior. I thought she might be able to figure out what's wrong with our pooch, here."

At Clyde's mention of him, Bixby flopped down alongside the table and rolled onto his back.

"Sure," Lila reluctantly agreed. "But is watching him during breakfast—which, by the way, I wouldn't have started eating had I known we were waiting for someone else to arrive—sufficient time for Alice to render a professional opinion?"

"Alice isn't staying for breakfast, so we needn't have waited for her. She's coming here to collect Bixby and her coffee and sandwich, and then she's bringing them all back to her farm."

"Her farm?" Lila's jaw dropped. "I'm responsible for Bixby, Clyde. I can't just let him go off with anyone. Even if they're a friend of yours."

"Now, now. It's just for the day. Alice will bring him back before we close up for the day."

"But Bixby doesn't know her."

"He'll get to know her. Alice is a licensed breeder and accredited dog trainer. Not only does she love dogs, but she has a farm full of animals she's rescued over the years. When I spoke to her about Bixby, she thought it might be a good idea to introduce him to other dogs to help ease his loneliness while Stella and Nick are gone and to help him socialize."

Lila folded her arms across her chest. "Bixby isn't lonely. He has me."

Clyde mirrored her pose and stared at her over the top of his glasses.

"Okay," she relented. "She might be on to something with the whole socialization idea. Being leashed to the cosmetics counter all day isn't ideal. He loves the pets customers give him, but it's not like being out and about playing, is it?"

"Alice has several acres where Bixby can play."

Lila breathed a heavy sigh and reached down to pat the dog's belly. "That would be good for him. When Stella and Nick are here, he gets a ton of outdoor time. More than I can give him. I just feel weird about letting a stranger take him."

Clyde reached across the table and patted her hand. "He'll be fine. Don't worry."

"But I do worry. Between the marriages and boyfriends, I wasn't always there for Stella when she was growing up. And now that she finally needs me to do something . . ." She threw her hands up in the air.

"Lila, you're doing a good job taking care of Bixby. You're also a good woman with a good heart. You have flaws like we all do, but you're there for Stella. She knows you are. She must, otherwise she and Nick wouldn't have opened their home to you now."

"Or they simply pitied me. I was in a fairly pathetic state when I first arrived."

"Dogs don't pity people. Look at how Bixby's taken to you. I bet you couldn't have rubbed his belly like that a couple of days ago."

"He smells the bacon and cheese in my sandwich."

Clyde flashed a rare smile. "Maybe . . . where was Bixby last night?"

She stopped petting the dog and took a long sip of coffee before answering. "With me. That's why I'm so tired. He's a bed hog. And he snores."

"I suppose he slept so soundly because he pities you."

Lila rolled her eyes. "Okay. You got me. I'll let Bixby go with Alice today."

"Good." Clyde uncrossed his arms and took a large bite from his sandwich.

Lila also took a bite of hers. "However, at some point I'd like to discuss these flaws of mine," she said after swallowing.

"Huh?"

"You told me I was a good woman, but that I have flaws."

"Yep."

"Care to tell me what those flaws are?"

"Nope."

"Why not?"

"'Cause I want to live long enough to finish my breakfast."

Chapter Twelve

For the first time since arriving in Playa del Carmen, Stella slept through the night. No doubt a combination of the house wine, lots of dancing, and the more relaxed atmosphere at the resort. Waking at eight, she was surprised to find Nick out of bed and waiting for her outdoors in the garden with coffee.

"Morning. When did you wake up?" She leaned over him and gave him a kiss before taking the chair on the opposite side of the bistro table.

"Seven."

"That's not early for you at home, but early for you on vacation. Everything okay?"

"Yeah, I'm just not used to all the traffic here. Our house is so quiet," he explained while pouring her a cup of coffee.

Stella accepted the cup of coffee from Nick and stirred in some milk, her face a question. "Traffic? There's not a car in sight."

"I meant foot traffic. Around three this morning I noticed the motion light outside the clubhouse was on. It shines through the window above our bed."

Stella nodded. "Desirée triggered it two nights ago trying to get her keys into the lock of her casita. But it wouldn't have been her who set it off last night, would it? The dance party was held here and it wrapped well before midnight."

"Yeah, I could have sworn she and Ruckert went to their casita together."

"Me too. Unless she snuck back out to meet someone."

"I couldn't say. I got up to check, but I didn't see anyone. Also, had she snuck out, the light would have gone off twice, wouldn't it? Once when she left and again when she returned. I was in such a light sleep, I'm sure I would have noticed it."

"Hmm . . . I wonder how close to the clubhouse you have to be to trigger that light."

"Why?"

"I'm remembering our prowler. They got as far as Georgina's

casita without the light switching on. And it definitely seemed as if I had interrupted them."

"You think they might have come back?" Nick asked.

"It would make sense. Except, what are they looking for? The police have already searched Georgina's casita."

"We'll have to test that motion light later tonight. Maybe after the costume party. It would give us a better indication of where the person in question was headed."

Stella agreed. "You mentioned traffic kept you awake. I can only imagine you meant more than just someone setting off the motion light."

"Yeah, after the motion light, it was difficult to get back to sleep."

"Because you knew something was wrong?"

"Yep. The motion light really played with my brain. I kept imagining someone lurking outside our bungalow. I did doze off for a short time, but before long, I heard the staff getting the pool chairs set up and ready. Then someone was jogging."

"That would be Ray Horrocks."

"I don't care who it was. The sound of their feet hitting the pavement as they ran laps around the pool drove me nuts."

"You're not usually that sensitive."

"I know, but between the light and this overdose business, my brain was working overtime. I don't know how you ever sleep when you're assisting on a case."

"I don't know either, but last night I crashed."

"I know. You didn't even wake up when the police arrived."

"The police? They're here now?"

"They got here a half hour ago," he confirmed.

"Why? Do you know what happened?"

"As we already discussed, I don't have your knack for eavesdropping, but as far as I could ascertain, Bernard Early tried to book a ticket back to the UK. Lenzana told him he couldn't leave."

"I'm not surprised Bernard wants to leave this place. It must be painful for him, what with all the memories here." Stella took a sip of coffee and swallowed. "And yet, Georgie's body hasn't been cleared to ship back home yet."

"What's the delay? Did Lenzana tell you?"

"The police still haven't found the oxycodone."

Nick reached into the napkin-lined basket of pastries on the table and selected a chocolate croissant. "Strange, isn't it? If Georgie was an addict, you'd think the stuff would be all over the place. Not in plain view, of course, but tucked into a dresser drawer, stashed at the back of the medicine cabinet, at the bottom of her handbag. You'd think she wouldn't want to run out of the stuff. And yet, by the looks of her casita, she had run out."

"I suppose she'd taken her entire supply. Maybe that's what killed her. The police are checking the trash for empty bottles and other paraphernalia."

"Yeah, what about that weird cleanup ordered by Luciana? Do you think maybe Georgie got her drugs from a member of the staff and the management tried to hide it?"

"Possibly," Stella allowed. "Although Georgie was all about image, wasn't she? She looked down her nose at the other guests. Would she actually ask someone at Caballero Cove for drugs? That would basically be admitting she had a problem. Wouldn't she be afraid of that information getting out to the other guests?"

Nick shrugged. "Addicts can be unpredictable."

"I don't know, Nick. Part of me thinks Georgina would have hated for anyone here to know that she had a drug problem. The way she spread rumors about the other guests, it was as if she needed to feel superior to them. She made sure she knew everything about everyone, just so she could have the upper hand. She needed to be seen as the queen of this place and a queen would never let others see her weaknesses."

"Not even the king?"

"Well, Bernard wasn't really the king, was he? At least she didn't seem to treat him like one."

"You think she made Bernard sleep in another casita to hide her addiction?"

"We can't be certain what Bernard knew or what he didn't. He mentioned Georgina seeing a doctor, but that doesn't mean much, does it?"

"No. One thing's for certain though, asking your husband to sleep in separate quarters is a pretty damning blow to a marriage."

"If she was, in fact, the one to make that decision. Perhaps Bernard suggested it."

"Oh, come on. I doubt Bernard initiated that move. You saw him on the bus to Tulum. He was like a wounded puppy."

Stella wrinkled her nose.

"Okay, he wasn't as cute as a puppy—still isn't—but he was definitely pathetic."

"True," she agreed.

"Yet another reason for Bernard to want out of here. Staying alone in that casita of his is a brutal reminder of how bad things had become in his marriage."

As a uniformed waiter dropped off a basket of freshly baked pastries, Inspector Lenzana came to join them. "I wanted to thank you both for coming to see me at headquarters."

"No thanks necessary. It seemed the right thing to do," Nick replied.

"It was more than the right thing. Because of you, I contacted Reverend Bailor's physician in England. He confirmed what the housekeeper told us. The reverend did not have high blood pressure, but low pressure. Not dangerously low, but enough to make him dizzy at times. He was shocked to learn that he had died of a heart attack."

"So this means . . . ?" Stella questioned.

"That we're labeling the reverend's death as suspicious and reopening his file. The UK authorities will be exhuming his body in the next few days. We contacted Georgina Early's physician. She confirmed that Señora Early had been taking hydrochlorothiazide for the past year and a half for high blood pressure. I received the records this morning. There was nothing in Señora Early's chart indicating that she had any pain issues. No chronic pain, no sharp pain, no mild pain, not even an ache. In the ten years she'd been seeing this physician, not once had she been prescribed oxycodone. The last exam Señora Early had was four months ago. The doctor found her to be in good health and with no complaints."

"So how did she get started on opioids? And how did she get the oxycodone?"

"I cannot answer the first question. She might have tried it in a recreational capacity and became 'hooked,' as you Americans say. It's a sad state of affairs, but Señora Early could have gotten it anywhere. There are many street dealers here who could have provided her with it, just as I am sure there are many dealers in the UK who could have done the same."

"So, was Georgina an addict?" Nick asked.

"Señora Early's physician claims she was not. She says that her patient exhibited none of the symptoms of opioid addiction. Her physical appearance had not altered much in the ten years she'd been seeing her. She had not lost or gained any vast amounts of weight, and her respiratory and heart rates were always strong, and her pupils normal. The physician claims that if Señora Early was using oxycodone, it was a very recent development, within the past three months. Even so, she still was skeptical."

"So, what's the theory?" Nick challenged. "Georgina decided to kick back and relax by the pool with a few oxycodone, but took one too many?"

"We've ruled Señora Early's death as suspicious, same as Reverend Bailor's. And we are searching through the trash removed from her casita for a suicide note or any other clues about what might have occurred."

"When did she die?" Stella asked. "I mean, she wasn't just lying there in the sun for . . ."

"No, no. She canceled her customary afternoon mojito at approximately four p.m. I believe your friend Señora Deville telephoned for help a few minutes past five. That means she died within that final hour."

"If we'd been back from Tulum earlier, we might have caught her in time."

"I do not think so, señora. The heart attack was sudden and fatal. You could have been standing at her side when it happened, but Señora Early would not have been able to have been resuscitated."

"So, her heart simply gave out?"

"In essence, yes. We are speaking with Caballero Cove guests to learn more about the afternoon Señora Early died and the circumstances surrounding Reverend Bailor's death. Since we are here . . ."

"You'll start with us," Stella filled in the blank. "Sure. Go ahead."

"As I understand, you were both with friends in Tulum the day Señora Early died?" Lenzana asked.

"Yes," Nick answered. "Bernard—er, Señor Early—made the trip with us. We left a few minutes before noon and returned a little after five. That's when we discovered Georgina."

"Was Señor Early with you the entire time you were in Tulum?"

"The entire time? No, but he was with us for the majority of the trip."

"Bernard met an acquaintance of his at the ruins," Stella elaborated. "A man who was staying at the hotel next door. They both went off to chat for a period of time."

"For how long?"

"Roughly twenty to thirty minutes, wouldn't you say?" she asked Nick, who gave a nod in response.

"And this acquaintance? Did you see him again?"

"We did, actually. He was boarding his private shuttle at the same time we were waiting for the hotel van."

"And at what time was that?"

"About four o'clock."

"While you were with Señor Early, did he mention his wife at all? Any problems between them? Any issues with her emotional state?"

"Yes, he did. He said that her overall mood had changed for the worse and that she'd become more irritable, more argumentative. He also said that he'd spoken to her doctor about it, but that nothing could be done."

"Did you believe Señor Early?"

"Yes, he seemed—how did you put it, Nick?"

"I said he seemed like an injured puppy. He acted as if Georgina had really hurt him with her behavior toward him and others."

"This is puzzling. I did not see anything in the physician's files about a consultation regarding Señora Early's moods."

"The NHS works differently than our American health-care system of referrals," Nick noted. "If Georgina had seen a private psychiatrist, it's possible that her physician may not have known."

"I will make some inquiries with the NHS," Lenzana said, making notes on his tablet. "When you arrived back here at Caballero Cove, did you notice anything unusual or out of place?"

"No, except that when Bernard called to his wife, she didn't answer. That's how and when we discovered she was dead."

"Was Señora Early alone by the pool?"

"Yes," Nick confirmed. "Everyone else was getting ready for dinner and drinks at six."

"Well, everyone except Ellie Sanderson and Kendal Chung," Stella added. "They were just heading into their casita when we arrived. Ellie waved to us."

"That's right," her husband rejoined. "They'd spent the whole day on the beach."

"How do you know they spent the whole day on the beach if you were not here?" Lenzana challenged.

"Because they told us they were staying on the beach that day, so that they could avoid being near Georgina."

"You told me, Señora Buckley, that no one liked Señora Early. Is this an example of that statement?"

"Yes. I witnessed three arguments between Georgina and other guests that morning alone. Then there were the other random comments she made during dinner the previous night."

"Would you mind detailing what you witnessed?"

Stella went on to describe Georgina's quarrels with Ray and Diana Horrocks, Ellie Sanderson and Kendal Chung, and Joseph Penrod.

"A lounge chair? A knitted blanket? These do not sound like serious matters," Lenzana judged as he typed his notes.

"You had to be here. It was all far more dramatic than it sounds. Georgie was completely unhinged about other people sitting in her seat. Ray tried to reason with her, but she was absolutely unreasonable. As for the afghan, Ellie and Kendal took Georgie's resistance as a sign that she disapproved of their impending parenthood and possibly even their union. Kendal was in great distress as a result, which as you know is not ideal for a pregnant woman."

"And Penrod?"

"That was quieter and far more subdued, but it was clear that Penrod was incredibly upset. It was in his body language. I couldn't hear what was being said, but Anika Banerjee overheard part of the conversation and they were supposedly arguing over some deal they had made."

"A deal?"

"Yes, Georgina supposedly worked in wealth management. Anika assumed that she was helping Mr. Penrod with some investments."

"Yes, on a recent questionnaire issued by Quintana Hospitalidad—the owners of this resort and the hotel next door—Señor and Señora Early both listed their occupation as independent investment consultants."

"Well, there you have it," Nick said. "They probably argued over money."

"Money can bring out the worst in people, yes," Lenzana agreed.

"I also ran into Jospeh Penrod in town before we left for Tulum," Stella said. "He completely avoided me as if I'd caught him in the middle of something."

The inspector continued to take notes. "You also mentioned that Señora Early made some remarks at dinner."

"She did. She insinuated that Desirée Hunt was seeing her dancing partner for something other than dancing. She tried to push Penrod into making the trip to Tulum with us by saying that at least he'd be away from her while he was gone. And she made some odd comment about swing dancing that didn't make much sense until we discovered that she's been going around starting rumors about the guests."

"Rumors?"

"Yes, Chip Ruckert heard from Georgina that Ray and Diana Horrocks and Anika and Manish Banerjee are swingers."

"Swingers? I do not know this term."

"Swingers are people who swap partners for an evening."

"Ah! Yes, I understand. Why would Señora Early say this?"

"Why would she say any of the stuff she said? She also told Ellie that something illegal was going on with the dancers and told everyone here that Señor Tugores had an illicit affair with a much younger employee."

"Many people indulge in gossip as they get older," Lenzana observed.

"It's a bit more than gossip when someone's out to destroy the reputations of the hotel manager and guests she's known for years."

"I'm not so sure she wished to destroy anyone. She only shared the rumors with those staying here at El Caballero, did she not?"

"But that's the just the thing. This is such a small, tight-knit group that Georgina had to know that the rumors she shared would eventually make it back to their subjects. What if one of those rumors she told hit a little too close to home?"

"I do not understand your meaning."

"I mean, what if one of the rumors she started wasn't really a rumor at all. What if it was true?"

"But why would she share it knowing it could hurt someone?"

"She might not have known it was true," Stella guessed. "Or she simply didn't care. I honestly haven't a clue. But one thing's for certain, it would have given someone an excellent motive for wanting Georgina Early dead."

Chapter Thirteen

Lila was counting the money in the Perkins' General Store till when Alice came by to return Bixby. Just as soon as Clyde unlocked the front door, Bixby barreled through the entryway, into the shop, and directly to the register.

"Someone missed his grandma," Alice noted.

Lila wasn't about to complain to the woman who'd cared for the rambunctious Lab all day, so she plastered on a smile and ignored being publicly deemed a canine grandparent. "So, how was he?" she asked, kneeling down to give Bixby a good scratch beneath his ears.

"Good as gold. Ain't nothing wrong with that dog."

"You mean he wasn't mopey or sad?"

"Nope. He played with my dogs and chased some of my chickens—which I put the kibosh on, but Bixby listened. Then he ate some treats and hunkered down by the fireplace for a spell before going out and playing with my dogs in the snow again. I'd say he had himself a good ol' time."

"So, you saw absolutely nothing wrong with him?"

"Absolutely nothing. He's a great example of his breed, plus a very good boy and a typical playful Lab. They're just full of love."

"Well, I'm glad you think he's okay. That takes a load off my mind. But what should I do if he exhibits sad behavior again?"

"It's most likely environmental. My farm is a new environment for him, so he had fun exploring and making new friends, but his home is filled with familiar scents, toys, and people. When some of those people go away, it could leave him feeling anxious and sad."

"Poor thing. I let him talk to my daughter on the phone last night, but it didn't seem to help him much."

"It's good that you let him talk to her, but that's not how dogs operate. There's a big difference between him hearing her voice and him being able to smell and touch her."

"That makes sense," Lila said with a frown. "Is there anything I can do for him until they return?"

"Just continue what you're doing now. He obviously feels safe and comfortable with you. Lavish him with attention. Don't leave him alone too often, as he's not used to it. Maintain his regular feeding schedule. And do whatever you can to make him feel happy and relaxed."

"I'll do my best."

"You already are. He's doing fine. You're doing fine. Really."

• • •

The police left Caballero Cove at approximately noon, leaving its patrons in a far less festive mood than they'd been in the previous evening. Donning their swimsuits and sunscreen, Stella, Nick, Alma, and Mills opted for a quiet day on the beach.

Be it due to the morning's excitement of having the police on-site or the determination that both Bailor's and Georgina's deaths had been deemed suspicious, the other guests also maintained a rather low profile, reading by the pool, quietly sunbathing, listening to earbuds, or swimming solitary laps.

The group was tense, yet still friendly toward each other, a fact borne out when Stella visited the clubhouse ladies' room following a quick dip in the pool.

Ellie and Desirée were standing in front of the sinks chatting about the latest news.

"None of it makes any sense," Desirée exclaimed as she refreshed her deep mauve lipstick. "To think that one of us—after all this time? I know Georgie could be a pain, but murder? It's ridiculous."

"Even more ridiculous is Reverend Bailor," Ellie replied. "The man ran a soup kitchen back at his church."

"He was an absolute gem."

The two women stopped talking and smiled at Stella.

"Bet you know what we're commiserating about," Ellie said, combing the knots out of her green-tinted bob.

"It's rather shocking news," Stella agreed. "Particularly for you all, having known each other for years."

Desirée nodded. "I know I've said it already, but I can't believe one of us would do such a thing. I honestly can't."

"I can't either," Ellie agreed. "I admit to wanting to punch Georgina in the face at times, but killing her?"

Stella joined the women at the row of sinks and checked her appearance in the mirror. "If Georgina could make someone like you want to punch her in the face, it's safe to say that someone more volatile, shall we say, could easily have gone a lot farther. Reverend Bailor is the question mark for me. From what I just overheard of your conversation, he seemed like a lovely man."

"He was," Desirée confirmed. "I can't imagine why anyone would want to hurt the man."

"Me neither."

"Was there a connection between him and Georgina? A close friendship?" Stella asked.

"No, Georgina wasn't close to any of us. I doubt she was even close to Bernard," Desirée remarked, fishing through her purse for a cigarette.

"That's true. She put a wall around herself. Never really talked about home or work or anything. She probably knew more about us than we ever knew about her," Ellie elaborated.

Stella's mind traveled back to that first day at the pool, when Georgina introduced herself. She did seem to ask an awful lot of questions. "I assume there were no rumors about the reverend."

"Rumors?"

"Well, this place seems to be awash with rumors, isn't it? We've only been here a few days and we've heard quite a few."

"No, there were no rumors about Reverend Bailor. How could there be?"

"Actually," Desirée spoke up, "there was a rumor about him once."

Ellie looked confused. "Really? I never heard anything."

"This goes back to before you and Kendal were coming here. Hell, I think even Gloria was still alive." She cast her eyes heavenward and shook her head. "It was when Reverend Bailor first came here. The rumor went around that the only way he could afford to vacation in a place like this was if he was stealing from his parishioners."

"Wow!" Ellie exclaimed. "How did I not ever hear this?"

"Because Joe Penrod shut it down. The reverend was understandably upset when the rumor got back to him. Joe, as his best friend here, made it clear that if he found out who started the rumor, he'd sue on the reverend's behalf. That shut everyone up pretty quick."

"Did Penrod ever find out who started the rumor?" Stella asked.

"No. Personally, I think it was Bernard."

Desirée's answer was surprising. "Bernard?"

"Yeah, I remember it clearly because I was so shocked at the allegation. It was wild enough to imagine this mild-mannered minister running off with the collection plate. But it was even crazier because Reverend Bailor had shown me a photo of his church. You'd be lucky if it sat a hundred people. He wasn't going to get very far on those funds."

"So, you didn't believe the rumor?"

"No. You, um, seem taken aback."

"A little. I thought Georgina was the gossip here at Caballero Cove."

"She was. But you asked who I heard that story from and it was Bernard. He and Georgina were getting along better back then. I swear she'd make up any old story and he'd repeat it. It was as if she'd say anything just to see how we reacted."

"And recently?"

"Georgina still made up her crazy stories, but Bernard didn't participate in spreading them around. It was if he'd had it with all her gossip, but then again, she'd kinda had it with him, hadn't she? Making him sleep in another bungalow." Desirée's newly painted lips broke into a smirk. "And now I have a question for you. I heard that you're here to investigate someone at the resort. Is it true?"

"No, it isn't true. I'm afraid that's just another one of Georgina's rumors."

"But Nick is in law enforcement," Ellie argued.

"He works for the Forest Service, yes."

"And Charlie's a cop."

"He's a sheriff, yes."

"And we saw the cops talking to you before they questioned us. Considering you weren't even here when Reverend Bailor was alive, that's kinda weird, isn't it?"

"Not really. Knowing we weren't here, Lenzana got our questioning out of the way first."

"Did he actually question you?" Desirée asked, smiling broadly.

"Yes, as a matter of fact, he did."

"Huh," she grunted. "Given your reputation, I'm surprised that he didn't ask you for advice."

"Advice?"

"Yeah, aren't you a supersleuth or something?"

Georgina, Stella thought. The woman had taken Charlie's comments and run with them.

"A supersleuth? Um, no. I've helped Sheriff Mills with a handful of cases, but that's it."

"Oh, come on. Tell us the truth," Desirée urged.

"That is the truth. I'm a fiber conservation and restoration expert. That's what I actually do for a living."

"So, Georgie made up the whole thing about you being a detective?" Ellie said. "She was crazy, but not that crazy."

"No, she didn't make the whole thing up, be she definitely embellished the truth. Like I said, I've worked on a few cases with Mills. That's all. We're all here for Alma and Mills's wedding. Honest." Stella crossed her heart.

"Okay, we believe you. But tell us, since you do have experience in these matters, what do you think's going on here? Do you think Georgie and Reverend Bailor were murdered?"

"It's looking very likely."

"But who would want to kill them? And why?"

Stella sighed. "I wish I knew. I really wish I knew."

Chapter Fourteen

By the time the guests at Caballero Cove met at six o'clock the mood was far more convivial—a mood no doubt enhanced by the occasion of the resort's traditional costume party. In light of recent events, the opportunity to pretend to be someone else, if even for a few hours, offered participants a much-needed escape from reality.

Demonstrating a wry sense of humor, Señor Tugores officiated the evening's festivities dressed as a circus ringleader.

Penrod, wearing his old army uniform, epitomized military punctuality by being the first guest to arrive. He was joined a few minutes later by Anika and Manish Banerjee, who had gone full-on Disney in Mickey and Minnie Mouse costumes.

"Look at you two," Penrod exclaimed with a laugh. "Well done!"

"We expanded upon a theme," Anika explained. "Things we would never like to see in our restaurant. Rodents were at the top of the list."

"I went along, because the costume involved shorts," Manish elaborated as he struggled to adjust his ears. "I had forgotten about the giant white gloves, though. I think these will come off soon."

"Oh, not yet. Not until everyone's seen you!"

"But I would like a drink, Anika."

"Señor Banerjee's usual," Tugores instructed a nearby server. "With a straw."

As the group laughed, Ray, dressed in a striped referee's jersey and black pants, and Diana, clad in a sequined basketball uniform, replete with metallic pink sneakers and basketball, arrived at the bar.

"Leave it to Diana to make a sweaty sport look glamorous," Anika said admiringly.

"I might look glamorous, but this costume is built for comfort. The elastic waistband on these shorts means I don't need to unbutton my pants after dinner."

Upping the sequin factor of the evening, Desirée Hunt appeared on the scene in a spangled purple spaghetti-strap top, a sparkly seashell necklace, and a metallic green mermaid skirt that resembled a tail. Even her makeup was magical, with green and purple gemstones lining the lashes of both lids.

While Ray sang the chorus of "Under the Sea," Diana whistled. "Girl, I think you might have just won best costume, and not everyone's here yet."

"Speaking of which, where's Chip?" Penrod asked.

"Oh, he took a call with his broker. I didn't want to listen to him talk numbers so I told him to meet me here when he's done."

Tugores served Desirée her customary martini and then looked up to see Alma and Stella arrive. Alma had sewn red hearts all over a black satin, flared skirt ball gown and encircled the neckline with a collar—not of lace but of playing cards. Her gorgeous auburn hair was pinned to the top of her head and crowned with a rhinestone tiara with a heart motif, and in her hand she clutched a red, heart-shaped scepter.

Stella, meanwhile, had also created her own costume. Taking a strapless pink satin gown that she had found at the local thrift store, she attached a wide bow at the back using similar fabric, donned a pair of elbow-length gloves that she'd dyed a matching hue, and finished it all off with a rhinestone necklace and silver sandals (also from Goodwill) and a platinum blonde wig.

"The Queen of Hearts and Marilyn," Penrod gushed. "Clever."

"Will Señor Buckley and Señor Mills be joining you?" Tugores questioned as he made sure that the ladies were provided with their favorite beverages.

"They should be here soon," Alma answered. "Stella and I kept our costumes secret from the guys. We worked on them together—or, I should say, Stella and her magic stitching skills worked on them—so we figured we might as well have some fun unveiling them."

"They're absolutely charming," Desirée remarked. "They look better than most rentals out there."

"Thanks," Stella replied. "Your costume is absolutely gorgeous, Desirée."

As the two women chatted, voices could be heard approaching the pool area. It was Mills, in his sheriff's uniform, and Nick, dressed in a red-and-white-striped shirt and hat, blue jeans, and a pair of thick-rimmed glasses. Around his neck hung a pair of binoculars.

"I should have guessed you'd wear your work uniform," Alma said to Mills with a shake of her head.

"Why should I go out and buy a costume?" Mills argued. "No one's seen me in this."

Meanwhile Stella addressed her husband. "Where's Waldo?"

Nick beamed. "I figured you like detecting so much that if you had to look for me, you'd find me more intriguing."

"I'll also find you perspiring. Denim jeans and a stocking hat in seventy-five-degree weather?"

"Yeah, I admit it felt better when I wore it in Vermont. Your costume, however, looks quite suitable for warm weather. In fact, I wouldn't be surprised if you were a bit chilly."

"No, I'm fine."

"Are you sure? I'd be happy to share my beanie with you." He playfully lifted his hat off his head.

"I'm sure you would be. Now behave yourself and tell Alma how lovely she looks."

Nick did as he was told and the four friends socialized with the group that had gathered at the poolside bar. They were joined moments later by Ellie and Kendal, who appeared to be dressed as two goddesses.

Ellie was wearing a green dress covered in all manner of artificial leaves, flowers, and branches. Her arms were covered in temporary tattoos of butterflies, and the headband holding her green locks away from her face was wired with tiny faux birds. "I am Mother Nature. And this is Mother Earth."

She motioned toward Kendal, who was draped in a toga that left her belly exposed. That rounded belly had been painted to look like the planet Earth. She too wore a headpiece—in her case a floral wreath that encircled her long black hair. "Since we are going to be mothers . . ." she explained with a radiant smile.

The group broke into applause.

"These are easily the most imaginative costumes I have ever seen," Tugores said. "So long as Señor Ruckert doesn't arrive dressed as a peacock, I would say the prize for best costume belongs to you both."

"You're safe," Desirée assured them. "Chip is neither that inventive nor that self-confident to pull off such a getup."

"Did I hear my name mentioned?" Ruckert asked as he sidled up to Desirée at the poolside bar. He was wearing a well-tailored yet very ordinary black tuxedo.

"Señor Ruckert, did you confuse tonight with our New Year's gala?" Tugores asked.

"Nope. This is my costume. The name's Bond. James Bond."

The group groaned.

"See what I mean?" Desirée posed to her fellow guests.

"Hey, I saved on the extra baggage charge by bringing one outfit for both parties," Ruckert offered in his defense.

"Safe to say you ladies won the contest," Diana remarked to Ellie and Kendal.

As Tugores presented Ellie and Kendal with their prize—a gift certificate to the spa at El Sueño del Mar hotel—the guests modeled their costumes for each other, exchanged compliments, and laughed. Amid the happy chatter, Bernard Early emerged from his casita. Wearing a short-sleeved linen shirt, shorts, and sandals, he looked as if he might have been headed into town if it weren't for the worn duffle bag slung over one shoulder.

The guests fell silent and glanced awkwardly at each other, as if wondering how to react to his presence. For better or worse, Ruckert put an end to their dilemma. "Bernard, good to see you. How you holding up?"

"Oh, um, hiya, Chip. Heya, everybody. I, um, I'm okay. You know . . ."

"We're all very sorry, Bernard," Desirée replied.

"Thanks. I know Georgie wasn't always nice to you all."

There were quick protests from the guests: "Not at all, Bernard." "Noooo, we loved Georgie!"

"No, no, now, don't dispute it. I saw it with my own eyes. But I want you to know that I don't believe for a minute what the police are saying. Suspicious death? It's absolutely bonkers. None of you would have hurt her. I know you wouldn't. It must have been someone from outside."

His fellow guests nodded.

"I am certain the police will find out what happened," Tugores assured him. "May I set a place at the table for you tonight, señor?"

"Thank you, no. I'm off to the gym. Need to burn off some nervous energy." Bernard shifted his weight from foot to foot.

"Oh, but the gym is closed for the day, Señor Early. It always closes at six thirty during the week."

"That's right. I must have lost track of the time . . ."

"Since you're out and about, how about a drink with us?" Ruckert suggested. "For old times' sake."

Early shook his head. "I couldn't. I hope you know how much I've always loved coming here and seeing everyone. But right now, all I can think about is getting back home and putting this behind me."

"We understand," Ellie said softly.

"The gym's closed, but I think I'll finally take your advice, Anika, and walk on the beach for a spell and then come back and read a book. You know, something to take my mind off things."

"I brought the new Louise Penny with me, if you'd like to borrow it," Stella suggested, recalling how Bernard said he loved crime fiction. "Unless it's not something you want to read right now . . ."

"I already have a book I'm reading, but thanks."

"Oh? Something good?"

"Um, yeah, the latest Lee Child. Reacher's my lad. Always has been."

"Yes, that is a good series," Stella replied before bidding Bernard a good evening.

"You okay?" Nick asked, noticing her frown.

"Yeah, I'm fine. Poor Bernard . . . he doesn't seem to be thinking straight."

"Oh, I know," Ellie commiserated, overhearing the conversation. "It's bad enough to lose your spouse, but to have to deal with a whole police investigation . . ."

"It has to be like Bernard said, right?" Kendal said. "It has to be someone from outside Caballero. None of us are capable of a thing like that."

"I meant to ask earlier, Ellie, but you and Kendal didn't see anything odd the afternoon that Georgina died, did you?" Stella quizzed.

"No, we were in the cabana all day. Didn't talk to a soul."

"But you must have left the cabana from time to time." She gestured toward Kendal's belly. "To use the restroom, for instance."

"Yeah, of course." Ellie's eyes narrowed. "I thought you weren't here to investigate anyone."

"I'm not. I already told you I'm here for the wedding."

"Oh! I get it. You couldn't say anything earlier because"—she dropped her voice to a whisper—"because Desirée was with us. This is all about Desirée and the dancers, isn't it?"

"Um, I don't—" Stella didn't have a chance to say otherwise.

"Yes, I did use the bathroom—twice, maybe three times. Desirée was by the pool each time I saw her, but not near Georgina. How about you, hon?"

"I didn't see—" Kendal threw a glance over her right shoulder. "You-know-who near Georgina, either. But I *did* see Chip Ruckert."

"Really?" Stella was surprised.

"I already told Ellie and the police about it. Ruckert looked like he was about to confront Georgina. He was in alpha male mode and went up to her and said, 'We need to talk.'"

"And?"

"That's it. She shut him right down. Didn't answer him. Didn't take her glasses off to look at him. Just went on with what she was doing. I didn't like Georgie all the time, but it was a seriously impressive diva move."

"What did Ruckert do?"

"He told her again that they needed to talk. Same reaction from Georgie, so he left. And he wasn't happy."

"Did he get close enough to Georgie to give her a pill or slip something into her drink?"

"He was definitely close enough. But I didn't actually see him do anything like that. I was on the way to our casita, so I only saw him from the back. He was leaning over her. It was a definite power move."

"How about Reverend Bailor? Did anything odd happen the day he passed away?"

"No, but his death was pretty odd in itself. He seemed fine at dinner. He chatted with me and Kendal," Ellie said. "The next morning, Renata went to clean his room and found the door locked. Reverend Bailor never locked his bungalow door. He said as a vicar, he didn't have much to steal. So, Renata notified Señor Tugores, who unlocked the door, only to find Bailor in bed, dead. He'd died in his sleep. The police said it was a heart attack . . . natural causes."

Kendal clearly sought to be reassured. "It still might be natural causes, right? The police are probably just double-checking."

"It could still be natural causes, yes," Stella confirmed, although she was more than a bit doubtful.

The dinner gong rang, calling the guests to the table beneath the pergola. Unlike the previous evenings' meals, this one was to be served buffet-style so the guests could chat and mingle. The period between dinner and dessert was to be spent dancing and playing games.

Stella, Nick, Alma, and Mills lined up with the other Caballero guests to fix their plates. There was a wide and tantalizing assortment of Mexican specialties, including grouper caught fresh that afternoon and braised in wine and topped with tomato, jalapeño, and olives, in addition to a selection of pastas and salads.

"Oh, I hope I can fit into my wedding dress," Alma cried. "There are still two days left until the wedding and this food is too delicious to pass up."

"I am certain you shall be fine. The snapper Veracruz is extremely light," Tugores advised.

"It's one of my favorites dishes here," Desirée added. "Not only does it taste fabulous, but I asked the chef and it's very low in calories."

"Sign me up." Alma went directly to the snapper and reached for the fish server. "May I get you some too, Desirée?"

"Oh, how sweet of you! Yes, please. A big portion. All this stuff with the police is so making me want to stress eat."

"I'll have some, too, Alma," Stella requested. "I know, Desirée. I was shocked to see the police here again this morning."

"Ugh. I don't get why they're here. I mean, I do, but like we were saying, there's zero chance Georgina was murdered by one of us. And the reverend? Puh-leeze!"

"Unfortunately, they need to investigate the possibility of foul play."

"Yeah, I know, but having them around makes me uncomfortable.

There has to be some other actual crime in this town they can focus on."

Desirée appeared awfully eager to see the police on their way. Did it have something to do with the dancers at the property? "Well, after dinner, you can dance away some of those tensions."

"I may need to borrow your husband for that. Chip isn't big on boogeying, in case you hadn't noticed."

Stella feigned ignorance. "Oh, that's right . . . there's no big dance party tonight, is there?"

"Nope, it's games and music with just us guests."

"Well, you can definitely borrow Nick for a song or two. If he doesn't mind. Although, he's probably not as good as your usual dancing partner."

"Sebastián? No, no one is quite as good as Sebastián," she said in a plaintive tone.

Why did someone and something that had provided her with so much pleasure just three days earlier now prompt such an expression of sadness?

"You made your lessons sound like so much fun," Alma said. "Maybe your Sebastián could give me and Charlie a lesson or two while we're here. We could dazzle the folks back home at the next police benefit dance."

"Sebastián isn't the person you want for something like that," Desirée warned.

"Oh? I thought you were happy with his classes."

"I was. Until I found out I was being billed incorrectly."

"Oh, that's too bad. Will the hotel make good on it?"

"I doubt it." Desirée was visibly uncomfortable.

"Don't be too disillusioned with Sebastián. Surely, he doesn't handle the billing."

"It wouldn't matter if he did. I'm through with it all," Desirée answered before rushing off to join Chip.

"Sorry," Alma apologized. "I didn't know I'd send her running."

"Yeah, she's more than a little spooked by something," Stella told her friend, *sotto voce.*

"I know. That's why I asked her about Sebastián," Alma confessed, her eyes dancing.

"What? I thought there was to be no detecting going on during your wedding trip."

"Bride's prerogative. I've seen you talking to everybody, asking questions, so I decided to jump in and join you."

It was Stella's turn to apologize. "Sorry, I can't help feeling that the answer to both Georgie's and the reverend's deaths is right under our noses."

"I can't either. Mostly because I know you. If you can't help but snoop when I specifically asked you not to, then there must be something important going on."

"I'm sorry, Alma."

"Nah, don't be. You've been great. You didn't say a peep to me and you didn't once try to bring Charlie into it. But I realized that this is more important than a wedding. I love Charlie and I'm getting married to him, no matter what. But those people who died . . . there needs to be some sort of justice. And if you can help—if *we* can help—get that justice by being involved, then so be it. *So*, what do you need me to do?"

"Just keep your eyes peeled and your ears open."

"I will. We do have an interesting vantage point that the police don't have, don't we?"

"Yes, and the people here never stop talking either," Stella informed her friend as Chip Ruckert approached. "Don't look now."

"Ladies," he greeted. "Quite the evening, is it not?"

"Yes," they agreed in unison before helping themselves to a gorgeous tossed salad bejeweled with nuggets of local mangoes.

"My Desirée tells me that your group is here on an investigation."

"No, we're not, Chip. I actually spoke with Desirée this afternoon and told her that we're simply here for Alma and Mills's wedding."

"But you are looking into what happened to Georgie and Bailor, aren't you?"

"I've told the police I would help them if I could. I'm sure you told them the same thing."

"Er, naturally. But as you know, the police in these places aren't quite what they should be."

"No, actually, I don't know that. I've found Lenzana and his team to be thorough, exacting, and entirely professional."

"Yes, well." Chip cleared his throat.

Stella braced herself for a round of mansplaining. She was not disappointed.

"When you've traveled as extensively as I have, you learn to see the signs of corruption and inefficiency. You'll soon learn that—"

She cut him off. "Do you somehow wind up in the police station in every country you visit? Perhaps I need to warn Lenzana about you and not the other way around."

Alma snorted while suppressing a laugh.

"Very funny," Chip scoffed. "But these police aren't even close to being on the right track."

"Oh?" Stella glanced over the buffet table for something else to accompany the snapper. She really wasn't interested in hearing any more about Ruckert's assessment of local law enforcement.

"Georgie was a teetotaler. An absolute straight shooter. She never would have taken that painkiller crap."

His words caught her attention. She reluctantly turned away from the gorgeous platter of saffron rice before her. "You're one hundred percent certain of this?"

"Positive," he asserted with a smug grin. "Georgie was a hard, hard woman to like, but she had her moments. I can't tell you how many times I offered to buy the Earlys a drink. Bernie—er, Bernard—always took me up on the offer. Likes his beer, he does. Georgie, on the other hand, always refused. Year after year, the same thing happened. I'd offer to buy a round; Bernard accepted, Georgie said no. A couple years back, I finally asked Georgie why. She told me that alcohol and drugs are poison. Poison to the body. Poison to the mind. And she needed to stay sharp. She told me she took high blood pressure medication—different ones through the years—but she would never take anything mind-altering. Never."

"So, you believe that someone administered the oxycodone to Georgina?"

"I do. And I know precisely who did it."

"You do?"

"Yes, it was Ellie."

"Ellie? Why her?" Alma asked.

"Because I saw her kneel down beside Georgie's chaise lounge the afternoon she died. It was only an hour or so before you folks came back here and found her."

"Did you tell the police this?" Stella questioned.

"No, they wouldn't know what to do with it."

She threw her head back and looked at the sky as a silent plea to the heavens for patience. "Well, I suppose I should be flattered you trusted me enough to share."

"You should. I was tempted to tell your husband since he's the law enforcement officer, but Desirée insisted you were the brains." He drew quotes in the air when mentioning her potential mental prowess.

"Yeah, thanks. Did you hear what Ellie and Georgina discussed?"

Ruckert shook his head. "You've seen enough of Ellie to know that she talks in that soft whispery 'I'm Okay, You're Okay' kindergarten teacher tone of hers. The girl's nice enough—or at least I thought so— but she needs to learn to enunciate. I can hardly hear her from the other end of the table, let alone the hot tub."

"Was Ellie angry?"

"No, she looked . . . confused, upset maybe, but not angry. She walked away and hurried back to the beach without a smile to anyone. That isn't like her at all. She's always cheerful to the point of being annoying."

"Did anyone else see her?"

"If they were looking out of their bungalow windows, maybe. I don't know what the weather was like in Tulum late that afternoon, but it threatened rain here. Everyone packed it in early and either went back to their casitas or to the clubhouse for a game of cards. It was just me and Georgina by the pool by that time."

"And you were seen just prior to that in a stand-off with Georgina," Stella revealed.

"Me? Who told you that?"

"I have my sources."

"Do the police know?"

"They do."

Ruckert breathed a heavy sigh and took a sip of his drink. It looked like straight Scotch. "Okay, yes," he admitted after several seconds had elapsed. "Yes, I went to talk to Georgie."

"From what I heard, it was a bit more than just a talk."

"Okay, maybe I was stern with her, but I was sick of it all. Sick of her and her ridiculous stories. All those things she implied about Desirée and her dance classes—they've taken their toll. Poor Desirée has said she never wants to dance again."

Stella frowned and stole a glance at Alma. Had Desirée lied to them about the hotel billing issues? Or was she lying to Chip when she blamed her newly developed aversion to dancing on Georgina's innuendo? Perhaps she was lying to them all.

"Funny, but I seem to remember that it was you making a big fuss over Desirée's dancing lessons at dinner the other night. Not Georgina."

"Because I bought into the poison Georgie was slinging. I'm a jealous guy and I reacted without thinking. I didn't give Desirée the benefit of the doubt."

Stella recalled the blonde woman teetering past their garden at three in the morning, stiletto heels in hand. Perhaps Desirée deserved more doubt than benefit.

"So, what did you say to Georgina?"

"I demanded that she stop terrorizing Desirée with allegations and innuendo. I demanded that she set the record straight by telling the other guests that she had lied and was wrong about the entire situation."

"What happened?"

"Nothing. She just sat there staring out at the harbor as she often did. At least I think that's what she was doing. She had her sunglasses on, so I couldn't see her eyes."

"She didn't say anything?"

"No, she just grunted."

"Grunted?"

"I'm pretty sure that's how you'd describe it." He mimicked the sound and it was, indeed, a grunt.

"How did you react?" Stella asked.

"How do you think I reacted? I was furious. I told her how her words had affected the woman I love and the most she could muster was a moan, a grunt, whatever that sound was. It was disgusting."

"What did you do then?"

"I demanded again that she stop her hurtful gossip about Desirée and told her that if she didn't, she could expect to receive a cease-and-desist letter."

"How did she react?"

"She didn't. She kept staring out at the boats or whatever the hell she looked at from that precious lounge chair of hers."

Chip's tone was intensely hostile. Stella wouldn't have been surprised if he had murdered Georgina himself. It was an idea unwittingly conveyed by her facial expression.

"I know what you're thinking," Ruckert said to her. "I can see it in your eyes, but I didn't do it. I never laid a finger on Georgie. Never even went near her. Señor Tugores was outside the clubhouse reviewing the dinner plans for the evening. He saw me. He'll back up my story. Also, need I remind you that I had no reason at all to want Reverend Bailor dead. Zero."

"Do you know of anyone who *did* have a reason to want Reverend Bailor dead?"

"No, no one that I can think of. It's strange, isn't it? He's the last person I would have expected to be murdered."

"Well, the police haven't officially declared it murder, just suspicious."

"It's only a matter of time. We all know it is."

Stella frowned. "Do you remember anything odd about the day the reverend died?"

"Just his death. I'd say that's odd enough, wouldn't you?"

"So, no disagreements between him and one of the other guests?"

"Not unless one of us went on a swearing spree in front of him," he said with a chuckle. "The reverend was one of the most mild-mannered people I ever met and this last trip was fairly ordinary. He arrived on the first of December, just as he always did. He hung out with Penrod, just as he always did. He ordered a gin and tonic, light on the gin, upon arriving. He . . . wait! Wait, there was something.

Something about his check-in."

Stella and Alma leaned in closer in anticipation.

Chip snapped his fingers. "I got it! Bailor switched casitas."

"Switched when he arrived?" Stella asked. "Or switched later during his stay?"

"It was when he first arrived. He always stayed in casita number two, but when Luciana called the porter to take his luggage there, he asked if he could trade with another one of the guests. Said his usual casita had been too noisy last year."

"Did he find someone to trade with?"

"Joe Penrod. Made sense with them being friends and all. It's also easier to relocate one person and their belongings than to relocate two people."

"Of course," Stella murmured to herself. Renata had said she'd always cleaned the reverend's bungalow, and yet when she had run into Renata just the previous morning, she was cleaning the even-numbered quarters. Moreover, it was Inés—housekeeper for the odd-numbered bungalows—who had packed up the reverend's belongings. With this new bit of information, the situation all made sense.

However, was the switch in accommodations an important factor in Bailor's death?

"The noise Reverend Bailor complained about," Stella prefaced, "what was it?"

Chip shrugged. "Plain ol' noise, that's all. Oh, he did mention the light outside the clubhouse waking him at all hours. Though, I don't know . . . Desirée and I were just across the way in number three and we've never noticed any noise. And we definitely didn't notice that light thing go off." He polished off his glass of Scotch. "I sleep like a baby every night."

Chapter Fifteen

Although clear and lovely, the evening turned chilly, with a cool breeze coming in from the sea, prompting the Caballero Cove guests to enjoy their supper by the fire Tugores and staff built in the giant terra-cotta chiminea on the croquet lawn.

Stella had just finished her plate of perfectly cooked snapper, salad, and saffron rice, when Anika Banerjee sidled up to her. "So, what do you think of all this murder talk?"

"Until the police obtain further information regarding both deaths, that's all it is. Talk," Stella replied, reflecting upon all the rumors and talk that had been circulating around the resort. Rumors and talk that might very well have contributed to the deaths of two guests.

"You mean you don't believe Georgina was murdered?"

"I think her death was deemed suspicious for a reason."

"I do too. In fact, I know it was suspicious."

"Excuse me, but if you have information, why are you coming to me? Why not speak to the police?"

"I did speak with the police, but I only just realized what I saw and what it might mean. And you . . . you came here to investigate someone. I think I know who that person is."

Stella was about to launch into another "I'm only here for a wedding" tirade, but she decided to just give in and listen. "You do?"

"Yes, it's Joe, isn't it? It has to be."

The mention of Penrod's name was jarring, as Stella had been ruminating on the bungalow swap between him and Bailor. And what it could possibly mean. "Go on," she urged.

"It looked like it was going to rain that afternoon—the afternoon that Georgina, you know . . ."

Stella nodded.

"Manish, Ray, Diana, and I went into the clubhouse to play a round of bridge. We could have played outside, under the awning, but the humidity prior to the storm was ridiculously high and the air-conditioning very appealing."

Again, Stella nodded.

"We took the corner table in the main dining room. My seat overlooked the pool area. There was practically a parade of people who went to see Georgina. Ellie was first. She knelt by Georgina's lounge chair and it looked as if she was praying or begging. Probably still wanted that knitted blanket for the baby, the poor thing. She knew how happy Kendal would have been to have had it."

"How did Georgina react?"

"I don't know. From the angle of my seat, all I could see was the back of her head, but she didn't seem to move much. And when Ellie left, it looked like she was holding back tears.

"After Ellie," Anika continued, "Chip, the bloated buffoon, came along and tried to intimidate Georgina. He stood at the foot of her lounger, hands on hips, chest out—white-man-in-control sort of stuff. It was comical in a way and yet—" She exhaled sharply.

"And yet?" Stella prompted. She did not want to put words in the woman's mouth.

"Chip's accustomed to getting his own way. I didn't always care much for Georgina or her behavior, but he was being a complete and utter bully that afternoon."

"Did he touch Georgina at all? Her body, her bag, her chair? Anything?"

Anika shook her head. "Nope, he just stood there, towering over her like some giant ape. I couldn't hear him, but he looked angry, like he was roaring and expecting her to comply. No wonder Desirée prefers to spend her time with those dancers. At least they don't behave like that. But all men can be trouble in some way, can't they?" Anika stared off into the fire, her mind focused on something—or someone—other than Georgina Early.

"Relationships definitely require work," Stella commiserated in an attempt to snap the woman from her reverie. "And patience. Speaking of which, how did Georgina respond to Chip's alpha male display?"

"I couldn't hear anything and I couldn't see anything but the back of her head. Whatever she did or didn't do, it really bothered Chip. It was glorious to watch him blow his top and then march off like a petulant child. It was very different from how Joe looked when he left Georgina," Anika continued to recall.

"How did Joe look?"

She searched her memory for the appropriate word. "Anguished?"

"Tell me what transpired."

"Joe came out of his casita—well, not *his* casita. He usually stayed in the one you and your husband are staying in."

"Yes, I heard Joe and the vicar switched bungalows. Something about noise and traffic."

Anika nodded. "The motion light sensor at the clubhouse gets tripped by the local wildlife. We have a similar problem back home. We live in the suburbs and our Ring camera is constantly getting switched on at night because some raccoon has decided to take a shortcut."

"Good thing that camera doesn't connect directly to the local police department," Stella remarked with a laugh before reminding Anika, "So, Joe's conversation with Georgina?"

"Joe went up to Georgina and sat down on the end of the lounger, by her feet. Again, I couldn't hear anything, but it looked like what he was saying was heartfelt. He appeared to be pleading, maybe? Not like Ellie did—not kneeling down and begging—but really speaking from his gut."

"And Georgina?"

Anika shrugged. "Who knows? She didn't seem to react, but I couldn't see her face. After a little bit of time, Joe seemed to give up. That's when he looked . . . anguished . . . pained . . . and maybe surprised and shock as well. It's difficult to describe the look on his face, but he certainly wasn't happy."

"At what time was that?"

"Joe talked to Georgina soon after Chip left, so a few minutes after four, maybe? We were finishing up our card game. Georgina was outside, alone. Señor Tugores had been in the pergola area preparing for dinner and talking on his phone, but he and everyone else had gone indoors—except for Ellie and Kendal, who were still in their cabana."

"How do you know Ellie and Kendal were still in their cabana on the beach if you were in the clubhouse?"

"Because I saw Kendal waddle up here by the pool. I imagine she came here to use the bathroom—even though their bungalow was closer, she would have tracked sand all over the place. When she saw Chip, she waddled back toward the beach as fast as she could. Later on, after we'd finished playing cards and returned to our bungalow, I saw Kendal and Ellie return to their casita."

Stella was satisfied with Anika's explanation. Indeed, her account corroborated both Kendal's and Chip's stories. "So why do you think Joe Penrod might be under investigation?"

"Because of the argument between him and Georgina. The fact that Penrod has money—money that Georgina might have been investing. Money is a great motivator for both good and evil. Also, where did Joe get that money from? Maybe it comes from some illegal activity."

"Do you believe Penrod earned his money illegally?"

Anika tossed her hands in the air. "I don't know what to believe."

"What about Reverend Bailor? What motive could Penrod have had for murdering him? They were supposedly good friends and Penrod looked inconsolable at dinner the first we were here."

"They were good friends. And I offer no reason for why Joe would want Reverend Bailor dead, except that he wouldn't. Unless it somehow had something to do with them switching casitas. The reverend was a creature of habit. He arrived here every year at the same time, stayed in the same bungalow, and then left at the same time. It was very strange for him to move."

"But the noise?" Stella argued.

"He was the type who would have preferred to put up with the noise than change his routine. He was . . . precise. Do you know what I mean?"

"I do. So, what was the real reason for the switch? And what does it have to do with Joseph Penrod?'

"I don't know." Anika threw her hands up in the air again. "I don't know why Joe would have killed someone who seemed to be his best friend. But I do know, without any doubt, that Joe was the last person to be in contact with Georgina on the afternoon she died. It must be him!"

"But that's not really true, is it?" Stella challenged.

"What? Of course it's true. I just told you . . ."

"You told me that you watched Penrod leave and return to his casita, did you not?"

"I did."

"Then, with all due respect, he wasn't the last person to have contact with Georgina. You, Manish, Ray, and Diane finished your card game after Penrod returned to his casita and then left the clubhouse, correct?'

"Yes, that's right."

"None of you could have left the clubhouse without walking right past Georgina. Even Señor Tugores on his way to the pergola and back to the clubhouse had to walk past her."

"That's true, but . . ."

"One of you might even have brushed up against her or touched her shoulder as you passed. One of you might even have slipped something in her water bottle."

"That's ridiculous. None of us had a reason to get rid of Georgina."

"No? Georgina was spreading rumors about Tugores. Ray and Diana had a rather noisy argument with her that morning. And both you and Manish refused to mourn her passing."

"That doesn't mean we killed her!"

"Maybe not, but it proves that everyone here at Caballero Cove that afternoon had an opportunity to drug Georgina. Anyone."

Chapter Sixteen

With Bixby in tow, a much-relieved Lila returned to the Buckley farmhouse where, after providing the dog with dinner, she secured the recently purchased Christmas tree in the stand Clyde had provided. With the tree securely in place and watered, she festooned it with white lights she'd purchased at a discount store that afternoon.

Pleased with her work and feeling she'd engaged in enough post-work activity, she heated her dinner—a delectable salmon in sake sauce with brown rice and braised greens—in the microwave. Breaking off a piece of salmon and rinsing it, she presented it to Bixby before sitting down to eat.

He devoured it.

Elated that her canine friend was behaving more like his natural self, Lila issued a silent prayer of thanks for Alice and her farm retreat. Suddenly recalling the advice she'd received about maintaining a relaxed and happy atmosphere, Lila requested her phone to play some vintage Style Council tracks and finished her supper.

Feeling fully relaxed for the first time in days, she took her phone upstairs, lit some candles, and drew herself a lovely hot bath with the homemade mulled wine–scented bath salts she had created for the holiday season.

Bixby, naturally, followed her into the bathroom.

"Grandma—er, I mean I can't tell you how happy I am that you're feeling better," Lila told the black Lab as he sprawled on the bathroom rug and watched as she sunk down into the suds. "Maybe all you needed was a little playtime. And a little extra TLC. I hope so. I so want you to be well and happy. Not just because you're a lovely dog and you are—you are a lovely dog—but because I once did a terrible thing to your mom. Your mom found a puppy and wanted desperately to keep it, but I gave it to the local shelter. I know—I know. You needn't give me that disapproving look. I know it was horrible; completely and utterly horrible. But my marriage with Stella's—er, your mother's father was disintegrating and I was overwhelmed taking care of Stell—I mean your mother. A dog at that time was simply too much."

Bixby gave a giant yawn.

"Yes, I'm sorry I'm boring you. Suffice to say I want to make it up to her. Maybe she's forgotten it, but I haven't. I feel as if I was too selfish, too self-centered. Proving that you're well cared for and happy is my way of making it up to her. I hope that makes sense."

Bixby yawned again.

"Okay, I got it. Enough soul-baring. When I get out of the bath, I'll reward you with some of those can't-resist dog treats from the shop. Clyde gave us the rest of the bag to take home."

Bixby began to roll around on the bathroom rug.

Lila laughed until the behavior continued for several seconds. Was the dog excited about the treats or was something wrong?

"Bixby," she called to him. "Bixby, are you okay?"

The Lab continued to writhe on the rug.

She leaned forward in the tub so as to get a better look at the possibly-ailing pooch. "Bixby?"

In an instant, he leapt onto all fours and charged toward the bathtub.

Lila's voice of concern swiftly turned to one of surprise as it became clear that he was headed directly toward her. "Bixby! Bixby, no!"

It was too late. The big black dog plunged headfirst into the scented bath, sending water splashing onto the walls and cascading over the sides of the tub.

"Bixby!" Lila shouted as the eighty-pound canine landed in her lap and placed his front paws on her shoulders.

He gave her face a good lick and then hopped out of the tub and into the hallway.

"Bixby! No! You're soaking wet. You'll get water everywhere!"

For Bixby, however, spreading the water everywhere seemed to be half of the fun as he ran into her bedroom and then shook himself dry.

Lila, a bath towel wrapped hastily around her torso, gave pursuit, but Bixby apparently thought it was a game of chase. As soon as Lila arrived in the doorway of her bedroom, he exited and sprinted down the stairs, leaving a trail of water and spicy fragrance behind him.

"Bixby! Bad boy. Bad boy!" she admonished, but the happy Lab exhibited no shame. Instead, he rushed into the living room and proceeded to roll his wet body all over the plush velour sofa.

"Bixby!" she cried one last time in an attempt to jolt the ill-behaved hound from the living room furniture.

He refused to budge, but contentedly sighed and went to sleep.

Lila pulled the towel tighter around her torso and surveyed the mess. "Well, I guess I should be happy you're no longer depressed."

• • •

Stella, Nick, Alma, and Mills retreated to the bungalow during the after-dinner, pregame lull under the pretense of freshening up, but not before Nick could conduct a test of the motion lights outside the clubhouse.

Nick had noted that said lights were always switched off for the after-dinner entertainment, but were left on the remainder of the night, including the evening meal—a fact borne out by the influencer couple who were caught taking photos by the pool.

While everyone was enjoying dinner and conversation, Nick slipped away and walked to the far end of the swimming pool. As expected, the clubhouse light switched on.

After what seemed like an eternity, it switched back off again. Walking stealthily, as a prowler might, he approached the clubhouse, waiting for the very second the light switched back on again. He passed casitas number nine . . . seven . . . five . . . three . . .

He had reached the garden gate of casita number three when the pool area once again became bathed in white light.

With his test complete, Nick rejoined the other members of his party and passed the results on to his wife, who nodded and appeared to mull them over with careful consideration. As the dinner broke up and the Caballero guests spilled back onto the lawn, Stella excused their group and led the way to their casita.

"There are two things that really bother me about this case," Stella announced as she shut the front door.

"Just two things?" Nick deadpanned.

Mills, meanwhile, had questions of his own. "Case? What case?"

"Georgina Early's death, honey," Alma explained.

Stella nodded. "The first is that we have absolutely no evidence that Georgina was even a drug user, let alone an abuser or addict. The second is that no one seems to have had a reason to want to kill Reverend Bailor."

"Wait," Mills urged. "Are you telling me that you three have been investigating this situation despite this being a strictly no-work trip?"

"Maybe," a sheepish Stella replied.

"It was mainly her." Nick pointed a finger at his wife.

"I officially joined in today, but I admit my mind's been buzzing," Alma confessed. "I'm sorry, Charlie, but we might be able to help the local police in some way. We'll have a terrific wedding regardless . . . so long as you're not too angry with me."

"I'm not angry, Alma. Gotta say, I've been watching the goings-on here with interest. Something's not right, though I can't quite put my finger on what it might be. But if this was my investigation, I'd start with those dancers. Someone said Georgina accused them of illegal activity. Maybe she was right."

"Desirée seems to have soured on them rather suddenly," Stella noted.

"If Georgina caught them out, that would be a solid motive for wantin' her out of the way."

"But what about Reverend Bailor?"

"Maybe he got wise to what was going on."

"Hmm . . . Bailor did change bungalows on this trip. Something he'd never done until now. He claimed it was because of the noise level, but what if it was because he'd heard something."

"Or saw something," Mills added.

"How do we find out what he or Georgina might have known?" Nick asked.

Alma cleared her throat and sat down on the living room sofa. "Fortunately, you have at your disposal someone of the right demographic for sleuthing."

Mills narrowed his eyes. "Who might that be?"

"Me!"

"You? These dancers go with older women with nothin' going on in their lives. You're a gorgeous, vital, successful woman."

"Awww, thanks, Charlie. But as far as they're concerned, I'm a woman of a certain age who's here with a significant other who doesn't like to dance."

"Hey, I like to dance," Mills argued.

"They don't know that. Anyway, we can just say that your back is acting up or some other nonsense."

"Alma, we came here to get married, not for you to go undercover on some sort of spy mission. Something could happen to you."

"What, calluses?"

"Um, I could join her," Stella suggested. "Besides, the dancers are here tonight, after our games and dessert, so you and Nick would be watching the entire time."

"Me?" Nick complained. "But I like to dance, too."

"Yes, but you're not very good at it. That will be my story to the dancers."

"So long as the only thing you complain about is my dancing."

• • •

After a few raucous rounds of charades and musical chairs, the group helped themselves to a decadent dessert bar before dispersing to the pool area for music and dancing. As anticipated, the dancers from El Sueño were on hand for a choreographed performance rife with flashing lights and sexual innuendo.

When the performance ended, they joined Caballero Cove guests and visiting El Sueño patrons—again, a gaggle of well-heeled middle-aged women in short dresses—on the dance floor.

Desirée shot a withering glance at the dancer she'd accompanied earlier in the week, then left to join Chip at the bar. Seizing her opportunity, Alma took the young man by the wrist before he could be snatched up by any of the other women. "Hola! I'm Alma."

"Alma?" He was disoriented at first, but promptly turned on the charm. "That means soul in my language."

"Really? How lovely."

The DJ, clearly playing to the crowd, put on Thelma Houston's "Don't Leave Me This Way," which elicited squeals of delight from the ladies of El Sueño.

"I am Sebastián." He took her hand and twirled her into the middle of the dance floor.

"Oh!" Alma exclaimed. She was genuinely surprised by the move. "I've never pulled that one off before."

"You dance with Sebastián, and you will learn all the right moves." Like all the dancers, he was twenty-something, of medium height, and handsome. "What is your costume?"

"I'm the Queen of Hearts."

"I am certain you are."

Despite the obviousness of the compliment, Alma still found herself blushing.

"Where is your husband? He does not like to dance?"

Mills had chosen a spot closer to the action and was watching Alma from a dark corner near the fenced-in trash area behind the clubhouse. "Oh, my fiancé doesn't mind dancing, but he hurt his back. It's an old injury."

"So, he often does not dance with you."

Alma could see where he was headed with this line of conversation. She played along. "Not as often as I'd like."

"Good thing Sebastián is here. I will teach you all the important moves."

He dipped her backward. This time she kept her composure.

"That would be wonderful. I would love to learn some new dance moves for my wedding."

"Sebastián will teach you. We start now." He twirled her again before launching into the hustle. "Do what I am doing."

Alma mirrored his actions.

"Good . . . good. You have excellent rhythm, Alma."

"Thank you."

"Sebastián can teach you the rumba, the samba, the cha-cha, the merengue. Every dance you could ever want to learn."

"That sounds wonderful, but I'm not sure I have time to learn all that. There are only two days left until the wedding."

"Two days? Alma, you need my accelerated program. We spend some time tonight, here on the dance floor, then we meet again tomorrow afternoon, tomorrow night, and then one last time, just before the wedding, to rehearse. We'll begin with the beautiful salsa— the dance of love." Sebastián punctuated this proposal by twirling Alma forward and then catching her in both arms.

She pulled away quickly and smoothed the skirt of her ball gown. The invitation was charming, but she was suspicious of his motives. Unless she was an eccentric rich aunt, a man of Sebastián's age shouldn't want to spend all his free time with a woman of her age.

Still, if he and the other dancers were somehow breaking the law, she'd have to get close to him. "That seems like an awfully short amount of time to see results," she replied. As much as she needed to keep close and observe him, she also didn't wish to appear too eager.

"You will see the results," he guaranteed. "You already see and feel them, don't you?" Sebastián pulled out a flamenco move, which Alma emulated.

"Yes," she said with a giggle. "Considering I've never made a move like that before, yes, I suppose I do."

"Then is Sebastián going to get you doing all the Latin dances for your wedding?"

"I guess we could give it a try." Alma looked across the dance floor at Stella, who gave the thumbs-up, despite trying her best to keep up with her dance partner, Eduardo's brisk tango.

"You are doing very well," Eduardo praised.

"Really? It doesn't feel as though I am."

"No, you really have excellent rhythm. It is a shame your husband does not like to dance with you."

"Oh, he likes to dance, he's just terrible at it."

Nick was back at their casita, listening in via the phone in Stella's clutch handbag. Although he could hear what was being said, his voice was muted. "Terrible?" he nearly shrieked. "We agreed that you'd tell him I wasn't very good, not terrible."

"That is the complaint of many women here at the resort. That is why we are here—to make your dancing dreams come true." He took her hand in his and kissed it.

"I don't think that has anything to do with dancing," she quipped, removing her hand from his.

"What's he doing?" a nervous Nick asked as he peered through the living room blinds. "If he's getting feely, I'll come out there and sock him in the jaw. Remember the code word for help, Stella."

Naturally, she couldn't hear him.

"I am sorry, but you make the most beguiling Marilyn Monroe."

"Thank you."

"Also, the tango is a dance of seduction and passion."

"Maybe we should try a different dance."

"But of course," Eduardo acquiesced with a smile. "What would you like to learn? The samba?"

"Um, sure."

"Where is your husband right now?"

"He's back at our casita sulking. I told him I was going to dance with you because he's not very good at dancing—"

Nick repeated the words. "Yes, that's right. *Not very good at dancing*, not terrible. Stick to the script"

"—and he became insulted and went back home."

"I hope you don't mind me saying, but he is foolish to let you out of his sight."

"Ugh." Nick faked a retching sound.

"He should take the lessons so he becomes a better dancer, rather than let you dance with someone else."

Stella fought the urge to roll her eyes. Eduardo's sentiments were correct, but his righteous indignation was well over the top. Did women actually fall for these guys and their shtick? "No, it's my fault. I probably shouldn't have been so hard on him."

"That's right," Nick agreed.

"You weren't hard on him for expressing your needs," Eduardo said.

Here we go, Stella thought. An opinion shared and voiced by Nick.

"Tell me. What would *you* like to do?" Eduardo asked, gazing deeply into her eyes.

"I would like to dance."

The DJ slowed things down with a soft Mexican ballad. "Then we will dance." He put his arm around her waist and began to sway. "When the DJ changes music, we'll try a samba or a rumba. You have great hip motion, so you should do well at both."

It was Nick's turn to roll his eyes. "Oh, boy."

"How long are you in Playa del Carmen?" Eduardo asked.

"Another five days. We're here for our friends' wedding."

"Then you and I have time to perfect our dance. Tomorrow, I will teach you how to move to the rhythm of the waves."

"Oh, I um, I'm supposed to visit a vanilla distillery tomorrow."

"Vanilla? I suppose your husband scheduled that."

Alma, the baker, was actually the person who'd made the arrangements, but Stella felt that a husband who couldn't dance and thought watching vanilla being made was entertaining would only incite Eduardo to further utilize his charms. "Yes, he thought it would be fun."

"Fun? A woman like you needs romance. Excitement. You go to your distillery tomorrow and when you come back, we will drink champagne and I will dance with you on the beach."

"Champagne? That sounds awfully expensive. How much are these dance lessons?"

"How much?" Eduardo drew a hand to his chest as if this question was a personal affront. "No, no. There is no charge . . . er . . ."

"My name is Stella."

"Stella," he repeated. "Star. That's what your name means—star. My star, our dance services are free. Complements of the hotel."

She was shocked by his answer. "Really? Señor Tugores pays you to entertain the guests?"

"Señor Tugores is an employee like the rest of us. We all work for Quintana Hospitalidad. Quintana Hospitalidad takes care of its guests. And what I provide is more than entertainment." He pulled her close and the pair took several paces back.

"Oh, yes, sorry. You are quite a talented dancer," Stella acknowledged.

"Thank you. Inside you there's a talented dancer, too. But we need to tap deep inside you to release her."

She cringed at Eduardo's choice of words. Meanwhile, Nick was shouting at the phone again. "The only tapping that will be done is on your head, Eduardo."

"Yeah, well, we might need dynamite for that," she said with an uneasy laugh.

"So, are we on for tomorrow?"

"I suppose it would be okay. But I'm afraid I have to cut tonight's lesson short. I should really talk to my husband and apologize."

"My star, you are making a mistake," Eduardo purred. "We have the moonlight, the music. Let him come to you."

"You know, I'm getting really sick of you, Eduardo," Nick said while watching out the casita window. He couldn't see the couple on the dance floor, but it helped somehow to be looking in that general direction.

"No, Eduardo," Stella insisted. "I apologize for my mistakes. I will see you tomorrow."

"At four o'clock?"

"Sí, at four o'clock."

He kissed her hand before she departed.

As Stella passed Alma and Sebastián, she could hear her friend also excusing herself. "I'm plain tuckered out. I'll see you tomorrow afternoon."

The two women convened near the bar, where they were joined by Nick. "There's about to be another murder at this resort."

Alma's face registered alarm. "Another?"

"Yes, Eduardo the Eager and his desire to uncover my wife's hidden talents, among other things."

"Oh, stop," Stella ordered him with a grin. "You knew I had to get close to one of the dancers."

"Yeah, so you could keep an eye on Alma, not so you filled your dance card, too."

"Call me crazy—"

"I think I just did."

"But I think it's better that Alma and I are both undercover on this. We can compare notes and see if there's some sort of widespread scam with all the dancers, or just one."

Nick pulled a face. "I guess you're right. I just hate that guy pawing at you."

"Pawing's the right word," Alma remarked. "I haven't had to fend off moves like that in over twenty years."

"Ugh, I know," Stella commiserated. "Believe me, Nick, I wasn't thrilled about it either, but I've already learned something. There's no charge for the extra lessons."

"Yes, that's what Sebastián told me, too."

Stella nodded. "Desirée's story about the hotel billing her incorrectly is a lie. So, why did she cancel her dance classes?"

"Maybe she got tired of Eddie the Fingers," Nick suggested, still showing his contempt for Stella's dance partner.

"Desirée danced with Alma's guy. And she seemed to like the attention—until now."

"Maybe she got tired of him referring to himself in the first person," Alma quipped. "Sheesh, is that annoying."

Stella laughed. "Everything Eduardo says is full of innuendo. It's ridiculously awkward. I honestly can't believe that the women here go for that sort of thing."

"Maybe they're tired of their 'plain vanilla' husbands," Nick said in a loud voice.

"Are you really upset about that? I was talking about a fictional being—a caricature of the insensitive, inattentive husband. Are you meeting Sebastián tomorrow?" Stella asked Alma.

"Yes, after our distillery tour."

"Same here. We're meeting on the beach."

"I'm meeting Sebastián in the ballroom at El Sueño."

"Hmm . . . maybe we can get them to meet us at the same place, so that the guys only have one spot to monitor."

"That's an excellent idea," Nick agreed. "I'd have no problem taking on Eduardo myself, but there is something nice about having backup. Speaking of which, where is Mills? Didn't he listen in on your conversation with his phone, Alma?"

"No, he preferred to stick close by and watch. Last I saw him, he was headed to the utility area behind the clubhouse. Said he could hide there. Knowing Charlie, he probably fell asleep," she added with a chuckle.

"We'd better go and wake him up."

Nick led the way toward the spot where the resort disposed of its trash and where its electrical circuitry was housed. Although the utility area itself was illuminated by a single light outside the clubhouse's rear door, the area outside the fence lay in heavy shadow, mostly due to the thick foliage designed to hide the spot from the pool area.

Nick switched on his phone's flashlight function. "Hey, Mills, wakey wakey."

His call was met with silence. Scanning the dark space near the electrical shed, he zoomed the light in on a folding chair that was used by staff during short breaks. From the chair, Mills would have had a clear view of the pool area and the dance floor.

The chair was empty, but a few feet away, facedown on the pavement, lay an unconscious man.

"Charlie!" Alma cried. "Oh, God, no! Charlie!"

Nick dropped down on his knees to examine Mills while Stella called emergency services.

Mills came to, groaning. "Nick . . . what happened?"

"It's okay, Mills. We're going to get you help. Just lie still."

"I'm okay. Help me to my feet."

"Nope. Not until you're examined by a doctor. You have a nasty wound on the back of your head." Nick removed his shirt and placed it at the site of the wound.

"I was here watching that dancer make time with Alma when I heard something rustling behind me. I stood up to take a look around and everything went black."

"An ambulance will be here soon. No more talking."

Nick gestured for a sobbing Alma to sit with Mills and apply pressure to the injury. Meanwhile, leaving his phone on the ground, he took Alma's device and with the flashlight function, examined the area surrounding the shed. A line of trees stood between the fence and the place where Mills had been seated. This line of trees ran from the pergola on one end to casita number one on the other.

Nick shook his head. Anyone on the property could have crept along the line of trees, snuck up behind Mills, and leveled the blow.

Stella returned with Tugores in tow. The pair had brought with them several beach towels, which they wrapped around Mills to stem the symptoms of shock.

Shortly after they arrived, paramedics were on the scene. Mills's wound did not appear to be critical, but he required a CAT scan and other tests before a doctor would release him. Alma rode in the back of the ambulance with Mills.

Stella and Nick followed closely behind in the backseat of Lenzana's patrol car. "Let this be a lesson to you that you need to leave the investigation work to the police," the inspector admonished. "Your friend was lucky, but that might not have been the case. It is obvious that whomever killed Señora Early and Reverend Bailor is determined to get away with it."

"Wait, did you say Reverend Bailor was murdered?" Stella questioned. "Did you hear something?"

"That Reverend Bailor also died of cardiac arrest produced by an overdose of oxycodone."

"My God . . ."

"Yes, we are dealing with an extremely dangerous individual, so no more playing detective. Please?"

"That's the thing, Lenzana. Sheriff Mills wasn't investigating anyone."

"What do you mean?"

"Mills hasn't been involved in the case at all. I'm the one whom everyone thinks is the detective. I'm the person with whom everyone shares the Caballero Cove gossip."

"Then why did this person assault your friend?"

Stella felt a hole in the pit of her stomach. "I haven't the foggiest idea."

Chapter Seventeen

Three hours after the ambulance transported him to the hospital, Mills returned with his fiancée and friends to Caballero Cove in Lenzana's squad car. The diagnosis of concussion with a minor intercranial hematoma was given with the advice that the patient rest, hydrate, avoid screen time, take over-the-counter pain medication, and to monitor for any changes. Mills was to check back with the emergency care physician in two days' time.

After thanking Lenzana for the ride, the couples made their way to their casitas. Stella and Nick made certain that Alma and Mills were both settled in and their casita fully locked before returning to their own bungalow.

Stella was bone-weary, but even after a hot shower she still couldn't relax. She and Nick got into bed and turned off the bedroom light, but she soon got up and wandered into the living room to keep watch out the large picture window. Nick soon joined her.

"I thought you were asleep," she said.

"I was and then I rolled over and you weren't there." He stood behind her and slid his arms around her waist.

"Sorry, I can't help but wonder if I could have done something to prevent the attack on Mills. If I'd stepped outside and called out to that shadowy figure, instead of slinking back behind the curtains, maybe . . ."

"Maybe that person would have attacked you and we'd have been rushing you to the hospital with a head injury instead of Mills."

"You're probably right."

"I am right. As always," he teased.

She gave a weak laugh. "Or so you think."

"That's better." He rested his chin on her shoulder and gazed out the window. "What are you looking for?"

"Answers. Why Mills? Was he simply in the wrong place at the wrong time? If so, what was happening at the time that he wasn't supposed to see?"

"I scanned the area where we found Mills. The line of trees that cover the fence where Mills was assaulted would have concealed his attacker. That line of trees starts at the clubhouse, meaning anyone here for the party tonight could have hit Mills. The line of trees ends at the first bungalow."

"Casita number two, where Joseph Penrod is staying. I have a lot of questions about that man. He seems to be everywhere, doesn't he? Swapping bungalows with the reverend, arguing with Georgina about some money deal, that weird encounter I had with him at the pharmacy, and now this."

"You think he might be our killer?"

"He's definitely suspicious. But I still don't understand why he would have killed Reverend Bailor. Or why he would have attacked Mills tonight."

"Hey, you don't think that the prowler was going to see Penrod, do you?" Nick suggested.

"Hmmm," she mused aloud. "I never thought of that. We did learn that the motion lights on that side of the pool aren't triggered until someone reaches bungalow number three, right?"

"That's right."

"That means the person I saw was headed toward Bernard's casita, Penrod's casita, or the clubhouse."

"I'd rule out the clubhouse," Nick stated. "There are other ways into that building that wouldn't have drawn as much attention. Like the door that leads to the utility area, for instance."

Stella agreed. "That leaves either Bernard's casita or Penrod's"

"Which once again places Penrod in the center of the action."

"Yeah, but what would someone be doing at Penrod's casita at three in the morning? What would they have been doing at anyone's casita at that time? Maybe the prowler is just that—a prowler. An isolated incident not related to the case."

"I'm not so sure about that. Bailor swapped places with Penrod because of traffic, right? That means the prowler you saw must have been skulking around that same area last year and triggering the motion light."

"Not necessarily. You forget, Desirée's been returning to her bungalow at all hours for quite some time now. Our fellow guests have seen her. Desirée and Chip are staying in casita number four, just across from Bernard's casita. I saw her trip the motion light when she came home the other night."

"What about Bernard? Maybe his friend from Tulum came to call on him."

"At three in the morning? After his wife died?"

"Then we're back to Penrod."

"And we're back to the beginning. Why would Penrod have killed Bailor? Why would he have attacked Mills? We're missing something here, Nick."

"I can't disagree with you there. All I can say with any confidence is that the attack on Mills coincided with you and Alma making friends with those dancing gigolos. Both Georgina and Mills were suspicious of them too."

Stella spun around to face him. "What did you call them?"

"Gigolos. I mean, they are kinda gigolos, aren't they? They're supposedly paid to dance, but their primary job is to keep guests company."

"You don't think they might be actual gigolos, do you?"

"They could be. I couldn't see you and Ready Eddie on the dance floor, but from what I heard, he was more than prepared to meet any needs you might have. And I mean *any*. So, I'd say there's a strong possibility there."

"Where is this judgment coming from? Gut instinct, life experience, or jealousy?"

"All three," he said with his usual cheeky grin. "But seriously, there's something up with those guys. We didn't get the full account from Alma, but they sold her on taking dance classes, too."

"Ah, but she wasn't sold, was she? The dance classes are supposedly free."

"Which, I gotta say, surprises me. If Rock Steady Eddie and the boys were being pushed to sell dance classes to tourists, I'd totally get it. But obviously they're selling something else."

Stella thought about Desirée and her array of body-conscious fashions. "Not sex. They're not selling sex. Desirée could find a willing partner just about anywhere. They're selling companionship and self-esteem. The question is what are they delivering?"

"Something that caused Desirée to become a very dissatisfied customer."

"Is she a customer, if dance classes are free?" Stella shrugged. "Which raises an interesting point. Why would Desirée cite a billing issue as the reason she stopped her classes? Lies often point to the truth. Maybe money was somehow involved."

"You mean maybe Desirée was paying for additional services?"

"Maybe. It's possible, right?"

"Anything's possible." Nick sighed. "It's late. You should try to get some sleep."

"I know, but—" She went back to gazing out the front window.

"You still want to keep watch."

"I don't want to be in our bedroom if that light goes off again. I want to see who's out there in case they decide they want to come in here."

"Lenzana has a guy out there on the beach standing guard."

"To keep people from coming in, but what if the killer is already here?"

"I understand." He pulled the cushions from the sofa and tried to make light of a tense situation. "Who needs Sweaty Eddie? I can accommodate your every desire."

"What are you doing?"

"Watch." He pushed all the cushions aside and transformed the couch into a bed.

"I didn't know this was a sleeper sofa."

"Every bungalow has one. It's in the online brochure. Look, it's already made up, too. Guess they were prepared in case we had an argument."

"Or you snored too loudly," she said with a wan smile.

"I don't snore," he maintained. "I'll go get the pillows from our bed and we'll be all set."

While Nick was in the other room, Stella stared at the pullout.

Every bungalow had one.

Chapter Eighteen

"Well, at least he ain't depressed," Clyde said upon hearing about Lila's night.

"That's what I thought, until I'd finished cleaning everything up. What a mess! I wish he'd find some happy medium." She sat at the break room table sipping the coffee he'd made for her. Bixby snoozed on the floor by her feet.

"I reckon he's like a kid. They cry when Mom and Dad first leave. Then, when they get used to the babysitter, they push the boundaries. That's what Bixby's doin'. He's pushin'."

"You know, you may have something there. I never looked at it that way, but he is sort of like a kid staying with a babysitter."

"Yup, he's staying with Grandma."

"A dogsitter," she corrected. "I wonder what I can do about it."

"Be stern with him. Don't take his guff."

As if in protest of Clyde's advice, Bixby got up and wandered off into the store.

"That's the opposite of what Alice recommended yesterday. She said to keep things calm and mellow."

"That was before the boy lashed out by soaking the house. The game has changed. So have the rules."

"I don't know, Clyde. It was just water. Maybe playing with all those other dogs brought out the puppy in him. He was just playing and nothing was destroyed."

"Nothing was destroyed, this time . . ."

Lila sighed. "Alice knows what she's doing. She at least got Bixby to come out of his shell. Maybe we should give her a call and let her know his behavior has changed."

"Alice is out of town the next couple of days. That's why I was in a hurry for her to see Bixby yesterday morning. But I can call in another fella who breeds Australian shepherds. Calvin knows his dogs."

"I'm not sure, Clyde. Maybe it's time to bite the bullet and take him to the vet."

"Is Bixby eating?"

"Yes."

"Sleeping? Going to the bathroom?"

"Yes, just like he normally does. He even went outside this morning and ran around for a good thirty minutes. He seemed happy."

Clyde nodded. "Let's call Calvin first. If he says Bixby needs to see a vet, I'll drive the two of you there myself."

While Clyde called his breeder friend, Lila opened the store for the day's business. It being a weekday, neither she nor Clyde anticipated a lot of customers—indeed, no one was waiting at the door for the shop to open, as they often did on weekends—but with the holiday season fast approaching, they also knew to expect few lulls in the flow of traffic.

"Calvin will be here in time for the lunch break," Clyde announced, entering the shop area from the break room. "Leonard will be here by then so he can help me look after the store while you two discuss Bixby's behavior."

With a plan to aid Bixby in place, Lila stepped behind the cosmetics counter, where the dog in question was slumbering in his bed. As he often did when in a deep sleep, he was on his back with his legs in the air.

After tuning the thirty-year-old stereo system to a twenty-four-hour Christmas station, Lila opened a packet of gingerbread cookies and placed them in front of the row of holiday-themed bath products she'd created, including the mulled wine bath salts she had hoped to enjoy the previous evening.

"I've gotta hand it to you, Bixby," she said while spraying herself with a smoky vanilla fragrance that put her in mind of cozy winter nights by the fire. "If any other male had disturbed my bath, they'd have gotten a real earful from me. You? I clean up the mess you created, feed you, play with you, and call a professional to figure out why you interrupted my bath in the first place."

The morning sped by, with Lila selling various lotions, salts, and fragrances to both tourists and locals alike.

At a quarter to twelve, a man approached the cosmetics counter. He was sixtyish with a gray beard, salt-and-pepper hair, and a black puffer jacket covered in animal hair. "Um, Lay-la, please?"

"I believe you mean Lila. That's me."

"Oh, I'm sorry. I'm Calvin. Clyde called me this morning about your dog."

"Yes, he did. Thank you for coming over with such little notice. Bixby, the dog Clyde told you about, is back here behind the counter in his bed."

"Good. I was worried that you called me about that dog sitting on the garage roof next door."

Lila laughed out loud. "A dog on a roof? I haven't been in Teignmouth very long, but such funny things happen here that I wouldn't be sur—" She had glanced over at the dog bed, only to find it empty. "That dog on the garage roof—what color is it?"

"Black. Looks like a Lab. Big one, too. Eighty pounds or so. What's so strange about it is that Labs aren't exactly the ballerinas of the dog world. They're full of enthusiasm, sure, but they're too clumsy to climb, so I'm not sure how he got up there."

"I know how he got up there. He's crazy, that's how."

• • •

Stella spent a restless night on the sofa bed. Nick did, too. She could feel the mattress—an excellent mattress for a sleeper sofa—spring up and then sink again every time he'd get up and check the door and window locks.

Stella, meanwhile, kept reviewing the facts of the case. The knowledge that every bungalow possessed a sleeper sofa shed a new and dramatic light on the Earlys' need for separate vacation accommodations. How bad were things between them if a generously proportioned casita didn't offer sufficient space for them to peacefully coexist? What had caused them to make the move from separate sleeping areas to individual dwellings?

Yet, Stella could easily understand the distance between them. Everyone at the resort had been a target of both Georgina's belligerence and her malicious rumors. Despite being first-time visitors, even Stella, Nick and their friends hadn't escaped unscathed.

So much drama, Stella lamented. So many rumors. But which if any of those rumors were rooted in reality? And which had been invented simply for Georgina's personal amusement?

With those questions at the forefront of her mind—and a resolution to find answers—Stella finally surrendered to the fatigue that had consumed the rest of her body. It was a few minutes before four in the morning. She slept straight through until seven thirty. Nick was already up and dressed when she awoke.

"Hey," he greeted, perching on the edge of the sofa bed mattress.

"Hey. Did you get any sleep at all?"

"A little. I checked in with Alma. Mills rested comfortably and is still asleep. Alma managed to sleep, too, which I was relieved to hear. I told her to text me once Mills is awake and we'll grab some breakfast in the clubhouse together. Until then, I ordered us some coffee."

"Perfect." She looked out the window. All was quiet and the sky was an ominous shade of dark gray. "Looks like rain, which seems appropriate after last night."

"Yeah, there are showers in the area this morning. It's cooler, too."

"Oh, you checked on Alma and Mills in person?"

"No, I texted Alma. I visited the scene of Mills's attack. Lenzana and his men were over there when I got up."

"And? Anything new?"

"Not much. Looks like the perpetrator hit Mills with a croquet mallet from one of the sets used on the lawn. The head of the mallet broke off in the attack, sparing Mills any further injury, thank God. Lenzana doesn't know where the handle went, but he's sure it will turn up somewhere, wiped clean of fingerprints, no doubt."

"Any footprints?"

"Not a one. It hasn't rained here in a couple of weeks so everything is bone-dry. On top of that, because the shed where Mills was sitting houses the electrical works, the land around it drains well."

"Is Lenzana questioning the guests?"

"His team took statements from everyone last night. They were all at the party, except for Bernard. He was still in town."

"Did he ask everyone about the rumors Georgina was spreading?"

Nick wrinkled his brow. "Huh?"

"I was thinking last night."

"I know. You kept tossing and turning."

She bit her lip. "Sorry."

"No apologies necessary. If I'd been asleep, I wouldn't have noticed."

She rose from the bed and slipped her kimono over her nightgown. "I was thinking about how Georgina's stories play into everything that's happened here."

"Do they? What about the dancing gigolos?"

"We wouldn't be checking them out if it weren't for Georgina's statements about them 'being up to something.'"

"You have a point there. So, what's the plan?"

"We confront everyone about the rumors we've heard."

"Confront? Um, need I remind you about what happened to Mills?"

"Mills didn't discuss Georgina's death with a single soul at Caballero Cove and still got clobbered over the head. And that's precisely why I want to talk to everyone. I want to find who did this."

"I do too." Nick looked down at the floor and Stella expected an argument, but she was surprised by his response. "Let's go ask some questions."

"*Let's*? Are you joining me?"

"You bet I am. I'm going to be at your side every step of the way."

"As a fellow detective? Or as my bodyguard?"

"Both. Unless the bodyguard job is already taken."

"Taken by who?"

"Let's-Go-to-Beddy Eddie."

"You're joking, right? And, by the way, that's the worst rhyme yet."

"No, I'm sure I could do worse than that," Nick said with a laugh. "Who's first on the list."

"The mystery man himself, Joseph Penrod."

• • •

"I'm not sure how I can help you," Penrod said as he held his casita door open for Nick and Stella to enter. He was dressed in a pair of khaki cargo shorts, a blue T-shirt, and a pair of house slippers. "I answered the police's questions last night. I was at the party with everyone else and didn't see who attacked Charlie. If I had, I certainly would have said something."

"This isn't about last night," Stella replied. "This is about the rumors that have been circulating around this place."

Penrod's face softened and he gestured them to sit down on the overstuffed sofa. "Ah, those. There have been rumors being spread around this place for years. Part of the vacation experience. I wouldn't pay much attention to them if I were you. There's nothing to them at all."

"So, there's nothing to the rumors that you're a very wealthy man?"

Penrod laughed and took a seat in the armchair opposite the couch. "I hadn't heard that one! No, I am not a wealthy man. I retired from the Army with a good pension and I managed to tuck away a tidy sum for our—er, my old age, but I am not what anyone would ever describe as wealthy."

"Then I suppose you didn't ever make an investment or business deal with Georgina Early."

Penrod leapt from his seat and rubbed the back of his neck. "No. No, I didn't have any sort of deals with Georgina. Where did you hear such a thing?"

"Someone overheard your argument with Georgina the morning of the day she died," Nick explained. "They heard you tell her that she needed to honor her end of a deal."

The color had drained from the older man's face as he anxiously moved his hand from the back of his neck to his face. "Damn this place! Damn it. It used to be a haven for us, for my wife and my family, and now it's just a hotbed of gossip and lies and everything else that's rotten. And it's all because of that woman."

He drew a deep breath and sat down again. "I suppose I might as well tell you. It all started with a conversation over dinner. It was my first time back here at Caballero Cove after my wife, Gwen, died. Reverend Bailor had checked in on me several times while Gwen was ill and I was at home, acting as her caregiver. We'd video chat and text each other. He knew how alone and hopeless I felt and helped to fill that void, all the way from England. He was an excellent friend and an even better human being.

"During that first dinner back," Penrod continued, "I lost myself, or it might be more precise to say that I found myself again. I ate, drank, and interacted with the other guests, not the way I used to, but they way I do now—as myself, a widower, and not a married man. I also laughed. I laughed at some ridiculous joke Chip told us. The sound of that laughter both surprised and alarmed me. It was the first time I'd laughed since Gwen's diagnosis. And it felt good. So good that I let my guard down when I shouldn't have.

"Later that same evening, I mentioned—quite briefly—how difficult caring for Gwen had been. Not just the nursing duties—I had some help for that—but dealing with the emotional side effects of the disease and its treatment. It was all Georgina needed to hear.

"During my next few visits to Caballero Cove, Georgina proceeded to question me about Gwen and her final months. Her inquiries were never too probing or ill-timed. I never felt as though she was grilling me. In fact, her manner was gentle and sympathetic. She made me feel as if I was confiding in a good friend. What a mistake that was.

"When I arrived this year, Georgina threatened to put it around that I helped to end Gwen's life. That I murdered the woman I loved because I was exasperated with her constant demands. If I didn't want to face a scandal, I was to pay her twenty thousand dollars."

Stella felt her jaw drop.

"What? You laughed her off, right?" Nick asked.

"No, I'm sorry to say I paid her the money."

"You paid her? Why?" Stella asked. "If you didn't harm your wife, then why would you give in to a blackmail demand?"

"Because I—I gave Gwen an extra sleeping pill the night she died."

Nick and Stella both sunk back into the sofa, clearly afraid of what they might hear next.

"Gwen was in discomfort the day she passed away—not pain, but discomfort. I must have adjusted her bed fifty times trying to find a position that worked for her. She was remarkably lucid, more so than she'd been in several weeks, so I had no idea it was the end. I only knew that she was having difficulty and that her requests to adjust the bed and complaints about the food I'd brought her were causing me difficulty. I was exhausted and needed to rest. So did Gwen, I thought, so I doubled her medication. Gwen passed away in her sleep and I . . ." Penrod's voice broke off as he fought back tears.

Several seconds elapsed before he spoke again. "I confided in Gwen's doctor almost immediately afterward and he assured me that the sleeping pill was not the cause of death. Nor did it speed things along. Gwen was already well along on her final journey; the extra dose only helped her cross that bridge peacefully."

"If that's true, then even more reason to ask: why did you pay Georgina?"

"Because I want to keep my family," Penrod answered without skipping a beat. "I wasn't around very much when our children were young. We moved from base to base for most of their lives. Germany, Italy, Japan. And I was often away on assignment. As a result, the girls— Jennifer and Arden—were extremely close to their mother. Even after they'd both married and started their own families, they still called Gwen nearly every day.

"When Gwen fell ill, the girls were devastated. They pushed us to move closer to one of them—Jennifer's on the East Coast, Arden in the Pacific Northwest—but I refused. It didn't feel right to leave our home just then. Not with Gwen needing treatment. She had her doctors and we had our circle of friends. The girls weren't pleased with my decision, but I stand by it. Still do. Packing up everything we own while in the middle of chemotherapy would have been insane. Also, Jennifer and Arden are both very busy juggling careers, marriage, and young children. I'm not sure exactly how much help they could have been.

"During one of Arden's check-in calls with us, I confessed that I was having a particularly rough day with their mother. Gwen had complained about every meal I'd prepared for her. I was in the kitchen practically all day, cooking something I thought she'd be able to enjoy, but to no avail. I was exhausted, both physically and mentally, and I made the unfortunate remark to Arden that perhaps it would be a blessing if their mother was to pass sooner rather than later."

"Surely they must have understood that you were under a great deal of stress," Stella said.

"Oh, they understood. Jennifer called me shortly afterward. After speaking with Arden, she'd arranged for me to see a psychologist so that I could discuss my 'negative feelings.' As if I had time to lay on some couch and cry my eyes out. And as for 'negative feelings,' my wife was fading away by the day, what did they expect from me?" Penrod was still angry. "Needless to say, I didn't react well to what I felt was needless interference. In fact, I was downright angry. Had Jennifer or Arden called me to discuss what I might want, that would have been a different story, but there they were, miles away, making arrangements that impacted my life and the care I could give their mother, without even asking for my input."

He drew a deep breath and calmed himself. "Since Gwen passed, I hear form the girls every now and then, but it hasn't been the same. They're cold. Distant. I'm positive that if they learned about that additional sleeping pill, I'd lose contact with them forever. That's what Georgina threatened. I didn't pay her to save face here at Caballero, but I paid her to prevent her from contacting my family. From our years of vacationing together, she knew about our daughters and their families. It wouldn't have been difficult for Georgina to track them down. I couldn't take that risk. It might be too late to repair my relationship with my daughters, but I still like to be able to see my grandchildren, even if it's only once or twice a year."

"You said you paid Georgina," Nick said. "Then why were you arguing the morning of the day she was killed?"

"Because she wanted more money. I refused to pay. As I already told you, I'm not a wealthy man. I did well in my career and was able to afford some of the trappings of success: a nice house, good health insurance, and the ability to send our girls to good universities. But Gwen's illness absorbed a vast portion of our savings. I downsized considerably in order to recoup some of that money. I receive a decent pension from the government, which enables me to take this two-week vacation once a year, but I also have to be careful what I spend to ensure I still have enough cash to live on the remainder of my days. And Georgina wanted to take that from me. After we'd already struck a deal! She said she was concerned about the high cost of living and financial security in her old age. What about my security?"

"Some might say that's an awfully powerful motive for murder," Stella remarked.

"That's why I haven't said anything until now. But I—I honestly cannot handle the stress any longer. I've always been a forthright person. That's gotten me into trouble, as I've explained, but I can't stand hiding things. Nor can I stand everyone going on and on about Georgina's passing when the woman was a complete and utter shrew. That woman was absolutely devoid of conscience."

"Do you believe Bernard knew about Georgina's extortion scheme?" Nick asked.

Penrod shook his head. "He might have, but I don't think so. Georgina and I never spoke when he was around. Also, I always figured Bernard as a pretty decent guy. No, the more I think about it, the more I believe he would have disapproved."

Stella hopped in with the next question. "The morning of your argument with Georgina, I ran into you at the pharmacy in town. You seemed shaken, confused. As if I caught you in the middle of something."

Penrod nodded. "I'm sorry about that. I was already rattled by my confrontation with Georgina, but then I had to go to the pharmacy because, despite my careful planning, I'd run short of my blood pressure medication. I could have sworn I'd had enough with me. That on its own was upsetting, thinking you're finally ready for the glue factory, but then when I picked up my prescription, I noticed that they'd given me capsules instead of the usual tablets. So, I went back in and spoke with the pharmacist in my broken Spanish. It wound up that the prescription was correct; here in Mexico, hydrochlorothiazide comes in capsules. But the events of the morning were enough to trigger my PTSD."

At the mention of hydrochlorothiazide, Stella flashed a glance at Nick. From what she knew about the drug, it was a widely prescribed blood pressure medication, but that both Penrod and Georgina should have been taking the same drug was an interesting coincidence. What, if anything, did it mean?

"Did you talk to Reverend Bailor at all about Georgina's demands?"

"No. I was sorely tempted to, but he was only here a day or so before he . . ." Penrod's voice trailed off. "It was so good to see him again, not on a video screen but in person, that I didn't want to mar the occasion. Had he lived, I know I would have eventually confided in him, but I never had the opportunity."

"You and the reverend exchanged bungalows. Why?"

"Didn't someone already tell you? You're obviously very well informed. We could have used more people like you in Intelligence," he said, a vague smile on his lips. "During last year's stay, Timothy— that was the reverend's first name—was kept awake at night by the clubhouse motion light. As my usual bungalow, the one you're staying in now, is farther away from the clubhouse, the light is less intrusive, so we traded."

"Have you been kept awake by the light?"

"I have two modes: asleep and awake. When I'm awake, I see the light switch on. When I'm not, I don't."

"When you've been awake, have you noticed what's been triggering the light?"

"I've looked out the living room window plenty, but I've never seen a damned thing. I figured it was probably a bat flying by or a raccoon getting into the trash."

"Can you think of any reason for someone to want Reverend Bailor dead?"

Penrod moved his head from side to side, mournfully. "Not a single one. Ever since the police ruled his death as suspicious, I've been turning it over and over in my mind and coming up empty. The only person here with that much evil in her heart was Georgina, but now she's dead too." He raised an eyebrow. "You think maybe she murdered Timothy and then killed herself?"

Stella provided an honest answer. "I never thought of that, but what reason would Georgina have to murder the reverend?"

"What reason did she have to blackmail me other than greed? Maybe she tried the same thing on the others and Timothy found out?"

"Maybe," she allowed, although she was truly doubtful. "But the police have yet to find a suicide note."

"That would be just like Georgina to play one last little trick. It would be just like her to commit suicide and let someone else hang for her murder."

Chapter Nineteen

After their meeting with Joseph Penrod, Stella and Nick went to the clubhouse for breakfast, where they met Alma and Mills. Despite his injuries, the sheriff's color was good and he appeared to be well-rested and relaxed. Alma sat beside him, clutching his hand.

Señor Tugores took it upon himself to personally fill their coffee cups. Except for their party of four, the dining room was completely empty. "Buenos dias. Señor Mills, it is so very good to see you with us this morning. How are you feeling?"

Mills rubbed his chin. "Like I went through a car wash on a bicycle, but otherwise, I'm okay. Happy to be alive, to tell ya the truth."

"I am so very sorry about what happened, señor. Tonight, at dinner, drinks are on the house for you and your party."

"Ah, apart from a sip of champagne on our wedding day, I'm afraid I'm on the wagon while I recover."

"Then please allow me to provide that champagne with my compliments," Tugores instructed. "Your fellow guests ordered their morning meal to be delivered in their casitas, so we held back on the buffet this morning. However, we still have a cooked-to-order breakfast available. Two eggs, cooked to your liking, salsa fresca, and your choice of tortillas or rye toast. I'll be back for your orders. In the meantime, Luciana will bring you some fruit and juice."

Luciana came directly from the kitchen to their table bearing a tray carrying four bowls of papaya, mango, and passionfruit. "Thank you. It looks as if you might be a little short-staffed this morning," Alma noted.

"Sí, although he"—Luciana nodded her chin toward Tugores, who was chatting with a member of the kitchen staff in the corner of the dining room—"doesn't like to admit it, many of our staff are frightened by recent events. We had three of our waiters call in this morning."

"That's terrible!"

"I'm sorry they were scared on my account," Mills apologized.

"Don't be. This has nothing to do with you. They were frightened the minute the police said both Reverend Bailor's and Señora Early's deaths were suspicious. Señor Tugores is a good man," Luciana stated, echoing the words of Lenzana just days earlier. "He doesn't deserve to have all this happen at his hotel. That's not to diminish the memories of the dead, especially poor Reverend Bailor, but Señor Tugores has worked too hard for this."

She walked back to the kitchen.

"She seems . . ." Alma struggled to find the right word.

"Enamored?" Nick offered.

"I was going to say dedicated, but yeah, I suppose enamored works, too."

Stella thought of the rumor circulating about Tugores and the younger employee. Was history repeating itself?

After ordering their breakfasts, as the foursome munched on the contents of their fruit cups, Stella and Nick revealed that they had resumed their investigation, starting with Joseph Penrod.

"I was going to ask if you still intended to get involved in the case. I'm glad you are," Alma declared. "I already told Charlie that if he's okay being left alone this afternoon, I'm keeping my dance class appointment with Sebastián."

"I'm keeping my dance class with Eduardo, too. But I'm going to call ahead and see if you and I can have our lessons together here by the pool so that Nick can keep an eye on us," Stella said.

"I'm still not so sure about this," Mills warned.

"I'm with you, Mills," Nick commiserated. "But if the classes take place out in the open where everyone can see them, I think they'll be safe. I also don't intend on letting anything happen to them."

"What about Penrod? You said you talked to him before meeting us. Did his story add up?"

"It totally added up."

"What's more, the fact that Penrod is also on hydrochlorothiazide reminded me of Georgina's disappearing medicine bottle," Stella said. "I don't for a second believe that Renata made a mistake. If she said that bottle was missing, then it was missing. The question is why?"

Tugores delivered their breakfasts and the four friends ate in thoughtful silence, grateful to have been spared from socializing with their fellow guests. At least for now.

When breakfast was over, Alma and Mills returned to their bungalow for a rest and a change of clothes as the cool, cloudy morning had evaporated into brilliant sunshine.

"It is good to see Señor Mills up and around," Tugores said to Stella and Nick as they left a tip for the morning meal service.

"Yes," Stella agreed. "For a while there last night, we weren't sure, but he was very lucky. Señor Tugores, you're a very observant man. You keep a close eye on everyone and everything around here, making sure that none of us want for anything."

"Thank you, Señora Buckley." He bowed deeply. "I do my best."

"You do more than that. Tell me, with that keen eye of yours, did you happen to see anyone near the utility shed at any part of the evening? Or even someone elsewhere on the property acting suspiciously?"

"No, I am sorry, señora. Dance party evenings are, as you can imagine, hectic for me and my staff. Between the Caballero Cove guests and those from El Sueño, it is difficult to keep track of everyone."

"Yes, I heard the dance parties were a new addition to the entertainment."

"Yes, the new owners came up with the idea three years ago to appeal to . . . how should I say? A different clientele," he explained delicately. "I am still unaccustomed to the . . . attention it draws."

"Yes, the dancers have a number of fans, don't they? Ardent fans," Nick said with a laugh.

Tugores also laughed. "As you say."

"I heard the entertainment used to be quite different," Stella said.

"Oh, yes." A proud smile crossed the manager's face. "Before Covid, we'd book different bands, all from neighboring towns. The locals would come and enjoy the shows with the guests. It was wonderful for everyone. The bands made a little money, the guests got to experience a little bit of local culture, and the locals got to socialize with people from other countries, not as servants or vendors reliant upon their money, but as equals. Everyone would dance and enjoy the music. Children would play together on the lawn. It was wonderful.

"I still try to provide culturally stimulating programs, but it's no longer an entire evening. Perhaps someday . . ." he added wistfully.

"I hope so. Everyone we've spoken to has such fond memories of this resort back in the day. Except . . ." She fell silent and cast Tugores a furtive glance.

"*Qué es?* What is it, señora?"

"Oh, well, as you're aware, Caballero Cove is positively rife with gossip."

Tugores cast his eyes heavenward. "This is sadly true."

"There has, unfortunately, been some gossip about you."

"Me?" he exclaimed, but the expression on his face told them that this wasn't the first time he'd heard allegations against him.

"Yes, some sordid tale about you and a young female employee. It sounded like it all happened years ago, but—"

She was interrupted by Luciana, who rushed in from the kitchen. "The tale is not sordid. That young female employee was my mother. And my father, Miguel Tugores, loved her very much."

Tugores put a finger to his lips and gestured that they sit at a table in the corner of the dining room, far from the kitchen, overlooking the pool. "I was nineteen when I met Luciana's mother, Lupe. She was just sixteen and I fell in love with her right away. We spent that summer here working at Caballero Cove. She was my parents' employee, yes, but I was their employee, too. We worked during the day waiting tables, cleaning rooms, and performing other chores. Any time off we had, we spent out there on Bandista Beach, swimming, fishing off the pier, and reading books beneath the shade trees in the town square.

"It never occurred to me that anyone would have reason to be angry with us or to disapprove. Three years isn't a big age difference, but when you're teenagers, it's enough. Lupe's parents complained to my parents about me. They felt that Lupe should be focused on finishing school and getting a good job. They thought she was too young to date anyone, let alone me. They complained to my parents, who were also concerned that I might not want to return to university if I had a *novia*, a girlfriend, here in Quintana Roo. And so, I was forbidden from seeing Lupe." He gave a faint smile. "If you remember your own youth, being forbidden from doing something makes it more attractive. So, Lupe and I continued seeing each other in secret. But eventually someone found out and told Lupe's parents. They threatened to have me arrested since, at sixteen, Lupe was under the age of consent. In ordinary circumstances, nothing would have happened to me, but because I was her employer's son, Lupe's parents would tell the police that I used my position to coerce her into a relationship.

"My parents explained to me that I would go to jail if I continued to see Lupe and even Lupe herself told me to let her go. I argued, but the decision was made for me. Lupe's parents moved the whole family to another state. I was devastated. I asked around to see if I could find out where they'd gone, but no one knew. Or they knew and wouldn't tell me. I went back to university and thought of Lupe often.

"Years passed," he went on, "as they do. I never forgot Lupe, but caring for my mother and father and running the hotel took all my time. Then, five years ago, I heard from Luciana. Lupe had died. Ovarian cancer." He reached over and clutched Luciana's hand as a single tear ran down her check.

"I had heard Mama talk about my father and Caballero Cove many times," Luciana said. "I wanted her to get in touch with Miguel many times, but she was married to someone else. Someone . . . not very nice. When she died, I knew I had to find my father. I went on the internet and found the hotel website, but thought that it had probably been sold to someone else. Yet, I still sent the email hoping that the new owner would know how to contact the former owners. You could imagine my surprise when I received an answer and it was from the same man my mother talked about."

"When Lupe moved away, I did not know that she was pregnant," Tugores explained. "I wish I had known. I would have been there for her, but when I found out about Luciana, I arranged for her to fly here so that we could meet. And I promised to make up for lost time."

"Yes, I got an apartment and started working here at Caballero Cove in charge of guest relations. It was difficult at first. I did not have hotel experience, but I think I have gotten good at it."

"You are terrific at it," Tugores gushed.

"I'm glad you both found each other," Stella said.

Nick echoed the sentiment.

"However, I'm confused as to why this rumor would have been started in the first place," Stella questioned. "There's hardly anything scandalous about it. Maybe fifty years ago, but not now."

Tugores nodded. "I believe it's because I never shared with the guests that Luciana is my daughter. Señora Early—I'm sure you know that she's the one who started it—she was always looking for the . . . the sins of her fellow guests. She must have heard something about Lupe and imagined that I had the same relationship with Luciana."

"Did she tell you that?"

"Yes, she said she knew what I was 'up to'—that was how she said it—with Luciana. She said I should be reported to the authorities."

"Did she threaten to report you herself?"

"Sí, she did."

"Unless?" Nick urged.

"She wanted a discount on her bill. I laughed at her. I could not believe she was serious. But, then she threatened to post on the hotel review sites and to tell other guests that I—that I once had a relationship with a minor."

"Unless you gave her a discount?"

"Correct."

"What did you do?"

"I gave her a small discount to make her happy."

"But why?" Stella asked. "There was no truth to the story she was spreading."

"But there was. Lupe was a minor when we met and I was nineteen. I should have known better."

"That was nearly thirty years ago and you were a teenager as well."

"Yes, but there are certain guests—none of them here now, but new guests looking for the El Sueño experience without the high price—who would not think well of me if they knew the truth. They like to have the vacation here—the sunshine and weather—but they look at us, us Mexicans, like we are animals. Even though Luciana and I are now united as father and daughter, a story like that . . . in their minds it would confirm their beliefs. I could lose my job here. I could lose this place. Apart from my daughter, Caballero Cove and that little piece of Bandista Beach are all I have."

"I overheard the two of you arguing with each other the day after Georgina's death. What were you arguing about?" Nick asked.

"My father found out that I told Renata to clean Señora Early's casita," Luciana confessed. "I told Renata to empty the waste bins and do a good cleaning before Señor Early went there to sort through his wife's belongings. The truth is, I'd already been in Señora Early's casita, searching."

"Searching for what?"

"Letters she might have written to other guests she knew, evidence she might have had to prove my mother was underage, notes she might have taken, emails she might have sent from her phone or laptop. Anything. I was desperate. Desperate to save my father. Renata caught me leaving the casita, so I made up an excuse. I told her I was inspecting it so we could rent it to someone else and discovered it needed a good cleaning. Part of me also thought, maybe by cleaning the casita, it would also erase any proof that I'd been there." She shook her head. "It was stupid."

"It was not smart," Tugores agreed, clutching her hand tightly. "But I know you did it for me. For us."

"I just have one last question," Stella announced. "When Reverend Bailor checked in last week, he asked for a different casita than the one he usually stayed in. Is that correct?"

"Yes," Tugores confirmed. "He complained about the motion light above the clubhouse door. He said it was constantly switching on at strange hours at night."

"I believe you live in casita number one, don't you, Señor Tugores?"

"Yes, I do."

"I tell him all the time to move in with me," Luciana commented. "I have an extra bedroom and plenty of space."

"I am happy here," Tugores replied. "And you and *tu novio*, Enrique, do not need Papa in the next room."

Stella smiled. "Casita number one is directly opposite casita number two, the casita normally occupied by Reverend Bailor, and like casita number two, it is adjacent to the clubhouse."

"That is correct."

"Are you ever bothered by the clubhouse light, Señor Tugores?"

"Me? No, I sleep soundly at night. Also, my mother and father designed the casitas so that the big window was in front, in the living room. The bedroom windows are high, above the eyeline, so you cannot see the casita next door and so no one can see you. They designed it this way so that guests could sleep with few distractions—sunlight, outdoor movement, heavy rain."

"Very clever. And very effective," Nick noted. "Each bungalow—*perdóname, casita*—feels like its own little world. The individual gardens help add to that feeling."

Tugores beamed at Nick's feedback. "Gracias, señor."

"It's true. So, did Reverend Bailor ask to be moved to a specific casita?'

"No, he asked to switch to another casita. He did not state which one."

"That is not the whole story," Luciana interjected. "Reverend Bailor complained about the light and asked me if I could move him to a casita on the other side of the pool."

"Wait, he specifically asked for a casita on the *other* side?" Stella confirmed.

"Sí, he asked for an odd—that is the right word, yes? Odd?—casita. Sergento Penrod was in numero nueve and said he would trade with his friend, so we moved the sergento's belongings and put Reverend Bailor there instead."

"Did you ask Sergento Penrod to move? Or did Reverend Bailor ask him?"

"Oh, the reverend did. He sent a text to the sergento and presto! The problem was solved!"

Chapter Twenty

Stella and Nick left the clubhouse and entered the pool area. The sun was sitting high in a flawless azure sky. As they had been on previous days, Ray Horrocks and Anika Banerjee were floating on inflatable loungers in the pool while Desirée and Chip were, once again, enjoying the hot tub.

The couple refrained from speaking to each other until they were back in their bungalow and away from anyone who could overhear what they were saying. Before they reached their front garden, they encountered Ellie Sanderson on her way back from the beach.

"Hey, how's Charlie?" she asked. "I hope he's okay. He and Alma came here to get married, not attacked."

"Mills is doing better than any of us expected. He still has to rest, but he has Alma by his side taking care of him. She's hanging in there. All she wants to do is make it to the wedding tomorrow evening," Stella explained.

"I bet. I remember marrying Kendal. I could not wait to say our vows and start our life together. Not that my love would have been any lesser if we hadn't married, but you guys get it." She gave Nick's arm a nudge.

"We do. Um, do you have a little bit of time to talk? In private?"

"Yeah, sure. Let me bring Kendal her green juice—they're short of staff today—and I'll meet you in your casita."

"Sounds good," Stella agreed.

Ellie showed up at Stella and Nick's door a few minutes later. "What do you want to talk to me about?"

Stella answered. "We've been talking to everyone about what's been going on here and—"

"It's true! You *are* here on an investigation."

"No, we're not. I mean we weren't, but now we are. Never mind. We called you here to tell you that you were seen kneeling beside Georgina an hour or so before Bernard discovered her dead."

Ellie's sunny disposition darkened. "Oh. That. God . . . I don't know what possessed me to do that. It was so very stupid of me. It was also exactly what Georgina wanted, me pleading with her. It made her feel powerful."

"Why were you pleading with Georgina? Were you hoping she'd change her mind about giving you and Kendal the knitted blanket?"

Ellie visibly shrank at the question, as if trying to fade into the background. "I wish. I went to see her about something else. Something from the past that I didn't want her bringing up again."

"Care to share?" Nick invited.

"Not really, but it's preferable to share with you than with the police." Ellie plopped onto the sofa.

Nick brought her a glass of water. "Tell us what happened."

Ellie took a long sip, placed the glass on the coffee table, and then spoke, her hands crossed in her lap. "I first came to Caballero Cove as a student. I didn't stay here. I stayed in a hostel across town, but I came here one night for a concert. A local band was playing and a traditional mariachi band started the show. The bar served Mexican beer at a reasonable price. For a couple dollars more, you could get a small plate of fabulous beans or tacos or grilled fish. Everyone—guests and locals—gathered here. It was magical. I decided then and there to return every year, and I have.

"The third time I came here, I brought along a boyfriend who decided this wasn't his scene and flew home on the second day. Alone and brokenhearted, I decided to party. It's embarrassing to think about now. I drank a lot and hooked up with a dancer. No, not the ones here," she responded to Stella's surprised expression. "The dancers here are . . . I don't even know how to describe them."

"Gigolos?" Nick offered.

"That's the perfect word for them! The way they're all over the wealthy middle-aged women in this place. It really does make you wonder . . ."

Nick flashed his wife a smug grin.

"Not that I should judge anyone. The way I behaved on that trip was abhorrent. I was absolutely obnoxious and more than a bit of obscene carrying on with that dancer the way I did. Ray, Diana, Manish, and Anika were here with their kids and I was like a crash course in what not to do while out of the country on vacation. But I guess after being dumped I was trying to prove something. Trying to prove that I was wanted and desirable. I was in my twenties, fresh out of school, feeling the pressure to live up to expectations while still trying to find myself and come to terms with who I really was. That's not an excuse for my behavior. Not at all. As soon as I sobered up—which was a few days before I was set to go home—I apologized to everyone. They were all so cool and awesome.

"Señor Tugores accepted my apology and invited me to return for a quiet stay. If I were him, I would have banned me!" she added with a laugh. "Joe shared an account of some his youthful exploits to make me feel better, even though he was fairly tame in comparison. The Horrockses and Banerjees told me about their drunken lost days before they became full-fledged adults with kids and a mortgage. And Reverend Bailor was just the sweetest. He didn't judge, didn't lecture. He pulled me aside and said that I was a special person who deserved to treat myself better than I had. He also said that I could talk to him at any time and that God didn't need to enter the conversation. He really cared, you know? I'm going to miss him not being here—his quiet presence. Do you know he gave us a baby gift before he died? That's the kind of man he was.

"Anyway, everyone was very understanding. Even Chip kept his mouth shut, which, given his conservative view of the world, was a miracle. Looking back, the only person who didn't say a word to me was Georgina. I should have known then that she was trouble. She liked to store these things away in her memory for use at a later date."

"Why?"

"It's as I said before: power. She liked to lord it over us all. Not even Bernard was safe."

"So, what happened when you spoke with Georgina?"

"I begged her not to say anything. I've always been open and honest with Kendal about my bisexuality, but I never told her about my bad behavior during that trip. The casual fling and the boyfriend and the drunkenness. In retrospect, I should have told Kendal everything from the start, before we even started traveling here on vacation. But I wanted to make new memories with her, instead of focusing on the past. I wanted to make this place our own little piece of paradise. It was a mistake, I know, but it definitely wasn't Georgina's place to correct it and it certainly wasn't the right time. Kendal's pregnancy hasn't been easy. She and the baby are healthy, thank goodness, but we've had a couple of scares. I told Georgina that. I begged her to keep quiet and let me tell Kendal in my own way and in my own good time."

"What did she say?"

"Nothing. She stared straight ahead, her jaw set, and didn't say a word. Now that I think about it, she might have been dead already. I don't know. I never checked. It never occurred to me that she might be anything but okay. She was always so formidable. I really didn't get a good look at her, either. She had sunglasses on and I had tears in my eyes, so my vision was blurred."

"Did Georgina ever try to use what she knew about you to make a profit or call in a favor?" Nick asked.

"You mean like blackmail? No, never. But I'm not sure we're rich enough for that. I mean, we both do okay, but babies and prenatal care is expensive, even with insurance. Georgina only did what she did with me as a means of control. She was queen of Caballero Cove and I was a mere peasant. Though, I wouldn't be surprised if she tried to blackmail some of the other guests. It's just another form of control, isn't it? And she did pass a comment when we first arrived about how business wasn't as reliable as it used to be. I assume she was talking about the business she runs with Bernard. Some sort of investment company."

"Did she go into specifics?"

"No, Bernard gave her the stink-eye and she changed the subject. That in itself was pretty incredible. Georgina actually paid attention to how Bernard felt about something. It was the first time I'd ever seen anything like that. She usually steamrolled right over him."

• • •

Lila stood outside the abandoned garage beside Perkins' General Store waving half of a rotisserie chicken in the air. "Go with the man,

Bixby. Go with the nice man and I'll give you chicken!"

Meanwhile, Calvin had propped a ladder against the building's side and had climbed up onto the roof, bearing the other half of the roasted bird.

"Bixby," Calvin whispered as he slowly approached the canine. Bixby was cautious, but otherwise relatively calm. He lay on the roof's peak, gazing around him in wonderment.

"Bixby," Calvin called again.

The curious dog, smelling the chicken, sat up.

"Good boy, Bixby. You stay. Stay. I'm coming to you."

Lila bit her fingernails as Calvin scrambled to the roof's apex and then, reaching up, clipped Bixby's leash to his collar. Traffic on Main Street had come to a halt as tourists and townsfolk alike stopped what they were doing to watch the daring rescue.

There was a smattering of applause among the spectators who had gathered in the snowy field just outside the garage. But Lila, as well as the majority of the crowd, knew the most difficult part was yet to come—getting Bixby down safely.

Just then, the Teignmouth fire department showed up in their bucket truck. "I knew those boys would eventually make it," Clyde remarked.

"It took them long enough," Lila remarked. "I don't know how much more my nerves would have taken."

"Yeah, well, they're slow but sure. I'm going inside to put together some sandwiches. I had a fire alarm go off a couple months back and these fellas cleared me out."

"Okay. I'm staying here until Bixby's down."

"Yep. Figured you would," Clyde replied before heading into the store.

A small team of firemen leapt from the back of the truck and cleared a path through the crowd to the garage. Once in place, the driver raised the bucket to the garage roof so that man and canine could step inside.

The entire rescue process took only a few minutes and was met with boisterous cheers.

"Bixby!" an elated Lila cried as she knelt down to welcome the dog rushing toward her.

Calvin followed closely behind Bixby. "So, tell me. What are your dog's symptoms?"

Lila laughed. "I told you. He's crazy."

"Nah, he's a good boy. Just your typical playful Lab. I reckon he chased a squirrel or chipmunk up there and then found himself stuck."

"Last night he hopped in the bathtub with me and dripped water all over the house. Today a garage roof. That sure is a lot of play."

"If you get him outside more, that should do the trick."

"Really? Because he was outside most of yesterday and he still caused mayhem."

"Labs will run and play until they're ready to collapse. Best thing you can do is tire them out."

"Hmm, I don't doubt you, but another friend of Clyde's recommended that I keep him and his surroundings calm. You see his owners—my daughter and son-in-law—are away and I'm at home alone with him."

"A calm approach with any animal is best, but when he's not relaxing, get him out running."

"I'll try. Thank you, Calvin. For everything. I can't believe you actually went up on that roof."

"Ah, I've been up on rooftops before. I was in construction for years before retiring and dedicating my life—and my clothes, as you can see—to the dogs. I don't know if Clyde told you but I'm not just a breeder. I also work in animal rescue. We've had cats stuck in some god-awful spots, so this wasn't anything new."

"Well, Bixby and I greatly appreciate your help. Is there some way I can compensate you for all you've done?"

"No, no thanks necessary. It's all part of what I do."

"Actually," Lila started, thinking of how valuable it might be to have an animal rescue volunteer help promote her products. "I've developed a line of all-natural doggie deodorizers that I'm launching tomorrow. The local paper is going to be there and I'm giving out samples as well as free dog biscuits. Oh, and human food too, although it's kind of a doggie gathering. You're welcome to join us if you like."

"You know, I might just take you up on that," he said with an easy smile.

"Great. I'll text you the details. After I take Bixby for a walk."

Chapter Twenty-one

As soon as Ellie left their casita, Stella and Nick changed into lighter clothing and set about their next mission. Nick, in a pair of khaki shorts and a linen-blend button-down shirt with a subtle hibiscus print, walked into town to see if he could grab a few words with Diana Horrocks and Manish Banerjee, while Stella in her swimsuit and cover-up went out to the pool to talk to Ray and Anika.

Stepping into the shallow end of the pool via ladder, she found the water a bit chillier than it had been during her last swim.

"It hasn't had enough time to warm properly. Go get a float," Anika encouraged from her raft.

"Yeah, join us," Ray said, welcoming her. "That sun is blazing. It shouldn't take too much longer."

She felt slightly guilty questioning people who were so warm and friendly, but remembering the attack on Mills, she tiptoed across the hot pavement to the equipment shed and selected an inflatable inner tube with an enclosed opening. She selected it over a nearby lounger as she thought the smaller, round design would make it easier to get into.

She was wrong.

After several seconds of attempting to ease herself into the tube while it was in the water, Ray came to her rescue and held the float so that it didn't slip out from beneath her bottom.

"Thanks," she said sheepishly.

"How's Charlie?" Anika asked. "I saw him and Alma head back into their casita. Is he okay?"

"He took quite a wallop but the prognosis is good. He just needs to rest."

"Thank goodness. I don't know what's going on around here, but Ray and I were just talking about how maybe we should go home."

Ray nodded. "I'd pay extra for a last-minute flight rather than be sent home in a box."

"The only problem is I doubt the police will let you leave. Not until both Georgina's and the reverend's deaths are explained," Stella said.

"Do they really think it's one of us?" Anika asked.

"They seem to think it's possible. And I can't help but wonder if it has something to do with all the gossip in this place. All the stories Georgina told."

"Georgie did like to gossip about her fellow guests. Desirée was the usual target. I don't know why Georgie seemed to have it in for her, but she was always commenting on Desirée and those dancers. I suppose Desirée does make a spectacle of herself at times, but it's no reason to be cruel."

"With Georgina, sometimes I think cruelty was the point," Ray said.

"Maybe, but I don't think that's entirely the case. Did she ever try to leverage gossip against you and your spouses for financial gain?"

"No, what gossip?"

"Georgina put around the story that the four of you are . . ." Stella wasn't sure how to gracefully describe the situation. "Well, that you're in the habit of, um, exchanging partners."

"Swingers?" Anika said in disbelief.

"Is that what she told everyone?" Ray asked. "Jeeze, what a twisted person. No, I had no idea she had done that."

"Neither did I. I can't believe it! As if she didn't already do her best to try to damage us."

"Anika," Ray chastised.

"Oh?" Stella remarked.

"A few days ago, Georgie came to us while we were here by the pool," Ray reluctantly admitted. "She said she had a photo to show us. Apparently, she and Bernard were out on one of their walks, when Georgie spotted Diana and Manish at an outdoor restaurant laughing and holding hands. She then proceeded to show us the photo she'd taken that supposedly proved they were having an affair."

"The photo didn't show anything compromising," Anika interjected. "The hand-holding she described was more like an affectionate high five, but there was something about their laughter and the way they looked at each other that raised a few questions."

"I can't remember the last time Diana looked at me the way she looked at Manish in that photo," Ray complained. "That's a sad thing to say given that it was just our wedding anniversary."

"Same with Manish. We're always so busy with the restaurant and now taking care of aging parents, that I don't think we've had a date night in years. I thought coming here on vacation and having some time to relax would spark some romance."

"It did. Just with the wrong person."

"You both believe that your spouses are having an affair with each other?" Stella questioned.

"No," Anika was hesitant. "Not physically, at least. But perhaps in an emotional sense."

Ray agreed. "I feel as though Diana and I have grown distant since the kids left the house. I think, maybe, she and Manish are connecting the way she and I used to."

"I feel precisely the same way about Manish. There's been some distance. Like we're more business partners than man and wife."

"So, why did Georgina show you this photograph?" Stella asked. "What did she expect you to do with it?"

"She wanted us to pay her money, otherwise she'd send it to our children," Ray said.

"She knew which universities our children attend. Once you know the email format for a company, school, or other organization, it's easy to plug a student's name and initials into that construct."

Stella was perplexed. "I don't understand. Why would Georgina come to you with the photo and demand blackmail money? Why wouldn't she show the photo to Diana and Manish and threaten to show the photo to the two of you unless they paid up?"

"I wish I knew," Ray replied, "but that's how it went down."

"We had until the end of the week to give her an answer."

Georgina's death certainly put a kink in that timeline, Stella thought. "Did Bernard know about her demand for money?"

"I don't know. If Georgina was with him when she took the photo . . ."

"Georgina was sharp," Ray argued. "I hate to say it, but she was far sharper than Bernard. She could have easily snapped that photo without him even noticing what she was shooting."

"True. Bernard also keeps to himself. It's difficult to see him getting involved in something like blackmail."

"How about Reverend Bailor? Do you think he might have known about Georgina's scheme?"

"Reverend Bailor was already dead when Georgie approached us. Why?"

"Just trying to figure out how the two deaths might be connected." Stella looked up from her raft to see Alma and Mills emerging from their bungalow to take in the glorious afternoon sun. They were greeted by Joseph Penrod, who had returned from his time on the beach.

As the group exchanged pleasantries, Stella couldn't help but notice how similar the two men were in appearance. They were the same height, with a similar build, and, although the color of their hair was different, they both wore it in a close-cropped, military-inspired fashion. The only visible distinction between the two was their age.

But that difference wouldn't be obvious on the darkened grounds of Caballero Cove.

Two men of similar build and height, both wearing a uniform. Was Mills the intended target of last night's attack or was it Joseph Penrod?

• • •

Nick returned an hour later and joined Stella as she sat at an isolated table on the lawn outside the clubhouse. She was on the phone with the front desk of El Sueño Hotel. "So, there's no way to move the lesson from the ballroom to the grounds of Caballero Cove? Ah . . . I see. Then Señora Deville and I will be at the ballroom at four o'clock. Sí . . . gracias."

"Well, I'll just have to go to the hotel with you. Leave your phone on and I'll listen in like I did last night," Nick resolved.

"You can't just linger in a hotel lobby," she argued.

"No, but I can hang out in the gym. I'll wear a pair of earbuds and use the treadmill, this way I'm ready to go whenever you need me."

"That's not a bad idea."

"Of course it isn't. I thought of it."

Stella groaned. "So, what did you find out from Diana and Manish?"

"Get this. Georgina was blackmailing them."

"Oh? Over a photo of them holding hands and laughing at a restaurant?"

"No, over a photo of Ray and Anika splashing each other while embracing in the pool. Although, according to Diana and Manish, the embrace was more playful than intimate."

"And Georgina threatened to send the photo to their children if they didn't agree to pay up."

"Yeah, by the end of the week. How did you know?"

"Because she did the same to Ray and Anika with—"

"The restaurant photo you mentioned," Nick filled in the blank. "Diana and Manish don't think the affair is physical."

"Ray and Anika don't think Diana and Manish's relationship is physical either. It's more of an emotional connection—"

"Due to distance in their respective marriages."

"Yep. Strange, huh?"

"Why wouldn't Georgina just blackmail each couple with their own photo by threatening to show it to their spouses? I hope that made sense because this is really confusing."

"I understood what you meant. I asked myself the same question."

"And?"

"Well, I haven't had a lot of time to think about it, but the only reason I could come up with is because none of them—neither of them?—none of them are actually having an affair. With each other," Stella clarified. "Who knows what goes on at home."

"I don't even want to contemplate it. I barely understand what you just said."

"Georgina didn't show Ray and Anika a photo of themselves splashing in the pool because they would explain that they were having an innocent pool fight in front of all the Caballero guests. Likewise, Diana and Manish could explain that yes, they were talking and laughing at a restaurant, but that they were high-fiving instead of holding hands. So, in order to create drama and coerce them into paying money, she made it all about protecting the kids."

"How could Georgina be so sure the two couples wouldn't just talk it out?"

"She probably heard about their lack of communication over dinner one night. Or even at the pool. She asked Alma and me a whole bunch of questions when we first arrived. Georgina knew far more about us than we ever did of her. From talking to the other guests, it was the same with them. They could tell me all about Reverend Bailor's parish and the soup kitchen he supported, but they knew very little about the financial company Georgina and Bernard supposedly ran together."

"You think that was on purpose?"

"I do," she replied as she got up and made her way to the pool. Selecting Georgina's favorite lounge chair, she lowered herself into it and gazed out at the view. From the spot, she could see the entire pool and, beyond it, Bandista Beach. To the right along the beach, Ellie and Kendal lounged in their cabana. Moving from right to left, the flawless sand was interrupted first by the wedding gazebo and then by the pier where the ferry and other fishing boats left for and returned from Cozumel. Behind the pier, a short distance away, stood Old Town Harbor and its collection of fishing boats.

"What are you doing?" Nick questioned.

"Trying to figure out why Georgina was so fixated on this spot."

"She said it was the view."

"Yes, and it's a lovely one too. But lovely enough to fight over?"

"Who said she fought over the view? Georgina didn't need much to start an argument. In this case, she was probably being territorial. She was the queen of Caballero Cove and this was her throne."

"You're probably right. It's probably nothing." Stella gave a sigh and gestured to her husband to follow her back to the secluded spot on the lawn. "I'll tell you what isn't nothing, though. While you were out, I noticed more than a passing resemblance between Joseph Penrod and Mills."

Nick bit his lip and thought about what Stella had said. "Resemblance? Huh . . . they do have the same body type and they're the same height."

"The same short haircut and the same gray sideburns too."

"Okay . . . so?"

"So, both men wore uniforms to the party last night, as well as a hat with a brim, which in the evening light would shield their faces."

"You're saying Mills was attacked by accident," Nick concluded. "But why would someone want to attack Penrod? It seemed like he came clean with us though, didn't it?"

"It did." Stella thought about the hydrochlorothiazide. "It's entirely possible that Penrod knows something but is completely unaware of the significance of what he knows."

Chapter Twenty-two

After a few hours of relaxation in one of Caballero Cove's seaside cabanas, Stella, Nick, and Alma changed clothes and prepared for their afternoon mission. Not wanting to be seen together, Nick, in his gym clothes, left for El Sueño Hotel at fifteen minutes before four. Along the way, he spoke with Stella, ensuring that their phone connection would still work in what might possibly be an underground gym.

Fortunately, he found the fitness center not in the basement of the building, but located at the end of a hallway adjacent to the hotel ballroom.

"Can you still hear me?" he asked before entering the exercise room.

"Sure can. And can you hear me?" Stella asked while applying a coat of mascara to her lashes.

"Yep. I'm going to keep my earbuds in but I'll mute myself."

"I'm going to mute for now, too. When we're on our way, I'll turn the volume back up. I'll text you when I do."

"Sounds good. Be careful. I love you."

"I love you too."

Nick tucked the phone into the back pocket of his shorts and entered the gym, where the attendant greeted him. He was athletic, deeply tanned, and in his late twenties. *"Buenas tardes, señor.* Are you a guest of the hotel?"

"I'm a guest over at Caballero Cove," Nick replied, handing the man the key to casita number nine.

The employee moved to the front desk and swiped the card. "Señor Buckley?"

"Yes."

"Hola and welcome. I am Jaime. Have you been to our fitness center before?"

"No, I haven't."

"I will show you the basics." Jaime grabbed a towel from the shelves behind him and emerged from behind the desk. "Here is your complimentary towel. We ask that you deposit it in the laundry basket by the door on your way out."

"Sure," Nick agreed.

"Electronic equipment—cycles, treadmills, ellipticals—are in this main room. Weights are through the door on your left and a speed bag and heavy bag are through the doors on the right. If you continue through the boxing area, there are lockers to hold your possessions. You'll also find a water bottle filling station and a variety of protein snacks for purchase in the locker area. Do you have any questions?"

"No, that pretty much sums it up. Thank you."

"You're welcome." Jaime glanced around the empty gym. "I'm probably not supposed to ask this, but what's going on over there at Caballero Cove?"

"What's going—? Oh, you mean . . . the deaths."

"Yes, the murders."

"Um, technically they're not murders yet. They're suspicious deaths."

"Police can call them what they want. We all know what they are. Is it true that one of them was a priest?"

"A vicar, yes, from England. And the other was a middle-aged woman. You might know her husband. He comes here all the time. The last name's Early."

Jaime shook his head. "It does not sound familiar."

"First name's Bernard," Nick elaborated. "He's an Englishman. In his fifties and about my height."

"No, I do not think I've met him."

"Really? He's been coming to Caballero Cove for years."

"No, he does not sound like anyone I know."

"Well, maybe another attendant has been on duty when he comes here."

"The only other attendant we have is part-time. No, if your friend comes here as often as you say, I would have met him."

• • •

Sporting the dresses they'd worn to their first dinner at Caballero Cove, Stella and Alma made their way to El Sueño's ballroom. Stella turned the volume up on her phone and ran another test with Nick. "You sound . . . breathless. What's up?"

"I'm on the treadmill. Although I did find out something interesting. I'll tell you later," Nick said before muting himself again.

"Wonder what that's all about," Alma said.

"Endorphins, probably. All that exercise," Stella teased, knowing full well her husband could hear their conversation.

"I've never understood people who said they feel good when they exercise. After exercise? Sure. But during? I tried a pilates video last week and I swore Charlie was gonna come home to my unconscious body knotted up right there on the carpet."

From the pocket of Stella's dress came Nick's muffled voice. "It's not endorphins. You're not the only detective in the family."

"Ah . . . someone put on his sassy pants this morning," Stella said.

"Yep. Tuning out again now."

The phone fell silent just as Stella and Alma approached the beautifully designed entrance of El Sueño del Mar. Stepping past the carport, one encountered a rill filled with tropical fish and spanned by a whitewashed stone bridge. The bridge led to a lush oasis featuring a variety of local palms, lilies, and bougainvillea.

At the end of this garden, a uniformed porter greeted them and held the door open so they could enter. With its high ceiling and plant-filled atrium, El Sueño's lobby successfully brought the outdoors in, creating the sense of a tropical paradise.

The two women followed the signs for the larger of the two ballrooms in the resort, taking note of the location of the gym where Nick lay in wait.

"Here goes," Alma whispered to her friend as they swung open the ballroom doors and moved inside.

They were immediately greeted by a dancer who called himself Luis, who was dancing with a woman who appeared to be in her early sixties. She was slender and dressed in a Diane von Furstenberg ballerina dress and stiletto heels. From the ballroom's sound system, a tango played.

"Buenas tardes. Are you beautiful ladies here for a lesson?"

It was clear from the welcome that all the dancers were trained from the same handbook. "We have appointments with Eduardo and Sebastián."

Luis let go of his dance partner's hand and retrieved his phone from the back pocket of his rather tight black woven trousers. Plugged into the bottom of his phone was an object Stella recognized as a credit card reader.

Luis typed something into his phone. Presumably a message to the missing dancers. "They will be with you momentarily," he announced and then resumed his lesson.

He and the woman were dancing dangerously close to each other. Far closer than the tango usually required. Apart from the proximity of Luis and his student, the situation held all the trappings of a traditional dance class.

"Hola," Eduardo greeted as he bounded through the ballroom's back door. "My star!"

Sebastián followed closely at his heels. "Alma . . . my soul. How are you today?" The dancer took her hand in his and gave her a twirl.

Eduardo, meanwhile, took Stella's hand in his and slowly kissed it.

Well, it did *have all the trappings of a traditional dance class,* she thought. "Um, yes, hello, Eduardo."

"Are you ready for our next lesson?"

"As ready as I'll ever be."

"No, no, no, my star. You need to be confident to dance the tango."

"I am confident. I'm confident that I'm as ready as I'll ever be."

Eduardo laughed. "My star, I did not know you could be so funny. But do not worry, soon you will be dancing the dance of passion and desire."

Stella didn't argue with him. She assumed it was part of the training that he speak provocatively to her. It was as if El Sueño had made a call to central casting when hiring their dancers. All of them were young, dark, handsome, and playing the part of the Latin lothario to the hilt.

She began mirroring his moves and actually found herself enjoying the lesson somewhat. Alma was nervous, but she appeared to be enjoying her lesson too.

After several minutes, the tango music gave way to a rumba. Stella was relieved that the dance of passion and desire had not elicited from Eduardo any attempts at passion and desire.

The third woman sharing the ballroom with them, however, seemed less than pleased with the change of music.

"Luis, more tango," she demanded.

"Cariña, there are other dancers here giving lessons. I cannot change the music."

"But Luis, you know how I love to tango with you. I absolutely *live* for it."

Luis leaned down and whispered something in the woman's ear. Something that made her break into a wide smile.

The scene reminded her of Eduardo's promise. "I thought we were having champagne on the beach today."

"Not today, my star. The first official lesson is always in the ballroom. To see how committed you are to your lessons."

Stella felt herself cringe. Committed? Did everything they said have to be so rife with innuendo? "So someday, we'll have champagne on the beach."

"Sí, my star. Someday soon."

As Stella continued her lesson, she noticed Luís escort the other woman out of the ballroom. Something about their body language suggested that it was not to say goodbye.

"I need to visit the ladies' room, Eduardo."

"Of course, my star. I will be waiting." He kissed her hand.

After giving Alma a quick nod as a signal that she'd be back, Stella emerged from the ballroom and walked toward the lobby as if looking for the ladies' room. There, in an alcove near the elevator bank, she spied Luis and the other woman.

They were fixed in an intimate embrace. An embrace that culminated with a kiss and the woman handing over her credit card. As Luis took his phone from the back pocket of his trousers, Stella removed her phone from the front pocket of her dress and recorded video of the dancer processing the card with the scanner attachment she'd seen upon first arrival.

Pleased with her work, Stella then snuck back to the ballroom without the couple ever noticing her presence. "I'm sorry about the interruption," she apologized to Eduardo upon her return.

"That is fine, my star. I understand."

"Thank you. I was afraid you'd question my commitment to the lessons."

"Not at all." He took her hand in his and kissed it. Then, with her hand still in his, drew his arm around her waist.

Stella might have thought it was an attempt at seduction if her arm weren't pinned behind her back.

"My star," Eduardo whispered in her ear. "I do not believe you went to the ladies' room."

She tried to laugh off the threat in the hope of diffusing the situation. "Yes, I did. Where else would I have gone?"

"You know where you went, Stella. I should have suspected you from the start. You weren't like the other ones. You're younger, prettier, but you're not any smarter."

The grip on Stella's wrist tightened. Remembering a self-defense class she once took, she kicked him in the shin just above the ankle, causing him to loosen his grip and stumble.

"Alma!" she shouted, prompting her friend to break away from Sebastián and run toward the door. "Nick! Nick, help!"

Stella didn't need to shout for Nick. She ran headlong into him as she and Alma tried to exit the ballroom. At his arrival, Eduardo and Sebastián escaped via a back exit through one of the hotel's kitchens.

Nick was tempted to give chase, but Stella begged him not to. "Let the police handle it."

"Lenzana's on his way. I texted the video you sent to me," Nick said, embracing his wife. "Are you two okay?"

"Shaken up, but fine."

"Same here," Alma echoed. "But what happened? Why did Eduardo attack you?"

Stella had just finished telling Alma about the credit card scan she'd witnessed near the elevator when Lenzana arrived on the scene. "My team picked up the dancers, Eduardo and Sebastián. They were running down the road as we were driving in. My officers have taken them to headquarters. They agreed to tell us everything."

"Prostitution?" Nick guessed.

"No, not that. Not yet. Credit card fraud. Female guests gave them tips for their services via card. But the card readers the dancers were using were actually skimmers that collected card numbers."

"That explains Desirée's complaint about the problem with her dance lesson billing. She realized her card number was stolen," Stella said.

"We will want to speak with Señora Hunt," Lenzana remarked. "A statement from her could be useful for the prosecutors."

"Good luck with that. Did the hotel owners know about this scheme? Or was it just the dancers?"

"We don't know yet. Quintana Hospitalidad is an esteemed national corporation, so I doubt they would get involved in something like this. El Sueño is known to be a hotbed of drug activity. High-end drugs for the elite clientele who stay here. But we've been tightening the noose on that activity recently. This credit card fraud ring is most likely an offshoot of that drug ring.

"When we find the bosses of both rings," Lenzana continued, "we've most likely found our killer."

"You really believe this fraud scheme is connected to Georgina's death?"

"*Absolutamente.* Señora Early suspected that the dance group was involved in criminal activity. She openly voiced this opinion and a few days later she is dead. I think it is a safe assumption that the two events are linked."

"And Reverend Bailor?" Stella questioned.

"You said Señora Hunt frequently visited El Sueño for their dance parties and returned to Caballero Cove in the early hours of the morning. Perhaps one of those mornings she was not alone when she returned? The Reverend Bailor might have seen her return with Sebastián or another dancer or maybe even the mastermind of the scheme himself. Reverend Bailor then became suspicious."

"Bailor did ask to switch casitas during this stay," Nick recalled.

"See? It fits into place. But we will know more when we speak with Señora Hunt."

Chapter Twenty-three

After giving their statements to Lenzana, Stella, Alma, and Nick left El Sueño del Mar in order to return to their casitas next door. El Sueño's building management, fearful of scandal, insisted that the police and witnesses enter and exit the building via a rear service door. The three friends were only too happy to oblige, as they didn't wish to get caught up in the mob of spectators and reporters who had been drawn to the resort by the sound of police sirens.

Making their way from the service entrance to the beach, they found a small crowd of curious onlookers, but it was a fraction of the size of the throng gathered beneath the hotel portico.

At the front of this beachside crowd stood a familiar figure. She was dressed in a gauzy floral-printed beach cover-up and a pair of gladiator sandals. She wore no makeup and from the redness around her eyes and nose, it was evident she had been crying.

"Hello, Desirée," Stella greeted.

"What happened? Has Sebastián been arrested?"

"Sebastián and Eduardo are in custody, yes. They're cooperating with police. I expect Lenzana to be calling you as well."

"Me? Sebastián was my dance instructor, nothing more."

"He might have been just a dance instructor to you, but you were a little more than that to him."

"I was?" Desirée's eyes were hopeful.

"Yes, I believe your credit card statements prove that."

With that sentence, all Desirée's hopes were dashed. "I was an idiot to believe he actually cared."

"But you clearly cared for him."

"I did. I still do. I had some good times with Sebastián. He made me feel young and beautiful again."

"You still are beautiful," Alma complimented.

"Thank you. If only Chip would notice every now and then."

"I'm sure he does," Nick offered.

"Then it would be nice if he said so or even acted on it." Desirée blinked back her tears. "It was so different when we were first together. He'd lost a wife and I'd lost a best friend so we talked a lot. Saw each other a lot. I know the other guests were shocked to see us together so quickly and I'm sure many of them thought I was after Chip's money, but it wasn't like that at all. We were friends and companions who could talk about anything. From that grew love. But lately . . . well, you can see for yourself. All Chip wants to do is golf. He's always loved a good golf course, but now he's obsessed. He uses it not as a pastime or sport, but a way to make business connections. And, when he isn't golfing, he's . . . drinking."

"Have you spoken to him about it?" Stella asked. "The drinking, I mean."

"I've tried, but he gets defensive. He says he works hard to maintain our lifestyle and therefore he deserves to play hard, too. I don't disagree, but I'd love if 'playing' included me from time to time." She stared off into the distance. "When I met Sebastián it was like an answer to a prayer. He complimented me on my clothes, my hair, my smile. I knew right away that it was part of the act, but beneath the act, he was charming. We actually talked about our childhoods, believe it or not. He's a local boy, grew up just outside Playa del Carmen in a city called Valladolid. He showed me the photos. It's beautiful—an old colonial city. But there's not much industry there and his family was poor. He taught himself to dance as a way to entertain the tourists. As a teenager, he'd busk on the sidewalks of Fifth Avenue after school. That's how he was recruited to dance at the hotel."

"Who recruited him? Quintana Hospitalidad or El Sueño?"

"Neither. From what I gathered, the dance group was contracted by Quintana to work at both El Sueño and Caballero Cove. It was organized by some man named Tomás. I never met him, but Sebastián mentioned his name once or twice. More in the context of 'Tomás would not like it if we did this or that.' Sebastián met Tomás on the streets. It's not surprising that he'd turn the dance group into a criminal racket."

"So, you don't think Sebastián had any part in coming up with this scheme?"

"No, he wouldn't. It just wasn't him. He was a good person

underneath it all."

"Yet he stole your credit card number," Nick noted.

"He did what he did to help his family. It was wrong and I condemn Sebastián for it, but who knows what we would do in his place?"

"Is that why you didn't report it to the police?"

"That and the embarrassment of it all." She began to cry. "But mostly because of Chip. He can't find out about this. He simply can't!"

"I hate to be the bearer of bad news, but the police already know that you were paying for sex, so——"

"Paying for sex? No! Sebastián and I kissed several times and held each other tightly, but that was it. The essence of our relationship was romance. Pure romance. That spark of first attraction. The possibility and excitement that comes with the beginning of a new relationship. I can't speak for any of the other women who took dance lessons here, but sex was never on the menu for me. Ever."

"Then why are you so afraid to tell Chip?" Alma asked.

"How would you go about telling Charlie that you were kissing and drinking champagne with a much younger man? Even more difficult is how do you tell the man you love that the magic has gone from your relationship? Even worse, how do you tell him that you think he's careening toward a drinking problem?"

"Perhaps a doctor could help refer him to a counselor," Stella suggested.

"You've met Chip. He's old school. He doesn't believe in counselors or therapy or psychiatrists."

"Then maybe you need to tell him that if he doesn't stop, he'll lose you," Nick said.

"But what if he wants to lose me? What if he's doing all this because he's unhappy with me?"

"Then you need to have a discussion with him to find out. Better that than to waste your time with someone who doesn't love you."

"You're probably right. I just love him so." She looked at Stella pleadingly. "Could you keep the police at bay until I talk to Chip? I'll talk to him tonight after dinner. Before he gets loaded."

"I'm not sure I have that power," Stella answered. "But I'll talk to

Lenzana and see what I can do."

"Thank you. I—I don't think Chip should find out about this from anyone else but me."

"I think you're right. Um, just one more question for you."

"Sure. What is it?"

"Did you ever bring Sebastián or any of the other dancers to your casita?"

Desirée shook her head. "Are you crazy? No. I'd be afraid Chip would see. Even if he was usually passed out in bed, I'd never take that risk."

Stella glanced at both Nick and Alma.

"Except . . ." Desirée added. "There was a night last year when I had a little too much champagne. I woke up at our casita the next morning wearing the dress I wore the night before. I still have absolutely no recollection of how I got there."

Chapter Twenty-four

Lila awoke at six a.m. Friday morning after a good night's sleep. The previous evening had gone well, both in regards to pre-launch party prep and Bixby's behavior. Arriving home from the store, she followed Calvin's advice and allowed the Lab a long play period in the snow, followed by dinner for them both. Post-dinner saw Lila finishing the tree trimming and tending to the baking of bone-shaped dog treats. Bixby watched with interest before falling off to sleep in his bed, not Lila's.

She smiled, knowing she'd provided the dog with the perfect balance of activity and calm. Then she prayed that she could provide the same environment today despite a houseful of people and pets.

There was only one way to find out.

Hopping out of bed, she put on the coffee maker and let Bixby out for his morning run before feeding him breakfast. As she sipped coffee, Lila carefully arranged her scented products on the dining room table, along with ingredient information and tester bottles so that dog owners could discover how each fragrance would smell on their own pet. She finished the display with a vase sporting an arrangement of dried flowers from a nearby nursery and then stood back and to assess her handiwork.

Perfect. The dried flowers echoed the hand-illustrated depictions of herbs and wildflowers on the front of the Posh Pooch packaging and echoed the organic goodness of the product line.

With the decorations and product in place, she showered, dressed, and set about readying the refreshments. Using the giant electric percolator that had belonged to her mother—and now resided in Stella's basement—Lila put on a giant pot of coffee, poured a container of orange juice into a pitcher, and arranged dog biscuits and an array of defrosted pastries from Alma's shop on silver platters.

She finished just as the first car pulled into the driveway.

Clyde, she said to herself. He had been scheduled to arrive early, but he had probably run into some last-minute questions or issues with the part-time employees he'd called in to run the store that morning.

Rushing to the door, she was surprised to see that it was Calvin. In his left hand he held the leash of a beautiful but very excited border collie. In the other, a bouquet of flowers. "These are for you. Congratulations on the product launch."

Lila felt herself blush. When was the last time anyone had brought her flowers. "Thank you."

"I'm sorry I'm early, I wanted to check in on our mountain climber." He knelt down and rubbed Bixby beneath his ears.

"He's doing great," she told Calvin as she unwrapped the flowers and placed them in a vase. "He had extended playtime yesterday evening and again this morning. It really seems to have helped him."

"That's good to hear. He's a great dog."

"Yes. I've never had a dog before, so it took some getting used to, but we're good friends now." She smiled and then remembered her job as host. "I'm sorry, here I am yakking away. Can I get you some coffee? Or maybe some tea? Wait, I can't offer you tea because I forgot to make it!"

Calvin laughed. "Coffee's fine. Can I give you a hand with anything?"

"No. No, thanks. Everything's done except for putting out a carafe of hot water." She set the kettle on the stove to boil.

"Well, how about I take Bixby out for another quick romp? Hermione here could use some exercise and it will keep them better behaved for your launch."

"Oh, would you? That would be wonderful."

"My pleasure." He flashed her a dazzling smile before leading both dogs into the backyard.

Calvin had just gotten the dogs outside when the other guests began to arrive. "Welcome! Welcome," she greeted, introducing herself and encouraging them to help themselves to the buffet as well as take advantage of the fragrance samples in the dining room.

A few moments later, the local press arrived with their cameras, encouraging Lila to pose with a bottle of Miss Dior for Dogs.

The party was in full swing and the air brimming with fragrance when Calvin returned with the two dogs. Bixby, as if possessed, came bounding into the kitchen and ran directly into the dining room.

Jumping up to lick her face, his front paws pulled down the décolleté neckline of her Michael Kors cashmere sweater dress, revealing the highly supportive black bra beneath it, as well as the ample cleavage it produced.

All the while, the newspaper's cameraman continued to snap photos.

"Stop!" Lila cried, hoping that either the dog or the newspaper employee—or both—might cease in their current activity. "Stop it! Bixby, down."

Calvin had finally caught up with the dog when Bixby took off and ran for the kitchen. "Bixby!"

Lila and Calvin gave chase. "Bixby. Come here! Now!"

But the canine wouldn't listen. Instead, he jumped up onto the kitchen table and surfed across its surface, sending croissants, Danishes, doughnuts, and doggie biscuits flying through the air. As he sailed along, Bixby caught whatever food he could in his mouth and endeavored to consume it.

For that brief moment, life seemed to be operating in slow motion. Calvin had leapt forward to capture the wayward animal, but he'd already moved on to the living room, where a handful of dogs and their owners had convened near the warmth of the woodstove to consume their morning treats and compare notes.

Calvin, with no dog in the room left to wrangle, fell unceremoniously into the piles of pastry left in Bixby's wake.

Meanwhile Lila, trailing behind Calvin, noticed that the kettle she'd started boiling upon the dog breeder's arrival was still on the stove and spewing black smoke.

As she raced to the stove to move the kettle, Calvin moved to the living room, where the pet owners were gasping at the sight of Bixby— the face of Posh Pooch designer doggie deodorizers—attempting to mate with the arm of the sofa.

Calvin corralled Bixby and put him in the downstairs laundry room while Lila, after scrambling to find a potholder, moved the kettle from the stove burner and into the kitchen sink. Unfortunately, she hadn't moved quickly enough and the black smoke had triggered the smoke alarm.

The press, the guests, and the dogs rushed not just for the kitchen door but for their vehicles.

As Calvin stood on a kitchen chair to deactivate the smoke alarm, Lila surveyed the destruction in shocked silence. "My launch . . . my deodorizer . . ."

"I'm sorry, Lila. I know how hard you worked and how disappointing this is."

Just then, Clyde arrived. He looked around, his mouth agape. "What in Sam Hill is going on here?"

"We can explain, Clyde," Calvin replied, "but right now, I think we have a more pressing matter. I really think we need to take Bixby to the vet."

• • •

Lila was fortunate that Dr. Lund, the only veterinarian in town, was both able and willing to examine Bixby on such short notice. He had seen Bixby for an introductory visit two short months earlier.

"I've taken blood samples and we'll get the results in a day or two. However, from everything I can see, there's nothing physically wrong with him," Lund explained. "His blood pressure is fine, his heartbeat strong, and his oxygen rate is solid. His pupils are a bit dilated, though. Did he eat anything unusual? You said you had guests at your home. Maybe someone fed him something they shouldn't have?"

"He wasn't in the house when the guests arrived," Lila explained.

Calvin had brought Bixby and Lila to the vet in his truck since Clyde had to return to the store to help customers. "He was running around with my dog in the backyard. You know as well as I do that there's nothing to eat out there. Not with all the snow we've had."

Lund frowned. "Then I have no idea . . ." The doctor paused and sniffed Bixby's head. "Have you been using incense or scented candles?"

"Yes." Lila's face lit up at mention of her products. "I've created a line of all-natural designer knock-off doggie deodorizers."

"Do any of your fragrances contain aniseed?"

"Yes, I have a riff on vanilla musk that's for relaxation. Oh, and a mulled wine scent. I made both of them into candles and bath salts as well as a deodorizer."

"I think I know the source of your problem. Aniseed is often referred to as catnip for dogs. Like catnip, not all dogs are affected by aniseed, but for those who are, it can make a dog extremely energetic and playful. When the aniseed wears off, however, the dog can become sleepy and lethargic."

"Wait. You mean all of this is because of my fragrances?"

Lund nodded. "We still need to look at the bloodwork, but it seems like the likely culprit. The party you threw—you said it was a launch, so there was lots of scent around, wasn't there?"

"Tons. You could scarcely breathe for the smell of it all."

"Yep, Bixby probably walked in from outside, took one sniff, and wham."

"I was so busy baking for the launch that I didn't light my candles last night. That's why he was so well-behaved."

"That adds even more credence to my theory."

"My God. So, all this time Bixby hasn't been sick or acting out or missing my daughter and son-in-law. He's been . . ."

"Stoned," Lund finished the sentence. "Bixby has been utterly stoned."

Chapter Twenty-five

Stella was seated at the garden table sipping coffee and gazing out at the shoreline when Nick came out to join her.

"Good morning." He gave her a kiss and sat in the chair opposite hers. "Today's the big day. Alma and Mills are finally tying the knot."

"Mmm," she answered distractedly.

"Mmm? That's all you can say about our best friends getting married?"

"Huh? No, I'm very excited. I can't wait for the ceremony."

"Yeah, I can tell. You're simply bubbling over," Nick deadpanned.

"I'm sorry. I can't stop thinking about the case."

"You mean the *closed* case? The case Lenzana cracked yesterday?"

"Excuse me, but who cracked the case?" she challenged.

"Aha! If you're fighting to get credit, then you believe it was cracked, too."

She folded her arms across her chest and sniffed.

"And you deserve the credit. You and Alma. You were both on the front line yesterday. But you have to admit, it all makes sense. The drugs, the credit card fraud—this is an organized crime ring, Stella. They'll remove anyone who gets in their way. Look at what they did to you just for taking a photo. I hate to think what would have happened if you hadn't kept your wits about you and used that self-defense move."

"And if you hadn't been down the hall, in the gym," she added.

"Yeah, speaking of which, I forgot to tell you something I learned yesterday. Something about Bernard."

"Oh?"

"Yeah, Bernard must have a girlfriend or something, because all those gym trips of his were phony."

Stella replaced her coffee cup in its saucer. "What?"

"It's true. I spoke with the gym attendant at El Sueño yesterday while waiting for you and Alma to arrive at the ballroom. He claims he's never met Bernard. Not even once. This is the primary, full-time gym attendant I'm talking about. If he's never met Bernard, then

Bernard has never been there." Nick picked up the coffee carafe and shook it. "Is there any left for me?"

"Sorry, no." Her mind had been so focused on the inconsistencies in the case that she'd forgotten to order more. "I'll flag a waiter down when I see one."

"No worries. I'll get it." He switched on his phone and began tapping the screen.

"What are you doing?"

"Ordering coffee. There's an app for service, remember?"

The app. She jumped from her seat. "My God, that's it!"

"What? What's it?"

She didn't answer, but instead ran through their garden gate and toward the pool.

Nick followed closely behind, fearing for his wife's sanity. "Um, you do realize you're in your nightgown and robe, right?"

"Yes, I know, but this can't wait." She arrived at the clubhouse end of the pool and began testing the seats surrounding the lounge chair formerly occupied by Georgina Early.

"What are you doing?"

"I was so busy trying to figure out what Georgina *could* see from her lounger that I didn't stop to think of what she *couldn't* see from the others. And . . . I've figured it out. Bandista Beach. Nick, call Lenzana and tell him that Bernard Early is our killer."

"What? How? He was with us the entire time."

"He didn't need to be here. In fact, it worked to his benefit that he wasn't."

"I'll call Lenzana and tell him about Early . . . even though I don't know how to explain what I'm telling him."

"Okay, I'll call him. You go find Early and make sure he doesn't try to make a run for it."

A passing waiter overheard Stella's remark. "If you are looking for Señor Early, he is gone. He checked out about an hour ago."

● ● ●

Stella and Nick once again found themselves in the back of Lenzana's squad car, this time driving hell for leather toward the

Cancun Airport, where Bernard Early, using a different passport, had been spotted.

"Bernard and Georgina were selling drugs to El Sueño's guests," Stella explained over the blare of the car's siren. "Georgina would watch the harbor for the boat bringing the drugs. Her chair by the pool is the only one with a totally clear view of both Old Harbor and the Cozumel pier. Once the shipment arrived, Bernard would go and collect it, bring it back to Caballero Cove, and then distribute it to their clients. Clients they carefully curated over the years of staying at Caballero Cove."

"That was pretty risky, wasn't it? Carrying drugs in an old gym bag?" Nick noted.

"It would have been if they'd simply been placed in the old gym bag. But Georgina was clever. Remember how her blankets were double-knitted so there were two layers of blanket and a space in between? The drugs were hidden in that empty space. If Bernard were stopped by authorities, he'd simply say he was delivering a homemade blanket knitted by his wife," Stella explained.

"That's why she wouldn't give that blanket to Ellie and Kendal."

Stella nodded. "Lenzana, you mentioned that you were tightening the noose on the drug sales occurring at El Sueño, which correlates with a comment Georgina made to her fellow guests about she and Bernard possibly losing business. Georgina was a cunning woman. And so, either to maximize her income, perhaps as a cushion until they could establish themselves elsewhere, or perhaps as an entirely new revenue stream, Georgina decided to pursue blackmail. It was a logical choice since she knew everything there was to know about the other guests and she enjoyed lording that information over them. She'd always spread rumors and stories, just for the thrill, but now she began tossing around stories in earnest, just to see what would stick, what was true, and what her fellow guests might be willing to pay to keep hidden.

"I don't think Bernard approved of Georgina's new business plan. The guests I spoke to who had paid money to Georgina all agreed that Bernard never repeated Georgina's stories and, therefore, most likely had nothing to do with the scheme. Why? Because it was incredibly risky. Bernard was already at risk, collecting and delivering drugs, and now Georgina was doubling that risk. All that was needed was a call from a disgruntled guest to you, Lenzana, and the whole operation would come tumbling down."

"So, he murdered Señora Early instead," Lenzana presumed. "But how?"

"He spiked her hydrochlorothiazide capsules with oxycodone."

"That's impossible. The hydrochlorothiazide was in tablet form."

"It was given in tablet form in the UK, but here in Playa del Carmen, it's a capsule. The bottle you found in Georgina's casita bore the label from the farmacia on Fifth Avenue and was dated from a few days ago. Yet, when you held it up for me to see, there were only a few tablets left in it. Why? Because those were not the pills from the farmacia. Bernard had removed the last of the tablets from Georgina's previous prescription and kept them aside, then he replaced the contents of the farmacia's capsules with the oxycodone, knowing Georgina would take one of them in the afternoon, as she always did. Only when she took the capsule on this specific day, he'd be several miles away in Tulum with us as witnesses."

"What about the man he met there?"

"Yes, the man . . . I thought at first that he might have been a customer of Bernard's, but if he had been, their so-called conversation would have been extremely brief. Just long enough to exchange merchandise for cash. No, I'm reasonably certain that the man was Bernard's boss or main supplier and the reason they met that day was to ensure that the plan to dispatch Georgina—the woman who was a threat to both their freedom and livelihood—was in play. Nick and I will provide a description of the man in case you want to put a search out for him."

"Yes, I will take care of that when we're back in La Playa," Lenzana confirmed. "So how did the pill bottle get back in Señora Early's casita?"

"Bernard put it there. When he discovered Georgina's dead body upon his return, he knelt beside her and put on quite the display of emotion, knocking over Georgina's bag in the process. While Nick was examining Georgina's body and the rest of us were calling for help,

Bernard took the incriminating pill bottle from the contents of the handbag and swapped Georgina's phone for his. Later on, while he was alone in his casita, 'grieving,' Bernard disposed of the tainted capsules and replaced them with the handful of tablets he'd kept aside to throw everyone off the track. He then returned the bottle to Georgina's bedside table—he most likely had a key—to create even more confusion."

"It worked," Nick remarked.

"You mentioned Señor Early taking Señora Early's phone," Lenzana questioned. "That was to cancel the señora's drink order, was it not?"

"That's right. When we were at Tulum, I suggested that we exchange phone numbers in case we became separated at the park. Bernard told us that he'd left his phone back at Caballero Cove in an attempt to unplug from life. That was partially true. He had left his phone behind, but instead he had Georgina's so he could cancel the drink order. If you have your tech people check, I'm sure you'll find that the request, although sent from Georgina's phone and her Caballero Cove account, was transmitted from a cell tower near Tulum and not one in Playa del Carmen."

"Very clever. And Reverend Bailor?"

"Reverend Bailor always stayed in the casita next door to Bernard Early. Except for this year when he made a point of complaining about the constant traffic. That's how he described it: constant traffic. While he stayed in his specific casita, he could not see who or what was triggering the motion light that kept him awake, because there are no side windows that allow an occupant to look out. This year, however, Reverend Bailor stayed in a casita on the opposite side of the pool— the casita we've been staying in. I have no doubt that Reverend Bailor, a self-described light sleeper, got up in the middle of the night and saw precisely what I did just a few nights ago."

"A prowler?" Nick guessed.

"No, Bernard Early. If you recall, it was Bernard who put the idea of prowlers into our minds at dinner the first night. But he was the only person who was actually on the prowl. El Sueño is a known 'party hotel'—even Chip Ruckert was aware of its reputation, which says a lot. Quintana Hospitalidad renovated the hotel so that it appeals to the young, attractive, and wealthy. Although I'm sure that Bernard made some daytime deliveries there—hence his so-called trips to the gym—a good deal of his money must have come from late-night calls. The clients who, mid-party, found themselves short of supply would call him and he would doubtless deliver, lest those clients find another supplier. I interrupted Bernard before he could return to his casita after one of those late-night deliveries, but I suspect Reverend Bailor, either already awake or awakened by the motion light, watched as the shadowy figure entered casita number four and then didn't go out again. If you check Bernard's belongings, you'll find the sneakers I described to you.

"As for Bailor, he probably suspected Bernard, as Nick originally did, of having an affair. Knowing how he cared for and sometimes counseled the other guests, Bailor told Bernard what he saw and offered his guidance as a friend and clergyman. In doing so, Bailor sealed his fate. Renata told me that the reverend never locked his casita door. It would have been very simple for Bernard to replace Bailor's low blood pressure medicine with the oxycodone."

Nick shivered. "Almost like a dress rehearsal for Georgina."

Stella nodded.

"What about the attack on Sheriff Mills?" Lenzana asked.

"Mills found himself at the wrong place at the wrong time, and in the wrong costume. The intended victim was Joseph Penrod. Everyone at Caballero Cove knew that Joseph Penrod wore his old army uniform for the annual costume party. It was a great source of amusement. As our killer wasn't at the party and only passed through briefly, undoubtedly on his way to another delivery, he didn't notice that Mills was also wearing a uniform. I caught sight of Mills and Penrod at the pool yesterday. They're of the same height and build and both have light-colored hair. Put them in a dark uniform in a dark corner of the resort, and it would have been nearly impossible to tell them apart."

"But why would Señor Early attack Señor Penrod?"

"Fear. Fear of what Penrod might know. Penrod was very close friends with Reverend Bailor. It wasn't inconceivable that the reverend might share what he knew about Bernard. Even if Bailor hadn't mentioned Bernard by name, Penrod knew why his friend had changed casitas. After all, that was the reason Penrod was now staying in the casita next door to Bernard! Penrod is in good shape—he runs, he swims. He's also retired military. If Penrod noticed the motion light switched on night after night, it was likely that he'd eventually dash outside to spot what had triggered it. Also, Penrod also takes hydrochlorothiazide. He was renewing his prescription at the pharmacy the morning I ran into him. He had received capsules and not tablets and thought the pharmacist had made a mistake. It was only a matter of time before Penrod, reading the news reports of Georgina's death and listening to you and the other guests' accounts, realized that the pills in Georgina's prescription bottle should have been capsules and not tablets."

"Wow," Lenzana uttered. "Wow."

They arrived at Cancun Airport, where airport security and local police were searching every departure gate for a sign of Bernard Early. After twenty minutes of intense activity, a call came from a member of Lenzana's team. Early had been captured just as he was waiting to board a flight back to the UK.

Lenzana, with Stella and Nick in tow, placed him in handcuffs.

"You're making a mistake. I'll call my solicitors," Early threatened.

"Go ahead," Lenzana countered. "But we know that you murdered your wife."

"I didn't!"

"No? Well, if you happen to beat these charges and are released, let me give you a little tip: never pretend to be a mystery reader. Lee Child no longer writes the Jack Reacher series. His brother, Andrew, does. But, of course, you wouldn't know that since you only claimed to be a mystery fan so you could get close to Nick and Mills and make sure they weren't in Playa del Carmen to assist in an investigation. An investigation of you and Georgie."

As Lenzana's team bundled Bernard Early out of the airport, Lenzana looked at Stella. "Wow. Wow."

Chapter Twenty-six

"I, Alma, take you, Charles, to be my lawfully wedded husband, to have and to hold, from this day forward, for better, for worse, for richer, for poorer, in sickness and in health, until death do us part."

Alma, wearing a sleeveless tea-length ivory silk dress, slipped a plain gold band onto Charlie Mills's left ring finger.

The justice of the peace gestured to Mills, signifying it was his turn. Taking the diamond band from Nick, he placed it on Alma's finger. He was handsomely turned out in a linen suit with white shirt. A single yellow rose was pinned to his lapel.

"I, Charles, take you, Alma, to be my lawfully wedded wife, to have and to hold, from this day forward, for better, for worse, for richer, for poorer, in sickness and in health, until death do us part."

"It is my great honor and proud privilege to pronounce you as husband and wife," the justice of the peace declared. "You may now seal your vows with a kiss."

The Caballero Cove guests applauded and cheered as Alma and Mills kissed. Señor Tugores, accompanied by Luciana, served flutes of champagne to everyone. "A toast to Mr. and Mrs. Charles Mills."

Stella wiped a tear from her eye and joined on the toast.

"Remind you of our wedding?" Nick asked as everyone mingled and congratulated the lucky couple.

"The sentiment, yes. The weather, no. I wouldn't have made it to our wedding if the limo driver didn't follow that snow plow."

"Yeah, and the reception had to be rescheduled. But the ceremony . . ."

"The ceremony was perfect. I was glad that only our immediate family was there."

"Me too." He touched his glass to hers.

"So, I was thinking of what you asked the other day."

"About visiting one of the cenotes tomorrow? They supposedly contain the bluest water you'll ever see."

"No, not that. Although I would love to visit the cenote. I was talking about the big question you asked."

Nick's eyes grew wide. "Oh. And?"

"I think it could be interesting to have another you running around the house, identifying trees and telling me the difference between altocumulus and nimbostratus clouds."

He broke into a wide grin. "Really? That's amazing." He kissed her and then made a face. "Wait."

"What?"

"I just realized we could have someone running around the house pointing out the clues that prove that Daddy finished off the rest of the ice cream."

Stella laughed. "We don't need clues for that. It's always you."

Desirée Hunt approached them, a full glass in her hand. "What a lovely day."

"It is," Stella agreed. "How are you doing?"

"Good, actually. I had a talk with Chip last night and came clean with him about everything. We had to talk through it, but we're both resolved to make things work. Together."

"I'm so glad."

"Me too. I know it won't be easy, but baby steps, right? Like this cider instead of champagne." She held her glass aloft. "If it helps him, I'm in."

"That's good to hear. Are you going to be around the next few days?"

"No, we're going to head home tonight. Chip's actually agreed to see a counselor, so wish us luck!"

Nick and Stella both gave her their best.

Ellie and Kendal came by next.

"This was such a beautiful service," Ellie gushed.

Meanwhile, Kendal wiped away her tears. "Sorry, hormones."

"Don't worry about it," Stella replied. "I cried, too, and I have no excuse."

A thought suddenly occurred to Stella. One that made her deposit her champagne glass on Señor Tugores's tray as he walked by.

"I thought you'd like to know that I told Kendal everything about my past," Ellie announced. "And she's been an absolute lamb."

Kendal shrugged. "Why wouldn't I be? That was years ago. You're not that person any longer."

"We're both glad to hear everything is okay between you," Nick said. "You have a lot to look forward to."

"That we do," Ellie agreed. "Oh, hey, did you decide to join us at the cenote tomorrow?"

"We did."

"Cool. We'll meet you at the clubhouse after breakfast."

Kendal spoke up. "It looks like they're setting up the buffet."

"Oh, we'd better go. It's only been an hour since you last ate." The couple excused themselves. "Talk to you later."

"Well, there you go. Not only are you a great detective, but you also seem to be a great mender of hearts."

"I don't know about that," she replied modestly.

"I do. Chip and Desirée and Ellie and Kendal. And look at the Horrockses and Banerjees. Both those couples look like they're on their second honeymoon."

"I noticed that. They're holding hands and snuggling—with their respective mates for a change. It's nice to see."

"Very nice to see." He slid an arm around her waist and drew her closer. "Nabbing bad guys, helping good guys. No wonder I think you'll be a terrific mother."

"I don't know," she sang.

"Well, we'll find out, won't we?"

She kissed him on the cheek and embraced him.

We will indeed find out, Nick, she thought. *And perhaps sooner than you think.*

About the Author

Author of the critically acclaimed Marjorie McClelland Mysteries, Amy Patricia Meade is a native of Long Island, New York, where she cut her teeth on classic films and books featuring Nancy Drew and Encyclopedia Brown.

After stints as an Operations Manager for a document imaging company and a freelance technical writer, Amy relocated to southwest England, where she was a featured author at Agatha Christie's Annual Greenway Literary Festival.

Now residing in Upstate New York, Amy spends her time writing mysteries with a humorous or historical bent. When not writing, Amy enjoys traveling, testing out new recipes, and classic films.